THE MUSIC HAS STOPPED...

Passed out, the bloody soak. Couldn't he have picked a less awkward place to sleep it off? Madoc gave the gross body a none-to-gentle nudge with his toe.

"Wake up."

Evidently he didn't speak loudly enough to do any good. The trombone player didn't stir. Madoc leaned over to give him a shake and found out why. It was a waste of time trying to wake somebody who had an icepick rammed into the back of his neck...

Charlotte MacLeod
WRITING AS
Alisa Craig

TROUBLE IN THE BRASSES

AVON BOOKS ◆ NEW YORK

TROUBLE IN THE BRASSES is an original publication of Avon Books. This work has never before appeared in book form. This work is a novel. Any similarity to actual persons or events is purely coincidental.

AVON BOOKS
A division of
The Hearst Corporation
105 Madison Avenue
New York, New York 10016

Copyright © 1989 by Alisa Craig
Published by arrangement with the author
Library of Congress Catalog Card Number: 88-91354
ISBN: 0-380-75539-4

First Avon Books Printing: April 1989

AVON TRADEMARK REG. U.S. PAT. OFF. AND IN OTHER COUNTRIES, MARCA REGISTRADA, HECHO EN U.S.A.

Printed in the U.S.A.

K–R 10 9 8 7 6 5 4 3 2

For Paula and Jim Francis
without whose help this would
never have happened

Author's Note

The Wagstaffe Symphony Orchestra does not exist in fact, nor has it been patterned after any other orchestra, Canadian or otherwise. Though every attempt has been made to create an authentic atmosphere, no actual person or place has been used as a model. Even Ace Bulligan is a figment of the author's sometimes overstrained imagination, though we rather wish he weren't.

Chapter 1

"Mother, what am I doing here?" whispered Detective Inspector Madoc Rhys.

"Shh!"

Madoc was not a whit surprised at Lady Rhys's reaction. He'd been asking her the same sort of question and getting the same sort of answer ever since she'd deemed him old enough to come with her and watch his father at work. It had taken him quite a while as a child to figure out precisely what Sir Emlyn was accomplishing by standing up on a little box in front of a lot of people dressed up as penguins, turning his back to the audience, and waving his arms around. It had taken his parents still longer to accept the realization that he, the second of their three children, was hopelessly, incontrovertibly, and quite shamelessly tone-deaf.

While his elder brother, Dafydd, warbled and preened his way toward operatic fame and even got to sing lead tenor in oratorio and cantata under his father's direction, Madoc had played cops and robbers with the kids in the neighborhood. In contrast to his younger sister, Gwendolyn, who'd cut her six-year molars on a clarinet reed and taken her place in some well-known chamber music ensembles before she'd felt the first swelling of a wisdom tooth, Madoc had devoted himself to reading *Renfrew of the Royal Mounted* and collecting his classmates' finger-

prints. When he'd gone all through school without learning
to tell a B-natural from a C-sharp, his parents had finally
announced they were washing their hands of him. He'd
thanked them politely and applied as a recruit to the Royal
Canadian Mounted Police.

Diplomatic relations were a good deal less strained now
that Madoc had got married and set up housekeeping.
However, Lady Rhys still hadn't got over her habit of murmuring vaguely on the rare occasions when her younger
son's name came up that Madoc had a position with the
Canadian government, in research. Now, out of the blue,
he'd received an urgent request to join his parents on tour
and not to bring Janet, and he still hadn't the remotest idea
why.

It was Janet herself who'd passed on the message. She'd
called him at work, as puzzled as he, to say that Sir Emlyn
himself had phoned, right after Madoc had left the house.
That was almost unheard of to begin with. Except on the
podium, that gentle little man was usually content to let his
wife handle the amenities, not to mention everything else
that had to be coped with. Used to unquestioning obe-
dience from his singers and musicians, Sir Emlyn had
merely stated in the kindest and sweetest way where he
could be found at which times of the day; and that he
hoped Madoc would lose no time in joining him and Sillie,
this being his pet and wholly nondisrespectful name for
Lady Rhys. He had added his regrets that it would not be
convenient for Janet to come this time, bade her a fond
good-bye, and hung up.

"But that's crazy," Madoc had replied. "Tad likes you
far better than he does me." Tad wasn't a nickname,
merely the Welsh word for *father*.

Janet had replied that he shouldn't talk foolishness, that
she'd worked out plane reservations which would get him
to Wagstaffe at twenty to eight, and should she confirm
them? She'd have his bag packed in half an hour, and what
time did he want her to drive him to the airport?

So that was that. He'd explained the situation to his

superior, and spent the day clearing his desk. There wouldn't be any organizational problem; he'd planned to take a couple of days off anyway because Janet's sister-in-law was already booked for a visit. He'd be sorry to miss Annabelle, but she'd be company for Janet. No doubt the two women would have a lot more fun than he would.

The plane had been a few minutes late, as planes so often were. He'd got to the hall by the skin of his teeth. A tight-lipped Lady Rhys had met him at the box office and hustled him up to her private box with no more than a "Hurry, the doors are closing."

Sir Emlyn was a stickler for starting on the dot and for allowing nobody to enter the concert hall while the musicians were performing. Back in England, he'd been known to keep certain members of the royal family standing outside until after the first number, though of course never the Queen Mum, of whom both he and Lady Rhys were particularly fond.

Early training had taught Madoc to endure with fortitude what his tin ear prevented him from enjoying. Police training and natural propensity were keeping him on the alert now. His mother had handed him a program but he hadn't bothered to find out what was being played. The pieces all sounded pretty much alike to him. The words, for there was always singing when Sir Emlyn conducted, wouldn't make any great sense; they never did. Since he was too prominently displayed to amuse himself spotting present or potential criminals in the audience, Madoc concentrated on the performers. At least one got a bird's-eye view of the stage from here.

He'd known the names of the various instruments from early boyhood, of course. Even though he couldn't tell them apart by their sounds, he'd never have passed up the chance to assimilate odd bits of information that might come in handy someday to the police detective he was going to be. Originally Madoc had been most interested in the oboes and bassoons, but only because he'd thought their skinny mouthpieces were drinking straws and those long tubes they were stuck into must be full of some delicious liquid that he wasn't getting a taste of and it wasn't fair.

The brasses had disgusted him because the musicians were, he thought, always shaking spit out of them. Somewhere along the line, he'd learned that it wasn't spit, merely condensation formed by the player's hot breath against the cooler metal that had to be got rid of so that the sound wouldn't come out as a gurgle instead of a moo. He'd asked his father once why a moo was any better than a gurgle, but had got only a sigh and a mournful glance in reply.

All things considered, Madoc and his father had always got on well enough. Sir Emlyn had made it plain that he felt his younger son was more to be pitied than censured and had been nice to him in small ways. He'd taken Madoc for little walks to visit the sheep and the hens while they were staying with old Sir Caradoc on the family farm back in Wales, as they often did. He'd listened to Madoc's reports of boyish exploits and tried to nod in the right places. He'd brought back presents from tours, usually the wrong sort of equipment for sports Madoc wasn't much interested in playing anyway.

They'd done their real communicating with shy smiles, handclasps, and the occasional embarrassed hug. Madoc was astonished to realize how much he loved the diffident little chap who could cause all that noise to be made up there. He was immensely relieved when the racket ceased in a tumult of clangs, bleats, and squawks and he could tackle his mother again.

"Mum, for God's sake tell me. What's this all about?"

Conscious of eyes upon her, Lady Rhys favored her son with a fond parental smile and leaned toward him with a playful manner, as playful as Lady Rhys ever got anyway, for she was always conscious of what she owed her husband's position. She was a handsome woman still; all the Rhyses were good-looking, even Madoc. Her hair was neither black like his nor silver like her husband's, but chestnut-brown without the aid of artifice and worn sleeked back into a chignon. As usual, she was wearing her diamonds and a floor-length black gown with elegantly flowing sleeves. Black satin for fall, Madoc noted; she wouldn't go into black velvet until around the first of December. In spring the gown would be black crepe or lace and in summer black chiffon. She bought replacements every five years or so, and saved the old ones to take along for emergencies. Her system saved a lot of fuss and bother on the road; there was always enough of that without adding a lavish wardrobe for the conductor's wife.

When she deemed the moment right, Lady Rhys raised her program so that it hid her mouth and murmured under its cover, "Your father's having trouble with the brasses. Keep your eye on the first trombone." She then sat back and waited for the applause to die down and her husband to start waving his arms again.

Madoc borrowed his mother's opera glasses, wondering what sort of trouble the brasses were giving and which was the first trombone. He assumed his mother meant in fact not the trombone, but the trombonist. There were three of them on stage at the moment: one a large, heavyset man of forty-five or so with a bright red face, one a smallish young fellow with a great deal of curly blond hair, and one who was medium-sized, neither young nor old, and had no particularly distinguishing feature about him. Professional instinct told him this was the man to watch, but it was the big chap who was giving the trouble.

Trouble there was, even though it might not be discernible to the eyes of untrained observers. The trombonist had something that looked like a long whisker hanging from the tip of his slide. A piece of fishline, perhaps, or gut from a snell. With this the man was contriving whenever he stretched out his instrument to its full length to tickle the neck of the flautist who sat in front of him. The flautist was a reasonably attractive, not-young woman. Like the other female musicians, she wore a long black dress. Hers happened to have a neckline that was scooped out a bit across the shoulders. Having that whiskerish thing dragged across her bare skin while she was trying to keep her place and hit the right notes must be maddening.

And that wasn't the worst. Every so often, during a pause, the trombonist would shake the moisture out of his instrument. Whenever he shook, Madoc could see the woman wince. Trumpeters and violinists were feisty by nature; one of these might have turned around and slugged him if he tried such a trick on them. Flautists were competitive but not likely to be combative; Madoc wondered for a moment whether his father had arranged this somewhat unusual seating in order to avoid any contretemps. But he couldn't see the ever-courteous Sir Emlyn Rhys penalizing a musician for being dependably well-behaved. Was it possible his father simply didn't know what was going on?

Yes, Madoc decided, it was more than possible. To begin with, Sir Emlyn didn't look at any orchestra, even the prestigious Wagstaffe Symphony, a great deal. He was primarily a choral director, and his first attention was always on his singers. He'd come to regard instrumentalists more or less as nice, steady workhorses who could be counted on not to throw temperaments, catch colds, or have babies at awkward times, all evidence to the contrary notwithstanding. Madoc had noticed years ago, when he'd been allowed to watch his father from the wings, that when there was no chorus to worry about, Sir Emlyn often led the orchestra with his eyes shut. When Madoc asked him why, he'd replied, "I can see better with my ears." That was another one which had taken the boy a while to figure out.

In any event, Sir Emlyn would hardly have sent out an SOS over a childish trick like this. What was going on here?

Madoc checked out the trumpets. Trumpeters were not the most sedate among the musicians as a rule, or so he'd been told, but this lot appeared to be behaving themselves well enough at the moment. The French horns were another matter. Nobody was doing anything wrong, but something definitely wasn't right. Two of the horn players were casting uneasy looks at the man between them, even while they ought to have been keeping their full attention on the score.

The one in the middle was puffing away, as he presumably ought to have been since Sir Emlyn had just pointed the baton in his direction. However, Madoc could see he was making awfully heavy work of it. Sweat was standing out on his forehead. His face was turning gradually from pink to yellow to stark white to a strange pea-green. Madoc nudged his mother and handed her back the opera glasses. She gave him another of her tight-lipped glances. Then she looked where he was looking, and her lips pressed even tighter.

Madoc thought he knew what was happening. Musicians, as he'd heard often enough, tended to have martyr complexes. Rather than miss a performance and thus concede that the show could go on without them, they'd drag themselves to work with broken legs and raging fevers. This chap must have been hit by a bug of some kind and had risked infecting the entire orchestra rather than desert his chair. Was he going to be sick on stage?

No, thank God, he wasn't. The intermission had arrived. Sir Emlyn was taking his bows, asking the orchestra to rise. The whole group must by now be aware of their colleague's plight. They let the horns go off first, the two who'd been sitting beside the sick man helping him off before any of the others. The maneuver was slickly accomplished; probably few in the audience noticed anything amiss. Lady Rhys waited until her husband made his final appearance and dismissed the orchestra, then she stood up and collected her furs.

"Let's pop backstage for a jiffy and let your father know you've arrived," she said just loud enough for those in the next box to overhear and understand that her going didn't mean they could, too.

Madoc hoped for his mother's sake that they wouldn't come upon the ailing horn player making a ghastly mess backstage, but he hoped in vain. The mess was already made, the musician lay face down in the midst of it. Some of his comrades huddled around, all of them looking pretty green, too. And these, judging from certain background noises, were the strong-stomached ones. Lady Rhys took command.

"Well, don't everyone just stand there. Frieda, go find Lucy Shadd and tell her to call an ambulance immediately. Joseph, fetch the stretcher from the first aid rack down the hall. We'll take him to the musicians' room until the doctor comes. Jason, find one of the stage crew. Tell him to bring some sawdust and a scrubbing pail. The rest of you clear out of here. Not you, Cedric. I want you to help carry the stretcher."

"Lady Rhys, can't you get the technicians to do it? My heart—"

"Fiddlesticks. The technicians are busy onstage and you're fit as a flea. Don't think I didn't notice you lugging that silly little blonde all around the swimming pool back in Atlanta."

"Wilhelm weighs a hell of a lot more than she did," grumbled the beefy man Madoc recognized as the jester of the trombone section.

"But you'll only be carrying half of him," Lady Rhys pointed out reasonably. "What's the matter with you, Wilhelm? Surely you haven't been silly enough to eat fried oysters again?"

Wilhelm didn't answer, or give any sign that he'd heard. Lifting her satin skirt and being extremely careful where she placed her satin slippers, Lady Rhys bent over him.

"Wilhelm, speak to me! Where does it hurt?"

"You'd better step back, Mother," said Madoc quietly. "The stretcher's here. Lay it down by his feet, sir, would you?"

He was fairly sure what ailed the French horn player. Wilhelm's feet offered no resistance when Madoc grabbed hold of the ankles and skidded him clear of the mess he'd made. Once the flaccid body had been rolled over on to the stretcher, everybody would know.

Cedric the trombonist was first to realize what had happened. "My God!" he exclaimed in what could only be described as a screaming whisper. "He's dead!"

"Cedric, this is no time for hysterics," snapped Lady Rhys. "Wilhelm's dehydrated himself and gone into shock, that's all. And bad enough, the silly man. He'll have to miss the plane and Lucy will be hopping. Take his foot end. Jason, take his head. Follow me."

Jason was one of the trumpeters who'd helped Wilhelm offstage. Madoc wondered momentarily whether his mother had forgotten she had a son available, or if she'd deliberately not asked him to help with the stretcher because it might impair his father's image to have a son doing manual labor in front of the musicians. No, Lady Rhys was not a foolish woman. She was used to bossing musicians around, that was all, and she'd done what came naturally.

A stagehand was hurrying along the corridor with a mop and bucket. He mustn't be stopped from doing what naturally had to be done. Madoc did what came naturally, too. There was a water cooler standing near the stage entrance, with a holder full of midget paper cups attached to it. As much by instinct as by intention, he used a couple of the cups to scoop up samples of the revolting mess on the floor, and sealed them inside one of the small plastic bags that were as much a part of his daily garb as his shoes and socks. Whatever had killed the horn player had started to do its job at least half an hour ago, maybe a good deal longer. Madoc put the little bag in his pocket and went to find his parents.

Chapter 2

"Why the police, Lucy?"

Lady Rhys's sharp question didn't cause the trim, elderly woman in the smart gray flannel suit to turn a hair. "Because that was the fastest way to get ambulance service, Lady Rhys. Besides, if it turns out there's something really wrong with Wilhelm, we'd have to call them anyway."

"Really wrong" was carrying euphemism to its outermost limit, Madoc thought. The poor chap was dead as last week's news; it needn't have taken the uniformed officer or the white-coated intern with the stethoscope to determine that. The young intern was straightening up now, turning to Lady Rhys as the obvious person in charge even though Sir Emlyn was now standing with his usual appearance of gentle melancholy a step or two behind her.

"He's gone, I'm afraid. Would you happen to know whether he had any history of chronic illness?"

"Oh yes," her ladyship replied. "Wilhelm had a terrible stomach, and he wouldn't stop eating things he wasn't supposed to have. Fried fish, you know, and heavy pastries and far too much coffee. And—"

Lady Rhys whipped a lace-trimmed handkerchief out of her sleeve and pressed it to her mouth. Lucy took over.

"Lady Rhys is quite right. It was chronic bleeding

10

ulcers, I believe. Poor Wilhelm was always a terrible glutton."

"You knew him pretty well, then?" the policeman asked her.

"I'd known him most of my life, off and on. We played together in the Champlain Symphony when we were both starting out, and later in the Sackbut Sextet. After I joined the Wagstaffe Symphony as a horn player quite some years ago, I played in the same section with him. I don't know whether you realize it, Officer, but an orchestra exists in a little world of its own, especially when it's on tour, as we are now. We get very close to each other. As director of operations, I'm the one who's supposed to keep our little world spinning, so I have to be aware of things like the special diet problems of certain orchestra members. I tried to keep Wilhelm off the fried clams and fried chicken and fried this and fried that, but he had a positive passion for grease. Lately he'd been stuffing worse than ever, it seemed."

"Did he show any other suicidal impulses?" the intern asked.

Lucy Shadd stared at him. "I'm not sure I know what you mean, Doctor."

"A person who has a known disability and persists in doing things that make it worse is playing Russian roulette with his life," the young man answered pedantically. "Usually it's because the person is depressed and has a subconscious or maybe even conscious urge to get his misery over with. Would you say your friend here was more down in the mouth than usual?"

Lucy looked at Lady Rhys, who shook her head.

"If he was, I certainly didn't notice. It seems to me he went right on telling his dirty stories and playing his decidedly unfunny practical jokes much as usual."

"He put a lump of plastic dog do in my instrument case only yesterday," a nearby violist volunteered. "I'd say he was still full of the old pep and vinegar."

Lucy scowled.

"Oh, you wouldn't see anything wrong with anybody if he dropped dead at your—" She choked a bit. "Actually, Doctor, I have to say Wilhelm had good reason to be depressed, even aside from his stomach. He was losing his embouchure."

"His what?"

"It's something that happens to wind players, particularly the brasses. One's lip muscles become so painful from the constant strain that one simply can't endure to play any longer. That's why I myself work backstage nowadays instead of out front. At least I was able to adapt when it happened to me, but Wilhelm was such a dunderhead—except about the horn. He was a superb French horn player. Nobody can take that away from him."

Lucy Shadd sounded rather fierce, and as if she'd just about run out of composure. Lady Rhys laid a diamond-laden hand on her shoulder.

"Let's see if we can find ourselves a cup of tea, shall we? What happens next, Doctor? Do we call an undertaker? Not to sound callous, but we have to push on to Vancouver right after the performance."

"There'll have to be an autopsy, I'm afraid," the intern apologized. "It's a matter of routine in a sudden death like this. Isn't that right, Officer?"

The policeman nodded. "That's right, ma'am. Could you give me the deceased's full name and address? Did he have a family?"

Lucy had got hold of herself. "His full name was Wilhelm Jan Ochs. I believe his only close relative is a brother in Manitoba. I have his and the brother's addresses in my files, but they're packed with the luggage. I can dig them out and call the police station with the information as soon as I find them, if that's acceptable?"

The policeman said that would be fine. The intern, the policeman, and the ambulance driver, who hadn't said a word the whole time, wrapped the body in green plastic and transferred it to the stretcher they'd brought with them. By now, intermission was almost over and the musicians had to hurry onstage. Nobody took any notice when Madoc followed the policeman out to the vestibule and handed him the little plastic bag of vomit.

"How did you happen to think of doing this, Mr. Rhys?" the man asked him somewhat suspiciously.

"I'd been reading a detective story on the plane."

That was no lie. Madoc had picked one up in the terminal to while away the flight. He'd found it hilarious. "The mess could hardly be left there, you know, with half the concert still to play, but I thought somebody ought to do something."

"How come you didn't put up a howl when they wanted to move the body?" The cop was finding him mildly amusing, too.

Madoc decided to take the question seriously. "Because I knew it didn't matter. You see, Ochs didn't just drop down dead all of a sudden. He'd been sick for quite some time. My mother and I were sitting in the front row and we could see him getting greener and greener. I didn't think he was going to hold out till intermission. The chaps around him were worried, too, I could tell. They took him between them and got him off as soon as they possibly could. I doubt whether Ochs would have made it on his own."

"Yes, I know. I have their testimony. Well, thanks for the doggie bag, Mr. Rhys. What do you do in the orchestra?"

"Nothing at all. I hadn't even met any of them, till just now. I popped up this evening from Fredericton for a little visit with my parents, whom I hadn't seen for a while. I have to catch them as I can, they're on tour so much of the time."

"I can imagine. Must be hard on your mother."

"Oh no, she loves throwing her weight about. The conductor's wife is always the power behind the podium."

"That figures. Are you a musician yourself, Mr. Rhys?"

"Not me. I have a rather tedious job with the Canadian government," Madoc replied disingenuously.

He was on ticklish ground, all too aware of what his

standing in the family would be if he let drop so much as the mere breath of an inkling that he might possibly be here on police business himself. Wilhelm Ochs's death by gluttony was something this nice fellow would easily accept. Wilhelm Ochs's sudden demise coupled with whatever it was that had driven Sir Emlyn Rhys to send for his son the Mountie might be enough to bring the tour to a screeching halt right here and now. Just finding out who he was might get the local authorities wondering. If they decided to hold the orchestra members here, bang would go Madoc's new-found popularity in the family circle.

That consideration alone would not of course have had any weight in striking a balance between his professional and his filial obligations. However, Madoc honestly didn't see why he should break his father's heart on the off chance that Wilhelm Ochs might have succumbed to something other than his own greed. Sir Emlyn was the humblest of men but he did have one boast: in all his years of conducting, he'd never once failed to show up on time for a scheduled performance. Why should this be an exception?

The autopsy and his little paper cup, if the police bothered to have it analyzed, should settle the matter. If there had to be any further investigation, it would be undertaken by the right people, namely people other than Madoc Rhys. If any of the orchestra members were needed, they'd be available. Nobody in this crowd was going anywhere except to the Fraser River Music Festival, where they'd been booked for over a year in advance. If it was somebody from outside who'd put an end to Wilhelm's career before his lip muscles gave out, then it wouldn't matter where the musicians were anyway.

All very rational, but Madoc still felt guilty. Blast it, why couldn't his father have come straight out and said what the trouble was? There'd have been no chance to talk to him about it backstage, even if the cop hadn't been present. Sir Emlyn was short a French horn; that would be tragedy enough for the moment.

Madoc could hear the tentative squeaks and blats which meant the orchestra was tuning up. He headed back to his seat, got an icy glance from his mother, and spent the latter half of the concert wondering how he might decently and reasonably get hold of that autopsy report on Wilhelm Jan Ochs.

Most likely nobody would be doing anything about it tonight, anyway. Depending on how many cadavers the pathologist had lined up ahead of Ochs, results might not be available tomorrow, either. If nothing came through by tomorrow night, he'd get the efficient Lucy Shadd to give the coroner's office a buzz.

From Vancouver, that would be. Madoc hadn't expected to be traveling with the orchestra. What he'd envisioned was a reasonably amicable meal with his parents in a comfortable restaurant before the performance, a fast but thorough briefing on the trouble with the brasses, if in fact that was what Sir Emlyn had called him about, and maybe a day or so spent sniffing around asking guilefully stupid questions. By that time, he'd assumed, all would be clear. The miscreant or miscreants would have been turned over to Lady Rhys for excoriation and, if their offenses were heinous enough, excommunication; and he'd be on his way home to Janet.

He hadn't even got any dinner, only a little box of semi-edibles described as a snack and a cup of lukewarm coffee on the plane. Lunch had been another sandwich, eaten at his desk, and a mug of stewed tea. Damn it, he was hungry.

Madoc had never been much of a pouter even at four years old, but he felt as if he'd be quite justified in pouting now. This was no way for a mother to treat her son. When at last the concert had whooped its lengthy way to a raucous end and Sir Emlyn was letting the musicians and singers take far too many bows for his liking, Madoc murmured to his mother under cover of the applause, "Can we collect Tad now and get supper somewhere? I'm starved."

His mother gave him yet another look. "Didn't they

give you something on the plane, for goodness' sake?"

"Something, yes. Goodness had nothing to do with it."

"Then why on earth didn't you stop for a bite at the airport?"

"Because I was running late and I didn't want to be any later. I was under the apparent misapprehension that Tad wanted rather urgently to see me."

"Of course he does, dear. Tad always wants to see you. I'm afraid we can't do much about food just now, but don't fret. Lucy will have sandwiches and things laid on once we get on the plane."

"Mother, you don't mean we're going straight from here? When are we supposed to leave?"

"As soon as we're ready is the best I can tell you. It's a private plane we've been lent, so they can't very well start off without us. I'll tell you what, dear, why don't you sit down with your father after he's finished changing and share his Ovaltine and biscuits? That will tide you over and give you two a chance for a nice, quiet little talk while the rest of us are out here slaving our heads off. You'd be no earthly use with the packing anyway. Come along."

Ovaltine and biscuits. Madoc should have remembered that on the days when Sir Emlyn was going to conduct an evening performance, he always ate a hearty breakfast and a generous luncheon, but no dinner because he got too strung up to digest. Mother would have treated herself to high tea at the hotel while Tad was having his rest, no doubt, and still be nicely replete with scones and lemon curd tarts. As usual, Madoc was stepping to the music of a different drummer. Suppressing a sigh that wouldn't have done him any good, he followed his mother's triumphal march backstage.

Here a kind of orderly pandemonium prevailed. Musicians were either packing their own instruments into the individual cases they themselves would carry or else reluctantly consigning them to heavily padded trunks that had foam nests to fit them into, especially the big, awkward ones like the cellos and double basses. These trunks,

Madoc gathered, were to be shipped by train in a specially air-conditioned car. So were most of the musicians and all of the chorus; a van and a couple of buses were already waiting outside to carry them to the station. The director of operations was running at full steam, making sure the instruments were being properly stowed, that everybody's luggage was accounted for, that nobody who was supposed to be bussed to the train would lag behind, and that those who were supposed to fly didn't get on the wrong bus by mistake.

Who went how, Madoc figured out after a while, was partly a matter of protocol and partly a question of time. Certain members of the troupe would be needed at the festival earlier than the rest: some to rehearse, some to arrange the amazingly complex details of getting everybody housed and fed and the concerts into rehearsal. Some of the principal players and all four of the vocal soloists would be on the plane with the Rhyses.

Not knowing what else to do, he concentrated on staying out from under everybody's feet until his mother gave him clearance to enter the conductor's inner sanctum. There sat his father alone at last, looking elderly and exhausted in the same tweed suit he'd worn for traveling since Madoc could remember. When he spied his son, he managed a smile.

"Ah, Madoc. Sit down, boy. Have a biscuit."

"Thanks, Tad. When did you start hitting the Ovaltine? Didn't it use to be hot milk and brandy?"

"Your mother decided brandy kept me awake." Sir Emlyn reached for the shabby leather briefcase that held his scores, pulled out a flat bottle, and poured a reasonable tot into each of the two plastic mugs that were sitting on the table next to the thermos. "Ovaltine's not bad, but I still find I like it better if my tongue's a bit numb. I'm glad to see you, Madoc."

"Sorry I couldn't make it sooner." The brandy was numbing his tongue just fine.

"And how is our sweet Jenny? She's not offended because I didn't invite her along?"

"Not at all. She has Annabelle staying at the house, so she couldn't have come anyway."

Sir Emlyn nodded. He was beginning to unwind a bit. Madoc didn't try to hurry him along. Whatever Tad wanted to say, it would come when he got ready.

It came. "This is a bad, bad business, Madoc." Sir Emlyn was pouring the hot Ovaltine as he spoke, being careful not to spill the tiniest drop. "What do you think about Wilhelm Ochs?"

"I'm trying not to think anything until we get the autopsy report, Tad. It sounds like a perforated ulcer. Ochs had a terrible medical record, I understand."

His father sighed. "They all have terrible medical records, or think they do. If they're not sick, they're complaining. If they are sick, they won't let you know it because they're afraid you might be glad of an excuse not to have them around. Ochs was all right at rehearsal this morning and he was all right when he got here this evening. I know because he was moaning to me about how rotten he felt."

"Maybe the chap was telling the truth for once. He could have eaten something at supper that disagreed with him."

"He wouldn't have eaten much since his lunch, I shouldn't have thought. Might affect the wind, you know. They were planning to eat a late supper on the train. Mrs. Shadd arranged for the dining car to be kept open."

"Is she the one they call Lucy?"

"Our director of operations, yes. A very efficient woman. She used to be a horn player herself, your mother tells me. Come to think of it, Ochs wasn't going by train, he'd have been on the plane with us. I wish we were going by train, too. It's the only civilized way to travel, in my opinion."

Sir Emlyn finished his Ovaltine with the determination of one getting a duty over with, and took a ginger biscuit to reward himself for the effort. "Now then, Madoc, I suppose you'd like to know why I asked you to come."

"It might be helpful," Madoc conceded.

"It wasn't about Wilhelm Ochs's death, of course. I wasn't expecting that." Sir Emlyn took another biscuit. "But I have to admit I was expecting something. I don't think of myself as a fanciful man, Madoc, but there has been an atmosphere around this place."

He ate his biscuit, then nodded as if he'd reconsidered the word and decided it was the right one, after all. "Yes, an atmosphere. Look you, son, there is nothing strange about musicians clowning around a bit. Ours is a stressful and taxing profession; a few laughs can help to break the tension. Some of the jokes may not be in the best of taste, I have to admit."

The conductor smiled wryly. "In fact, most of them aren't. The brasses are the worst, as a rule. Chaps who make their careers out of blowing high-toned farts, as Ochs himself far too often called them, have a natural affinity for bathroom humor. One understands and makes allowances."

"Even Mother?"

"Your mother has great skill at not noticing what it's wiser to ignore. So have I, but one can't keep on walking around with one's head in a bag forever. There has been unpleasantness, Madoc."

Chapter 3

This, for Sir Emlyn, was a remarkably strong statement. Madoc decided he'd better tell his father about the trombonist with the fishline on his slide. Sir Emlyn thought it unfunny, also.

"Cedric Rintoul is a fine trombonist, but I know nothing to recommend him as a human being. To torture poor little Loye, who's a bundle of nerves at the best of times, was the act of a wretch. Do you know that plucky woman never missed a note or wobbled off pitch through the entire concert? She'll have screaming nightmares tonight from the strain, no doubt, and keep the whole train awake. It's happened at the hotel twice already."

Madoc shook his head. "I don't think Mrs. Loye is going on the train. She wasn't lined up for the bus with the others, and I'm quite sure I heard Mrs. Shadd say something to her about the plane."

"Ach, then she'll keep us awake instead." Sir Emlyn shoved the last of the biscuits toward his son. "At least your mother will be on hand to soothe her down. Loye's fits are one thing even Mrs. Shadd can't cope with. I only wish Rintoul weren't flying with us, too. I'm surprised your mother let this happen."

"Maybe she thought she'd better have them both where she can keep an eye on them," said Madoc. "What else has been going on, Tad?"

"A great deal that I don't know about, I expect. There's been, as I said, an atmosphere. Ill-will. Fighting. Not among the singers, they wouldn't strain their throats screaming at each other. Anyway, singers are too involved with their own larynxes to think much about what goes on around them. It's the orchestra. By fighting I don't mean fisticuffs, look you, but insults and arguments much worse than the usual more or less amiable teasing and bickering that one always hears among musicians. Ochs was one of the worst. When I first took over the orchestra he was a good-natured clod, gross in his habits and worse in his language, but not a troublemaker like Rintoul. For the past week or so, Ochs had turned into a real curmudgeon, snapping and snarling and accusing his colleagues of dreadful deeds."

"With any justification?"

"Yes, unfortunately. For one thing, his horn was switched."

Sir Emlyn leaned across the table. "Now mind you, son, this may not sound all that serious to you, but you must realize a musician's instrument is virtually a part of himself; not only his means of livelihood but his treasure, his beloved, his constant companion. Unless he plays the harp or the piano, of course."

It wasn't much of a joke, but Madoc did the best he could with it and his father plucked up the spirit to go on.

"Anyway, there we were, ready to go onstage. Ochs opens his case and begins to yell. 'Where's my instrument?' he's yelling. 'Who's got my so-and-so instrument?' His language was awful, I tell you. We had a terrible time shutting him up."

"There's no chance he made a mistake?"

"Madoc, would you mistake another woman for your wife? Of course the horn in the case was not his. We found out later that it belonged to a student who'd been rehearsing with the Youth Symphony. The kid had gone off with Ochs's horn in all innocence and brought it back as soon as she realized there'd been a switch. Ochs insisted she'd taken his horn on purpose and there was a hell of a scene, even though anyone with half an eye could see the poor child was simply the victim of a tamned tirty trick."

Sir Emlyn's Welsh accent had never altogether deserted him, and tended to get a bit out of hand in his rare moments of extreme agitation. "And that wass not the worst," he went on, abandoning all efforts to keep his consonants under control. "You would not know this, but brass players have to keep putting stuff on their lips. The pressure of the mouthpiece irritates the skin. They all have their favorite ointments, like the singers with their throat sprays and cough lozenges, bless them. Ochs swore by a certain patent remedy which is normally applied to a different part of the person and ideally adapted to the sort of coarse japery which is so popular among the brasses."

He coughed delicately. "Anyway, somebody got a tube of the stuff and injected it with red pepper juice or some tamned thing, and sneaked it into Ochs's pocket. The next time Ochs salved his lips, he almost went crazy from the smarting. The stuff raised such blisters that he had to play the Saturday concert with a cotton wool mustache stuck to his upper lip. Now, was that a decent thing to do to a man who was already beginning to have trouble with his embouchure? And of course that ass Rintoul had to keep riding Ochs about how lucky he was that he hadn't used the salve on the end it was intended for. Madoc, tell me the truth. Do you think Ochs's death could have been due to some other beastly joke?"

"Anything that beastly would hardly count as a joke, Tad. Do you have any idea who doctored the pile medicine?"

"Well, naturally, I thought of Rintoul because he's such a nasty rogue and your mother doesn't like him either, but I couldn't very well go accusing him without evidence, could I? He'd be just the kind to raise a big stink with the Musicians' Union, and I don't have to tell you how the director and the trustees would feel about that kind of trouble. Besides, I may be wrong. Rintoul himself found his mouthpiece stuffed with garlic the other day. Not that it wasn't poetic justice. He always has a breath on him that would make a horse gag and God help the poor wretch who sits close to him. I'll have to move Loye; she's suffered enough. And people think all a conductor has to do is stand up there and wave a little stick!"

He wrestled with his feelings a moment, then made his final plea. "Madoc, I've always thought I was a reasonably adequate disciplinarian. I've never had much trouble with an orchestra before, but this is beyond me. Even the orchestra manager has ratted on me. She's supposed to have come down with some particularly horrid sort of flu, but I think it's plain funk. She'd been looking pretty grim lately. So Lucy Shadd's been trying to cope single-handed. Your mother's helping all she can, but I'm stuck with the lot of them until after the festival. I simply don't know what to do, Madoc. That's why I sent for you, and that's why I didn't want Jenny here. I'd send your mother away if I thought she'd go, and that's the first time in our married life I've wished my Sillie were somewhere I was not. You can see the state I'm in, son. Can you possibly help me out of this?"

"What you're asking is pretty much what I do for a living, Tad. I shouldn't think we'd have too much trouble pinning down the joker, or jokers. It's pretty well got to be one or more persons connected with the orchestra in one capacity or another, and it doesn't look as if there's any particularly subtle mind at work. Tell me more about the dirty tricks."

What Sir Emlyn had to tell certainly was unsubtle. The so-called practical jokes had been mostly of the sorts that disgust rather than amuse. The string section hadn't been bothered a great deal; the woodwinds had suffered minor harassments. It was the brasses who'd taken the brunt; the flutes, neither brass nor wind, had got it, too. Frieda Loye, like Wilhelm Ochs, had been a particular target.

"Loye asks for it, I suppose." Sir Emlyn sighed. "She's such a stoic while she's being teased, then she has those screaming fits later on. I blame myself very much for having put the poor woman in front of Rintoul tonight. I'd thought she'd be safe enough right under my nose. Fishline on his slide had simply not occurred to me."

"It wouldn't have occurred to me, either, Tad. I'm sure you had far more than Frieda Loye's nerves to think about. Not to worry you further, but what will you do for another French horn?"

"That's the least of my problems. There'll be musicians enough around at the festival; we'll be able to pick someone up. Well, son, I expect your mother will be looking for us. You brought some extra clothes with you, I hope?"

"Yes, Jenny packed me a bag. Which reminds me, I want to give her a ring before we go. Is there a telephone I can use?"

"Oh, we conductors are lords of the earth. They give us everything but peace of mind. Right over there in the corner, *bach*. I'll leave you to it, shall I?"

"No, stick around and say hello. Jenny'd rather talk to you than me any time."

"You wouldn't be trying to make me feel better?"

Madoc was trying, and he was succeeding. He was only a little bit reluctant to turn the telephone over to his father once he'd got through explaining to his wife why she'd better not expect him for a few days. Then his father took over, then Annabelle got on the extension phone, then Lady Rhys came in to see what was keeping her menfolk, and they had a jolly interfamily round robin. Madoc had no idea who was going to get stuck with paying for this lengthy call and he didn't much care. Sir Emlyn was looking a great deal less frazzled by the time they rang off; that was surely worth a few dollars of the orchestra's expense money.

"And now," said Lady Rhys, "we really must get cracking. Lucy wants us all aboard the bus to the airport. We've already kept her waiting, I'm afraid, but it was worth it. Your Jenny is such an absolute love, Madoc! If only Dafydd could find himself another one like her."

Another woman like the former Janet Wadman, assuming there ever could be one, would have more sense than to get herself tangled up with Dafydd, Madoc thought. However, he wasn't going to jeopardize his recent promotion to fair-haired boy by saying so. He went to pick up his unpretentious suitcase, discovered Mrs. Shadd had already organized a flunky to carry it out for him, and reconciled himself with no great difficulty to acting the undistinguished son of a V.I.P.

There were fewer than twenty of them on the bus. Madoc didn't know who they all were but he couldn't see where there'd be much chance for getting in any detection here, so he settled himself for a brief nap. Early in his career, he'd learned the invaluable knack of grabbing a few winks when an opportunity presented itself. Hence he was among the most alert members of the party when they boarded the aircraft.

This was not a big plane, there were barely enough seats for their party; but it was a customized Grumman, lent for the occasion by a very rich patron of the orchestra. The regular passengers' seats were comfortably padded armchairs, one on each side of the aisle. The four chairs in the tiny forward cabin were real lounge chairs on swivel bases, with headrests that popped up and footrests that popped out when the sitter leaned back. He and his parents got three of these, naturally.

The fourth went to the concertmaster, an incredibly distinguished-looking Frenchman of fifty or so with one dramatic white streak in his black hair. Monsieur Houdon made one or two agreeable remarks to the Rhyses, then settled down with the score of a Beethoven violin concerto of which he'd be playing the solo parts during the upcoming festival. From then on, he rehearsed his music on an imaginary instrument, no doubt with surpassing skill, all the time he wasn't stopping to eat or drink.

Madoc had at first thought Lucy Shadd might be planning to take that seat for herself, but it didn't look as though the director of operations intended to do any sitting whatever. They were hardly airborne before she was around with a tray of champagne in plastic goblets. This was a gift from another generous patron, she informed everybody up and down the aisle. Then she served out assorted sandwiches, then coffee with or without caffeine as desired, then little pastries and cakes, then fruit and cheese, then liqueurs. Finally she came again with a vast box of incredibly expensive chocolates, still another gift from yet a different patron whose name Madoc didn't bother to catch since none of the chocolates appeared to be stuffed with arsenic. After the chocolates, she distributed damp, hot finger towels and blankets and pillows to all who wanted them. At long last, she sat down in the front seat of the rear section and put her feet up.

They were taking a more northerly route than had been planned. This, the co-pilot had explained over the public address system somewhere between the champagne and the pastries, was on account of some turbulence that had unexpectedly manifested itself to the south of them. Their plane, though a good plane and a safe plane, was not a new plane, a large plane, or a powerful enough plane to climb above the weather. It wasn't a fast plane, either, as planes went these days. They still had a few hours' flying time, and the altered route would delay them still further.

Madoc didn't care. The chair was comfortable, the food had been more than ample, the passengers behind him had either quieted down or couldn't be heard above the roar of the engines. His mother and father, experienced troupers that they were, had already nodded off with their heads on their headrests and their shoeless feet on their footrests. He was thinking seriously of following their excellent example when he became aware that the turbulence was no longer to the south of them.

The co-pilot came on again. "Sorry folks, we thought we'd be able to give you a smooth ride by changing course, but it looks as if the storm's caught up with us. We may be experiencing some real roughness for a little while."

He was absolutely right. The roughness they were experiencing was like no tossing around any of them had been through before. The co-pilot was still jovial. "Hope you've all got your seat belts securely fastened, folks. Better return your seats to the upright position and make sure your tray tables are put away and locked. We'll be out of this in a—"

The plane dropped what felt like a thousand feet straight down, and then began to buck. Madoc could feel the belt cutting into his stomach as his body was hurled clear of the seat. It was like being inside a crazy-mad brahma bull. He could hear the engines straining for altitude. They were going up, higher, higher—now they were dropping, hitting, lurching like a car in a skid on the side of a cliff. The lights went out. The engines cut off. The co-pilot said, quite clearly in the sudden stillness, "Jesus!"

"Everybody fasten your seat belts, quick. Put your head on your knees and your arms around your head. Sorry, but I guess we're going down."

Madoc couldn't see his parents, but he knew they'd be hunched over as bidden; Tad in his shabby tweeds, Mum still in her black satin and diamonds because she'd been too busy to change before the luggage was sent off. They'd have their arms around each other, he thought. He smiled over at them through the blackness, tucked down his head, sent a great wave of love to Janet, and waited.

They landed quite gently, all things considered. It was still pitch dark, and a few people were screaming. Madoc pulled out his little pocket flashlight and flicked it on.

His parents were all right, blinking at him and trying to smile, still with their arms entwined. Jacques-Marie Houdon sat up, nodded, and played something on his imaginary violin. Mrs. Shadd looked not only terrified but outraged that her schedule had been disrupted. Madoc got rather shakily to his feet and walked the few steps to the cockpit. The pilot and co-pilot were sitting there like a pair of statues, both of them stark white in the faces, both of them with their eyes wide open, staring straight ahead. Madoc was the one who managed to speak.

"Nice job, you two. My father has some brandy in his briefcase."

That joggled them back to life. They all three started to laugh. It was the funniest thing that had ever happened. The pilot reached down beside him and picked up an emergency lantern. The co-pilot lifted a sliding door on the wall and hauled out half a dozen ordinary flashlights. Still giggling, Madoc took five of the flashlights along with his own, switched on a couple, and went back into the cabin.

"Here, Tad, have a light. Could you spare a little of your brandy for the pilots?"

"Give me that torch. I'll take it to them. There's plenty of brandy." Now that she had something to do, Lucy Shadd was calm enough. She unscrambled herself from her seat belt and began to bustle.

"Just as well." Sir Emlyn was smiling his gentle, familiar smile. "I was planning to finish off that brandy myself. Straight from the bottle. Eh Sillie? Care to join me?"

"Oh, you dreadful man!" Lady Rhys was laughing, adoring.

Madoc went along into the main cabin. "All right, folks, it's safe to come up. We're on the ground. I don't know where and we don't seem to have any electricity, but we're all in one piece, aren't we?"

"You mean we don't get to play 'Nearer My God To Thee'?" That was, oddly enough, Frieda Loye, looking quite cocky and pleased with her own joke, such as it was. So was everybody else. Laugh and the world laughs with you, Madoc thought. Thank God there'd be no weeping alone this time around. They were all climbing up from between the seats, checking their instruments, counting their fingers. First things first.

Lady Rhys was out in the aisle now, helping Lucy Shadd carry around the drinks. Sir Emlyn was sitting quietly in his armchair, leafing through his scores and sipping at his brandy. Madoc distributed the rest of the flashlights at strategic points and went forward again to the cockpit.

"Any idea where we are, gentlemen?"

"If you're looking for a simple yes or no, the answer's no," said the pilot. "I don't know what the Christ we ran into, but it tossed us clear to hell and gone and knocked out our whole damned electrical system. I suppose that's why the engines quit. Unless they fell off, which is also possible. The radio's not working, nothing's working up here except my wristwatch, and that's probably wrong because I don't know which time zone we're in. We'd been flying on instruments through solid overcast for quite a while, which you probably didn't realize."

"My God! How did you find the ground?"

"I think it must have been angels," the pilot replied in all seriousness. "When the engines cut out and the lights went off, the clouds broke and the moon came out just long enough for me to spot a smooth open strip. We'd dropped out of the turbulence into a nice, steady tailwind, so we just glided in. Angels are the only reasonable explanation."

He was probably right, Madoc thought. "Why don't we open the door and see if they're still around?"

"Great idea. God, I'm wobbly."

"I'll get the door, Mac," said the co-pilot. "You brought us down. Here, drink the rest of this brandy."

Together, he and Madoc got the cockpit door open and the steps lowered. It was cold, almost bitter. That tailwind was really going after the clouds now. The moon wasn't at the full, but it was casting enough light to show them a landscape straight out of a Lex Laramie novel. Behind the aircraft was only open plain; in front were the Deadeye Saloon and the Miners' Rest Hotel, both of them shut tighter than a drugstore cowboy's Levis.

The co-pilot snorted. "Boy, our luck's really holding. We've hit a ghost town. This place is dead as a doornail."

"It's dead all right," Madoc agreed, "but I'm not sure it's a genuine ghost town. Looks a bit slick for that, wouldn't you say?"

"Hell, yes, now that you mention it. This is probably just a movie set, a lot of false fronts with nothing behind 'em. The Hollywood guys are doing a lot of their filming in Canada nowadays, you know. Come on, we might as well know the worst."

"Perhaps we'd better put on our jackets first, and close the plane door," Madoc suggested. "The cabin will cool down fast enough without our wasting what heat there is."

And the plane might be the only shelter they'd have for who knew how long a time? Madoc wished the co-pilot hadn't mentioned a movie set. As they got closer, that was exactly what the place suggested.

Chapter 4

But that wasn't what it turned out to be. The fronts were in
fact falsely mock-pretentious, but the modest frame build-
ings behind them were solid enough. There weren't many:
the hotel, the saloon, which was probably a restaurant also;
a somewhat anachronistic nickelodeon which had posters
of old Tim Holt and Tom Mix Western movies out front; a
few tightly shuttered gift and clothing shops; a general
store; a so-called museum with a badly carved life-sized
wooden mule tied to a hitching post out front. There was
the sheriff's office, of course, with a big gold star painted
on the door; the barbershop with its striped pole and a sign
in the window reading SHAVE AND HAIRCUT 2 BITS. TEETH
PULLED 25¢ EXTRA.

"No sign of a watchman around," Madoc remarked.

"Who the hell would be willing to stay?" grunted the
co-pilot. "I have a hunch I know where we are. Somebody
was telling me about a speculator who'd reopened one of
the abandoned mining towns as a tourist trap. Somewhere
up toward Dawson Creek I think he said. I'm not sure
whether it was on the Alberta or the British Columbia side,
but I'll bet you a nickel this is it. They only open the place
up about three months a year, I believe. Nobody'd come
anyway, once the snows begin. We must have been blown
a hell of a lot farther north than I thought we were. Now
what do we do?"

"Burglarize, I think," said Madoc. "The hotel would be our best bet. They probably have a dynamo and some kind of battery-operated teleradio affair, shouldn't you think? Not to mention a stove and possibly some food. Are there any tools in the plane? They've got deadbolts on the doors, but we could probably jimmy a shutter off one of the ground-floor windows if we had something to pry with."

"No problem. I'd better tell the passengers to stay put till we know where we stand here, hadn't I? I must say I'm surprised they haven't all come piling off the plane already."

"The singers and the winds are worried about the night air on their throats," Madoc explained, "and the rest have probably gone back to sleep. Go ahead and talk to them. I'll poke around for a likely place to break in. By the way, what's your name?"

"Ed Naxton. My partner's Steve MacVittie. And you're Sir something-or-other, like your dad, I suppose. Sorry, I'm not up on that nobility stuff."

"I'm not so hot on it, either. Anyway, my father's only a knight. You have to be a baron or better to count as a peer. Call me Madoc, why don't you?"

"Sure, Madoc, long as it doesn't get me slapped in the family dungeon. I'll be right back. God, I hope there's a stove in that dump."

It was cold here, really cold. Perhaps Ed was minding it more because the plane had been kept so hot for the benefit of the various hypochondriacs on board. Madoc himself was feeling the chill. He'd only brought a mackintosh to wear over his suit; he'd thought it would be plenty when he left home. Now he wondered whether Janet had thought to pack him a pullover.

He also wondered whether Ed and Mac would be able to open the Grumman's luggage compartment if the passengers were going to be on the ground for any length of time. But mostly he wondered how they were going to get into the hotel. The answer seemed to lie in a somewhat wobbly shutter on the side of the building next to the Deadeye Saloon.

By the time Ed showed up with some airgoing equivalent of a wrecking bar, Madoc had managed to joggle a few screws loose enough from the dried-out wood of the window frame to slide the bar underneath. After that, it was a piece of cake. Ed, being much the larger, boosted Madoc through the window they hadn't even had to smash, and handed him the flashlight they'd been sharing. Madoc flickered his way through a dusty hallway that was cold as banished hope into an even colder expanse that must be the lobby. He found the front door and released an assortment of bolts and bars in order to let in Ed and a little more cold.

"Now to find that radio, eh? It ought to be here behind the desk, shouldn't you think?"

"Nope," said Ed. "It'll be through that door marked NO ADMITTANCE so's the tourists' kids can't monkey with it."

Ed would be right, of course. Madoc decided he himself must be even more tired than he'd thought he was. At least his skill at housebreaking hadn't yet deserted him. The door was locked, but the lock wasn't much. There was, as expected, a radio, a highly modern and sophisticated affair totally out of keeping with the Wild West decor. Its batteries were dead. There was no way to recharge them, and no spares were to be found.

They did manage to locate a flossy black iron parlor stove with a lot of curlicues on top, though. It was sitting smack in the middle of the lobby, with a heap of ready-cut stove wood beside it.

"Wouldn't hurt to get a fire going," Ed grunted. "Some of 'em are acting pretty restless back there."

"I don't suppose there's any hope of your getting the plane's radio fixed any time soon, is there?" Madoc asked.

"We won't be able to find out what went wrong with the electrical system till we get enough daylight to see by. As to whether we'd be able to fix it, that's another question. Maybe we'd better just figure on camping here for the time being, don't you think?"

After a trial run with a few wadded-up newspapers and a handful of kindling to make sure the chimney hadn't been blocked up for the winter, they managed to get the stove throwing out some heat, and none too soon. Lady Rhys led the pack.

"Ah, good!" She set down the overnight case she was carrying and rubbed her hands together in the glow from the isinglass-paned door. "At least it's one step in the right direction. Where's the kettle, Madoc?"

"One might also ask where's the water, Mother. I'll go see what I can drum up."

"I'll come with you." The director of operations left the doorway, where she'd been shepherding in the stragglers off the plane, and darted to Madoc's side before Lady Rhys could get there. "Men can never find anything. Which way is the kitchen?"

How was he supposed to know? Madoc was beginning to feel that it might be possible to work up a fairly vigorous dislike for Lucy Shadd, but of course he owed it to his father's position not to show any such ungallant sentiment. "Back here, I should think," he answered mildly, wondering just how either of these efficient women thought it would be possible to balance a pot of water on top of all these wrought-iron exuberances.

He led the way to the kitchen unerringly, since there were so few places it could have been anyway. The room looked to be fairly well equipped with kettles and pots of various kinds. There were plenty of plates and mugs, and a supply closet stocked with various dried and canned foods, along with canisters of tea, sugar, salt, and other staples. Water was a different matter. Lucy Shadd was at the sink, turning the taps without any luck.

"What's the matter with these things? I can't get the water to come out."

"No, it will have been shut off before the owners left," he managed to explain without laughing in her face. "That is common procedure when a place is closed up for the winter. Water left in the pipes would cause them to freeze up and burst."

"Well, how was I supposed to know? I'm not a plumber. Do you have to just stand there gaping? Turn it back on, can't you?"

"I don't know whether I can or not. I expect this place has a drilled well. That means the water has to be pumped up by means of a generator. I don't know where the generator is. I will find it and get it working if I can. I would say it is unlikely anybody in your party will have died of thirst before somebody finds us. It is, however, quite probable that some of your charges would appreciate having beds to lie down on. Since you feel obliged to make yourself useful, why don't you go and check the bedrooms? You will no doubt find them upstairs. The stairs are to your right as you face the desk in the lobby, in case you were about to ask."

"Thank you."

Lucy Shadd didn't flounce away, she simply went. Madoc was sorry he'd been rude, but not sorry enough to call her back. He found the generator in a shed behind the kitchen. It was supposed to run on propane gas. There were no propane tanks to be found. He went back to the sink, investigated an antique hand pump that he'd thought was intended as a part of the atmosphere, and found after some experimental fiddling that it worked just fine. He filled a large tea kettle and carried it into the lobby all by himself without help from anybody.

"Here's your water, Mother."

"Thank you, Madoc."

Lady Rhys picked up a square pad of folded canvas that had been left sitting on top of the woodpile and used it to grasp the curlicues. The ornaments came off in one piece, leaving a neat round hole just big enough for the kettle in the top of the stove.

"Set it right here, dear. Did you find any cups and saucers?"

"Plenty of mugs. And tea, sugar, and dried milk. I'll bring some, shall I?"

"I'll help." Astonishingly that was Sir Emlyn's soprano soloist, Delicia Fawn. Madoc couldn't think why some of the male musicians snickered, until he got to the kitchen. Delicia was not a shy woman.

"What do you say, dark and delicious? Care to try out for the semifinals?"

Madoc knew that singers did breathing exercises, and that deep breathing tended to stimulate pectoral development, but did all sopranos breathe as deeply as this one? It was disconcerting, feeling those twin thumps on his waistcoat every time she inhaled. He said, "Semifinals for what?" and knew right away that he'd made a potentially serious mistake.

"Look, sweetie," she drawled, running her fingers through his hair without being invited, "you can't tell a musician by the size of his piccolo, can you? Before I make any decision about who's going to play my organ for the rest of the tour, I hold auditions, that's all. Saves a lot of fuss and bother, eh. Drop by my room in a while, assuming I get one."

"Yours will be the one with the queue outside the door, I assume. And I'll be the chap who's not standing in it. Thank you for your flattering offer, Miss Fawn, but my parents are fond of my wife, and so am I. Besides, I'm not staying with the tour once we get to Vancouver," he hoped, "and you'd only have to run the auditions over again after I left. Here, take the teapot and canister to my mother, will you? I'll bring the mugs."

Of whom he'd passed up the chance to become one. So this was why his mother wouldn't let her husband travel alone. Unchaperoned, poor old Tad would have been torn apart by some sex-starved maenad long ago. Here was a side of his parents' life that he'd never imagined to exist, much less thought to be experiencing. He picked up a trayful of thick white mugs with "Thar's gold in them thar hills" painted on the sides, and carried them back to the lobby in a state of considerable bemusement.

These people didn't really need tea, Madoc thought. They'd been stuffing on one thing and another since they left Wagstaffe. What he supposed his mother thought they did need was the feeling of having found a safe shelter that the homely hot drink would help to create. Considering the circumstances that had got them here, she was probably right.

It was interesting to see his mother being Mum to a planeload of musicians. However, Madoc didn't feel he had time to stand around admiring the gracious manner in which Lady Rhys was dispensing the mug that cheered but did not inebriate, to the possible regret of Cedric Rintoul and a few more like him. There were oil lamps in the kitchen; a few of them had better be got going before somebody broke a leg rushing up those stairs to where the line would hypothetically be forming.

Madoc supposed he ought to find out how Miss Efficiency was making out with the beds, too; nobody else was showing any inclination to be useful. Delicia Fawn, having done her bit with the sugar bowl, had got herself a mug of tea and was snuggling up to the stove. Warming up for the main event, no doubt. Madoc went back to the kitchen and started filling lamps.

Once he'd set a lighted lamp on the desk and another one on the landing to illuminate the stairway, the dingy lobby began to look almost cheery. Madoc carried a couple more to the second floor and set one of them on a bracket in the upstairs hallway that had most likely been installed for that very purpose. Then, still carrying the other lamp, he followed the gleam of the battery lantern Lucy Shadd had commandeered to a linen closet where she was snatching blankets and pillows off the shelves with the concentrated zeal of a deacon counting the Sunday morning collection.

"We have water from the hand pump in the kitchen sink," he informed her, "and oil lamps with which we'll have to be careful. There are candles also, but I don't think

we ought to risk them. It will not have escaped your notice
that this place is a firetrap."

"What happened to the electric generator?" was all the
thanks he got, and that in no dulcet tone.

"Nothing to run it on."

"Rats! Well, I suppose it's not your fault," the woman
admitted grudgingly. "It's just so cursed maddening, when
I'd thought I had everything going like clockwork. What's
happening down in the lobby?"

"My mother is giving them tea. How many bedrooms
do we have?"

"Only ten. People will have to double up. I suppose
they'll start yelling about the lack of privacy. And what in
God's name are we going to do about the bathrooms, with
no running water?"

"Walk, I suppose. Since this place appears to go in for
authenticity, maybe they haven't torn down the old privy
yet."

"But the singers can't go trailing out back in the cold!
Think of their throats."

Madoc was damned if he'd think of the singers' throats.
"What about chamber pots? Surely there must be some
around here. I expect they use them for soup tureens," he
added helpfully.

That actually got a laugh out of Lucy. "I shouldn't be a
bit surprised," she agreed. "Come on, let's look in the bedrooms. Here, give me that lamp. You take the blankets. I
hadn't bargained for being a chambermaid on top of everything else, I must say."

"Can't you ask some of the others to help you?"

"And have the Musicians' Union down on my neck?
That's not the way things are done in this crowd."

"Then don't ask. Just leave the bedding in the rooms
and let them cope or not as they see fit."

"You are naive, aren't you? However, I suppose it's
worth a try."

She darted in and out of the rooms, Madoc at her heels
dispensing blankets as directed. The rooms were pretty

much as he'd thought they'd be; little boxes with roughly plastered walls and softwood floors studded with the dents of many boot heels. The furnishings were rag rugs, mismatched iron beds with old-fashioned coil springs and nice new foam mattresses wrapped in plastic against the possible forays of wintering rodents, rickety chests and washstands in that cheap yellowish wood that ages so ungracefully. There were chipped enamel pitchers and basins on the stands and, yes, enamel pots under the beds.

"Let's hear it for authenticity," said Lucy with a wry sort of gratitude. "Now how the bloody hell do we heat water enough for everybody to wash in?"

"We don't," said Madoc. "Those who are willing to settle for cold water can bring their pitchers downstairs and fill them at the pump. Those who aren't can damned well stay dirty. We'll manage something in the morning, if we're still here."

"It's already morning. My watch says half past three, for whatever that may be worth. I suppose I'd better go down and talk to them. Are there lamps enough to go around?"

"No, but if it's that late they won't be needing any in another hour or so. Come on, then."

In the lobby, Lady Rhys was collecting mugs. Most of the others were sitting around looking glum, a few were nodding off in the not very comfortable wooden chairs. Lucy stood on the second step from the bottom, holding her lamp like Florence Nightingale.

"There are beds upstairs for any of you who want to lie down. They're not made up, but I've managed to find blankets and pillows. Most of us will have to double up, so please take the roommate you had in Atlanta. Whoever that might have been," Lucy added with the merest hint of a glance at Delicia Fawn.

"It's not too awfully cold up there; the stove's beginning to take the chill off and it will be kept going. Unfortunately the generator doesn't work, so there's no running water in the bathrooms. If you want cold water to wash with, Mr.

Rhys tells me you can get some from a pump in the kitchen. He'll help you work it. The rooms do have rudimentary facilities, and I'm afraid we'll just have to make the best of them for this once. If you'd rather stay down here by the stove, of course, feel free. I apologize for the inconvenience."

"Why should you?" Lady Rhys demanded. "It wasn't your fault. For goodness' sake, Lucy, go get some rest yourself. You must be worn to a frazzle."

"Thank you, Lady Rhys. I'll put a lamp in your room, and see about getting your bed made up."

"Nonsense, Madoc will do all that. Good night, Lucy."

Chapter 5

While doing his stint at the pump, Madoc at last got to sort out his fellow castaways. They'd seemed a crowd in the cramped lobby; in fact there weren't all that many. What they boiled down to were the three Rhyses, the four singers, the concertmaster (who was, as always, the principal violin), and seven of the other principals: viola, cello, flute, clarinet, oboe, trumpet, and trombone. Wilhelm Ochs would have been the eighth. The other principals had opted for the train, either because they detested flying or because they wanted to be near their cumbersome instruments even if they couldn't take them out of the trunks en route.

Lucy Shadd turned out to be the only one of the ten staff members traveling with them. The media director had gone on ahead some days ago, luckily for him. The orchestra manager, of course, had been forced by her malady to miss the flight. The luckless woman who bore the impressive title of assistant to the music director had been banished to the train because Sir Emlyn didn't much like having her follow him around telling him what to do. More importantly, neither did Lady Rhys.

The two pilots had been persuaded to leave their increasingly frigid aircraft by the warmth of the stove and Lady Rhys's persuasion, not to mention Delicia Fawn's. If in fact the soprano was their goal, though, they might be in for a bit of a letdown. Joe Ragovsky, the principal violist, had already confided to Madoc that he'd be well advised not to waste his time, as if he'd been going to anyway.

"As soon as you got inside the door, she'd hand you a surgical mask and a bottle of some god-awful-tasting antiseptic mouthwash. You'd have to gargle and put on the mask or nothing doing. Delicia comes on strong enough, but when push comes to shove, she thinks a damned sight more of her voice than she does of her men."

If any of these chaps still had enough stamina left for a sociable gargle after a night like this one, more power to them, Madoc thought as he waggled the pump handle up and down, up and down.

His first customer had been the contralto, a comfortably padded woman of forty or so with a spiritual expression, a heavy braid of dark brown hair, and the almost certainly adopted name of Norma Bellini. She hadn't spoken all evening, as far as he knew, except to say "Dank you" in a low, thrilling tone when he'd filled her pitcher. She'd had the air of somebody who just wanted to take out her hairpins, slip off her shoes, and lie down; and who could blame her?

The bass was Carlos Pitney. He'd be called a black man, Madoc supposed, though in fact he had nothing black about him except his well-polished shoes. His skin was the color of walnut, his hair a uniform steel-gray, his eyes a lighter shade of brown than Madoc's own. He was gravely courteous in his demeanor, stately in his address, and quite willing to pump for himself, though he couldn't get the knack of the quick little jerk at the top of the upswing which made all the difference between a gush and a hollow gurgle.

The tenor, on the other hand, made no effort to lift a finger but chatted pleasantly enough about what a pity it was that Madoc's brother Dafydd had not succeeded in attaining the pinnacle of excellence which he himself had mastered in some particular aspect of vocalization. As far as Madoc was concerned, the man might as well have been talking Choctaw.

He hadn't bothered to introduce himself, no doubt taking it for granted that Madoc would know the name of anyone famous enough to sing for Sir Emlyn. Madoc had found out easily enough from Delicia Fawn, who'd dropped by to get some gargling water and to find out whether Madoc might care to reconsider. The man was Ainsworth Kight, he was older than he looked, his impressive head of chestnut-colored hair was mostly toupee, and he'd never even made it to the semifinals. Ainsworth was as good a singer as he said he was, though, so none of the rest mattered.

The two brasses came together, one with the pitcher and one with a water pistol that needed filling. The obnoxious Cedric Rintoul did not become less so on closer acquaintance. The principal trumpeter, Jason Jasper, didn't impress Madoc all that favorably, either, even though he offered to show Madoc his impressive collection of whoopee cushions if they ever reconnected with the wardrobe trunks. Nothing was supposed to go into those trunks except the clothes worn for performances, but obviously a good many extraneous articles did, and some necessities didn't. Madoc remembered that onstage Jasper had been wearing black socks pulled over his tan shoes and a white tie deftly folded out of toilet paper. He hadn't been the only orchestra member in makeshift attire; Madoc had gathered they didn't do it to be funny.

Jacques-Marie Houdon, the concertmaster, had been impeccable onstage, and still was. He took his filled pitcher, nodded affably, and went away. Joe Ragovsky, the violist, a likeable chap from the wheatfields of Manitoba, offered to pump and succeeded. Joe even pumped for the cellist. This was Helene Dufresne, whom Lady Rhys had alluded to as a most agreeable woman even if she did walk bowlegged, as cello players tended to do. Tonight Miss Dufresne had on a voluminous gray wool dirndl and floppy leather boots, so Madoc couldn't tell much about her walk, but he assumed his mother was right. She generally was.

Frieda Loye, the flautist, gave Madoc a nervous little

smile and gasped, "Oh, that's enough. You mustn't bother about me," when her pitcher was less than halfway filled. The clarinetist, Corliss Blair, settled for a mug since she was to share Helene Dufresne's room and hence her pitcher. The oboist didn't come to be pumped, but Joe Ragovsky said his name was David Gabriel and they'd be bunking together.

Sir Emlyn and Lady Rhys would share a room, of course. The self-sacrificing Lucy Shadd was apparently going to take on Frieda Loye and her nightmares as part of the job. The two brass players would be together, as would the two male singers and the two pilots. Theoretically, that meant the concertmaster and Norma Bellini would have rooms to themselves, since it didn't seem likely that the contralto would care for a ménage à trois with Delicia Fawn and whoever might have won the toss tonight.

That would appear to take up the ten rooms, with none left over for Madoc Rhys. However, this would not be the case, according to the informative Mr. Ragovsky, since Monsieur Houdon would in fact be paying his respectful attentions to Madame Bellini although nobody was supposed to notice. The way things looked right now, there'd probably be at least one spare bed in the pilots' room, too.

While the rest got themselves sorted out upstairs, Madoc occupied himself building a fire in the big kitchen range, filling the hot-water reservoir on the back, and setting a copper washtub of water on top. That should be enough for the morning ablutions. He put more wood in the lobby stove, shut down the dampers, and went to seek what rest he might obtain.

By now, it was getting on toward five A.M., or not as the case might be. Four or three, maybe, according to how many time zones they'd been blown across. The Grumman most likely had not yet been reported overdue, its flying time was probably longer than a commercial plane's. The train wouldn't be due in for ages yet. There was nobody out here to report a downed aircraft without any lights; nobody would be looking for them.

Back in Fredericton, Janet and Annabelle would be thinking about getting up even though they didn't have to; they were both early risers by habit. They'd sit a long time over the breakfast table, planning their day, talking family, catching up on Pitcherville gossip, of which there was never any dearth. They'd go over again the details of the cozy chat they'd had last night with Madoc and his parents.

Madoc was humbly thankful his Jenny would have that to think about instead of a phone call from some reporter wanting to know the details of the crash and how it felt to be a widow. She'd feel a little bit let down if he didn't call her again tonight, but she wouldn't really start to worry for another day or so.

He found a room with sagging twin beds and nobody in either one of them, shed the three-piece tweed suit he'd been wearing to placate his mother, and wished he'd had the foresight to bring a separate overnight case as all the other passengers appeared to have done. He could borrow Tad's shaving things in the morning, and perhaps even a change of linen. Keeping his socks and underwear on, he wrapped himself in a couple of itchy blankets and stretched out on one of the beds. Luck was with him; he got almost a full hour's sleep before the screeching began.

"My God, what's that?"

The voice was not his own. In the grayness of almost-dawn, Madoc was interested to see that he'd acquired a roommate. MacVittie must have won the semifinals; Ed Naxton was in the other bed looking startled, as well he might. The noise was dreadful.

"As an educated guess, I'd say it's our flautist having her customary nightmare," Madoc explained. "My father told me Mrs. Loye puts on quite a turn when she gets going."

"I'll say she does. Sounds like a pig getting its throat cut."

With the speed of much practice, Madoc was already into shirt, coat, and trousers. "I'll go. My mother seems to have elected me general handyman."

Grateful that he'd opted to keep his socks on against the desperate chill of the mountain night, he slid his feet into his shoes and tied the laces. The lamp he'd brought to light the narrow upstairs hallway was still feebly aglow, doing its small best against the approaching daylight. Madoc knew just how it felt. Why couldn't the confounded woman have taken to insomnia instead of nightmares?

He was not the first on the scene. Lady Rhys had beaten him by a whisker, surprisingly colorful in a long robe of russet, green, and yellow velour. Madoc supposed she must sometimes get sick of all that black. She was standing over another twin bed like the one Madoc had just got out of, shaking a slender woman by the shoulders.

"Frieda, wake up and quit screaming. You sound like a runaway train. Sir Emlyn needs his sleep, you know."

"Mother," Madoc said gently, "that's not Frieda."

Lady Rhys groped among her gaudy swathings for the ever-present silver chain around her neck, found her Victorian silver lorgnette somewhere along the line, and flicked it open. "Why, so it isn't. Lucy, whatever is the matter with you?"

"I—he—water, please!" The voice was croaky and almost incoherent.

"Madoc, get her some water. He what, Lucy? Who did? Here, drink this." She held the thick mug Madoc had filled from the pitcher to the hysterical woman's lips. "Now then, what's this all about?"

"My throat. He—"

Lucy Shadd wasn't shrieking anymore, but her roommate was.

"Madoc, go get that lamp," his mother ordered. "Quickly. Frieda, stop making those ghastly noises. Do you need some water, too?"

Frieda cut herself off in mid-yelp. "Lucy woke me up." She made the accusation in something of a self-satisfied tone, as if it were a triumph for her not to have been the waker this time.

"But you were screaming right along with her," Lady Rhys pointed out.

"I was screaming at Lucy to tell me why she was screaming."

"You were not!" cried Lucy. "You were screaming at him, too. You were just as scared as I was."

"Was I? I don't remember being scared. Him who?"

"I don't know." Lucy fell back in exhaustion upon her slipless pillow. "I'm sorry, Lady Rhys. It was too awful."

"What was?"

"Being strangled. If Frieda hadn't begun to yowl and frightened him off, he'd have killed me. He meant to, I could feel it. You saved my life, Frieda, truly you did."

"Did I really? I'm so glad, Lucy. What—what did he do?"

"He put something around my neck and pulled it tight. I could feel it cutting into my skin. I suppose I must have made some kind of noise. I don't know. It woke me up, the pain and choking. Then you piped up and I felt the thing slacken and he ran off."

"He who?" Madoc prodded. "Did you get a look at him?"

"No, everything was blurry. I think he'd put something over his face. One of those stocking masks. You know."

"But you're sure it was a man?"

"It must have been. His hands were so strong."

"That doesn't mean anything," said Lady Rhys. "All instrumentalists have strong hands, they exercise them so much. You of all people ought to know that, Lucy. Bring the lamp closer, Madoc, so I can get a look at her throat."

Madoc's younger, keener eyes had already taken note of the thin line around Lucy Shadd's none too swanlike throat. Fishline, he thought, remembering that small but effective instrument of torture he'd seen attached to Cedric Rintoul's trombone during the performance. That had been sadistic enough, but this was something else. He was not yet sure what.

"Mrs. Shadd," he said, "would you mind sitting up, or

at least rolling over so we can see the back of your neck?"

She obeyed without question. The red line was there, too.

"You say the garotte was already around your neck when you woke up?"

"Yes, it was. Don't make me say it again!" Her voice was rising.

"I'm sorry, Mrs. Shadd. I know this is unpleasant for you. I'm just trying to understand how the would-be strangler managed to get his line all the way around your neck without waking you. You would have been lying down with your head on the pillow, would you?"

"Yes, certainly. I don't sleep standing up. I suppose the answer is that I was totally exhausted and it took something really drastic to wake me. You must remember, Mr. Rhys, that I'd been stuck for the past several days with the orchestra manager's job as well as my own, which is taxing enough at the best of times. I've had a tremendous lot of responsibility and very little rest. And last night wasn't exactly peaceful, with that awful business about Wilhelm and having to get the orchestra off. Not to mention just missing a plane crash. That was the closest brush I'd had with death until just now, and I have to say two in one night are a bit much."

"We quite understand," said Lady Rhys. "Now you'd better just lie there and try to get some more sleep. Don't worry, Lucy, we'll make sure nothing else happens to you. I have some tablets, if you'd like something to calm you down."

"I haven't got time to be calm. What about the bathwater?"

"It's all taken care of," Madoc told her. "You'd better take the tablet. You'll be no good to anybody if you wear yourself out completely."

"That's easy for you to say. Who's going to manage the breakfast?"

"Oh, for goodness' sake, Lucy," Frieda protested, "quit

trying to be Superwoman. You can't even boil an egg, you
said so yourself."

"I'll get a tablet," said Lady Rhys, and the matter was
settled.

It was odd, Madoc thought, that still none of the others
had come to see what the screaming was about. They must
all be more used to Frieda Loye's nightmares than he'd
have thought possible. But as Lucy Shadd had just pointed
out, the lot of them had been through a colleague's sudden
death and a near-crash after a hard evening's work and half
a night of travel. Maybe their disinclination to leave their
hard-won beds wasn't so strange, at that. While his mother
went for the tablets, he took up the lamp and started nosing
around for what he might discover. It didn't take him two
seconds to spot the length of thin wire thrown down beside
the bed.

"That's not just wire," Frieda said when he held it up.
"It's a violin string. An A-string, I should say, but I'm no
authority. Joe or Helen could tell you. Or Monsieur Houdon, I suppose, if you had nerve enough to ask him."

"Oh, I'm a nervy sort of fellow," Madoc assured her.
"Are violin strings hard to get hold of?"

"Not particularly. Stores that sell musical instruments
have them. Or you can send away for them, or borrow one
in a pinch. String players always carry extras. One can
break or go false on you and have to be replaced."

"What happens to the broken ones? Can they be
mended?"

"Oh no, that wouldn't be worthwhile. They just get
thrown away. Unless a person took a notion to twist them
into flowerpot hangers or something. I must say I've never
heard of anybody who did. Strings are no big deal, Mr.
Rhys. I've bought them often enough myself, as a favor."

Frieda Loye emitted an odd little snort of laughter. "I
remember years and years ago, when I was still at the con-
servatory. I was waiting for a bus to go to the music store. I
had a bunch of errands for some of the crowd and when the
bus pulled in, this girl who'd stopped to talk with me

yelled, 'Don't forget my G-string.' Everybody looked at us as if we must be a couple of strippers or something. I was so embarrassed, I got off the bus before my stop. You do silly things when you're young. And sometimes when you're old enough to know better, too."

She sounded awfully bitter. Madoc wondered what she'd done that was so foolish; however, it could hardly be germane to the matter at hand.

"You saw nothing of this intruder?"

"No, nothing at all. As Lucy says, we'd had an exhausting trip and I was glad to get to bed. I just wish I'd been able to sleep longer; I feel like a worn-out dishrag. Though naturally I'm glad I woke up in time to save Lucy's life," Frieda added in an almost laughably polite little-girl voice.

"It's funny I didn't see him go out, though," she went on. "He must have been awfully quick. Maybe I did see him and just don't remember. I could be in one of those fugue states Freud used to go on about. Do I mean Freud? I read something once he wrote about a boy who'd been scared by a rooster. Unless I'm thinking of somebody else. I'm not much of a reader, I have to admit. Except music, of course."

"When you read music, do you wear glasses?"

"If you mean do I need glasses to see, why don't you say so? I'm not particularly thin-skinned, you know. One can't be, working with an orchestra. Yes, I need glasses and so does Lucy. We both wear contacts. What do you want to bet the reason everything looked blurry to her is that she just didn't have her contacts in? Lucy's eyes are much worse than mine," Frieda added rather smugly.

"That's right, Frieda." Lucy spoke wearily, as if her throat was bothering her a good deal. "I'm so used to my contacts that I just didn't remember having taken them out. I must be even more exhausted than I thought I was. First Wilhelm, then the plane, now this. I don't know how much more I can take."

"You don't have to take anything, Lucy. Except this."

Lady Rhys was back with the tablets. "They're quite mild, really. It's just to help you get back to sleep. Madoc, pour her some more water. Frieda, don't you think perhaps you ought to take one, too?"

"Here? In this room?"

"Now Frieda, you don't honestly believe that chap would dare to come again in broad daylight? But I'll sit right here with you if you're nervous."

The flautist appeared to find Lady Rhys's offer more nervous-making than the prospect of a return visit from the strangler. "No, really, Lady Rhys, I couldn't think of putting you to the trouble. I'll be all right. I can always scream if anything happens. I'm good at that, you know."

Frieda Loye managed a twitch of a smile. "But would you mind terribly explaining to Sir Emlyn that I wasn't the one who screamed first this time? I know it's silly, but—"

"Nonsense, dear. I know just how you feel, and I'll certainly tell him. But you mustn't worry, my son won't let anything happen to either one of you."

"Your son?" croaked Lucy. "What can he do?"

"Madoc can do whatever is necessary, I assure you." Lady Rhys drew herself up to her most imposing stance, took a deep breath, and bit the bullet. "My son," she announced in full, rich, pear-shaped tones, "is a policeman."

Chapter 6

After one incredulous snicker apiece, Frieda and Lucy accepted Lady Rhys's declaration. It was not possible that the conductor's wife would have joked about a thing like this.

It had had to be done, of course, but Madoc rather wished his mother hadn't chosen that particular moment to be noble. Now that his cover had been blown, there was no hope of sneaking back for another forty winks.

Madoc did, however, return to the room he'd been using, found Ed Naxton sound asleep, and decided to leave the poor chap to it. He thought it unlikely that either of the pilots could be involved in what was happening to the orchestra, though it was axiomatic that one never knew. He tucked in his shirttail, put on his waistcoat under his jacket, ran his pocket comb through his hair, cursed the lack of a toothbrush, and went on the prowl.

His parents were at the far end of the corridor, on the front of the building. Madoc didn't bother going into their room. He could hear through the ill-fitting door his mother explaining in a portentous whisper what had happened, and his father replying calmly, "Don't fret yourself, Sillie. Madoc will handle it."

He smiled a little and touched his knuckles lightly to the door across from theirs.

He got no reply, only an agreeable rhythmic, rumbling noise. He pushed open the door—there were no such re-

finements as locks up here—and saw two beds, each with
a rather handsome male head on a far from handsome
striped pillow tick. One head was fair, one was dark. One
was snoring tenor, the other bass; though Madoc could not
be expected to know whether they were on pitch. It was a
scene of perfect repose. Madoc surmised that men who
sang opera and oratorio as often as Pitney and Kight did
were accustomed to hearing loud soprano shrieks and could
shut them out at will. He shut himself away from the two
singers and moved on to the next room.

A light tap was answered by an "ungh." Madoc opened
it and stuck his head in. Joe Ragovsky was awake, though
just barely. The man in the other bed either wasn't or was
pretending not to be. This must be David Gabriel, the
oboist. No wonder Madoc hadn't been able to remember
what Gabriel looked like; he had the kind of face that was
designed to be instantly forgotten, and was quite wasted on
a woodwind. It would have made a pickpocket's or a swin-
dler's fortune. He said, "Sorry, wrong room," and closed
the door again.

He tried the same tactic on the door across the hall, got
no response, and opened it a crack, careful to lift up on the
knob so the hinges wouldn't squeak.

"Get out of here or I'll yell the place down."

The voice was Corliss Blair's. The clarinetist was sitting
bolt upright, clutching two handfuls of blanket around her.
She had a headful of pink foam rollers; her pink flannel
nightgown had a frill around the neck. It was a pity Lucy
Shadd's gown hadn't one. Madoc stepped into the room
and closed the door behind him.

"Don't bother, that's already been tried and it hasn't
seemed to work. I'm sorry to barge in on you ladies, but
my intentions are strictly honorable."

"Shucks," said Corliss, "I was afraid they might be.
Sorry, Madoc, I thought you were one of the happiness
boys. We've already had to throw Cedric Rintoul out of
here once. What's up besides you?"

"There's been an unfortunate incident down the hall."

"What sort of incident?"

"Somebody apparently tried to strangle Lucy Shadd with an A-string."

"Should have used a G-string," mumbled a voice from under the blankets in the other bed. Helene Dufresne emerged slowly from her cocoon. "Good God, is it daylight already? What time is breakfast?"

"Oh shush, Helene," said Corliss. "Aren't you the least bit curious about who tried to murder Lucy?"

"No, I'm curious about whose A-string they used. There was a D-string missing out of my cello case. I noticed it last night when I was packing my cello. You're sure it's not a D-string, Madoc? They're rather hard to tell apart if you aren't a string player yourself."

"I'm not sure of anything. I thought at first it was just a piece of wire. Frieda Loye told me it was a violin A-string, but she didn't have her contacts in. Maybe you wouldn't mind giving me an expert opinion later on."

"I'd be delighted. Is the string still around Lucy's neck?"

"No, I found it on the floor under the bed. The assumption is that the assailant slipped the string around Lucy's neck while she was still asleep, then crossed the ends over and pulled."

"What a splendid idea. Cheap and easy. Only I gather it didn't work. I'm surprised Lucy let the person get away instead of showing him how it ought to be done. She doesn't usually stand for inefficiency. So that's what all the howling was about just now? I thought it must be Frieda having another nightmare."

"Frieda insists Lucy began screaming before she did, but Lucy claims it was Frieda's screams that scared the intruder away. I suppose it's possible Frieda did in fact have a nightmare at the opportune time and start yelling before she woke up. There's a good deal of confusion as to the actual sequence of events. They both appear to have been sleeping very soundly when the room was entered."

"You talk like a policeman," said Corliss.

"That's because I am a policeman."

"You're kidding. I thought you must be a folk singer."

"No, I just need a haircut. In point of fact, I can't tell one note from another."

"That needn't prevent you from being a folk singer."

"I'm afraid I wouldn't know. My tone-deafness is a greater affliction to my parents than it is to me, so perhaps you'd be kind enough for their sakes not to spread the word around. Anyway, my mother's given me orders to find out who attacked Lucy Shadd and make him stop trying to kill people, so would you mind telling me whether you've been aware of any homicidal maniacs strolling around the hallway during the past half hour or so?"

"Not offhand, no," said Helene. "But then we haven't been watching. What do they look like?"

"Well, you see, that's the problem. One can't always tell. Quite seriously, ladies, have you heard any stealthy footsteps, anything of that sort?"

"Lord, yes, stealthy footsteps by the bucketful. People have been stealthing all over the place," Corliss replied. "Mostly in Delicia Fawn's direction, as usual."

"Which is where?"

"Madoc, don't try to tell us you haven't dropped in on her yourself?"

"My mother wouldn't let me. Come on, Corliss, left or right?"

"Right, then. You're actually serious, aren't you?"

"That's the impression I've been endeavoring to convey."

"You're really and truly a policeman?"

Madoc fished in his pocket and found one of his cards for her.

"Detective Inspector, RCMP? My gosh, what are you here for?"

"To spend a little time with my parents; at least that was the idea when I came. I had to be in Wagstaffe on business, you see, and they thought it might be fun for me to join the company and snatch a free ride out to the festival. Now that we've run into a spot of trouble, my mother's decided I may as well make myself useful. So I'll welcome any cooperation you're willing to give me."

"You honestly believe somebody tried to murder Lucy Shadd just now?"

"There's a nasty red mark around her throat that adds a certain credibility to the assumption. I shouldn't advise your going to look at it just now, though. My mother's given her something to quiet her down. Frieda Loye has also expressed hope of getting a little sleep, though I don't know how well she's going to succeed. She seems a nervy sort of lady."

"I'd be pretty darned nervy trying to sleep in a room where my bunkie's just missed being strangled," said Helene. "For Pete's sake, Madoc, couldn't you have found someplace else to put them?"

"That aspect of the matter didn't seem to bother them much," Madoc replied. "And frankly, in a ramshackle old place like this, I don't see that changing rooms would make much difference. I have a feeling Lucy was determined to tough it out and Frieda was reluctant to put anyone to the bother of switching. I understand she's already caused some of you to miss a bit of sleep on your previous stops."

"I'll say she has," said Corliss. "She's been hooting off like a calliope about every third night lately. I don't know why, she never did before."

"You've worked with her for some time, then?"

"Oh yes, we principals are all old hands with the Wagstaffe. It's one of Canada's finest orchestras, as your parents must have told you, so once they hire us, we're happy to stay on. You know, I suppose, that Lucy used to be principal horn player? She bucked for Wilhelm to take her place when she had to retire."

Madoc gave the cellist one of his gentle smiles. "Retire sounds like an odd word for someone who works as hard as Lucy Shadd does."

Helene shrugged. Her nightgown was short-sleeved,

and Madoc could see how muscular her arms were. "I know, but being on the staff isn't like being a member of the orchestra. I'd hate getting shoved off the stage, myself."

"You're safe enough, Helene," said Corliss Blair. "We winds blow ourselves out sooner or later, but the strings go on forever. Look at Pablo Casals."

"Yes," said Madoc, "why don't you? By the way, Helene, I was wondering how you happened to be on the plane last night? I'd been given to understand that the players usually preferred to travel with their instruments. You didn't bring your cello with you?"

"No, it's on the train, where I thought I was supposed to be. They'd already taken away the instrument cases and I was getting on the bus when Lucy ran up and told me I was on the list for the plane. God knows why, I loathe flying. I assumed it was some sort of mixup, but Lucy's been having such a hellish time trying to do two jobs that I didn't want to make a fuss. Besides, I have a favorite cousin in Vancouver and it looked like my chance to grab some free time with her. You just can't count on anything, can you?"

"Sometimes it seems that way. But my mother is counting on me to find her a clue, so I'd better get cracking. Thank you for your help, ladies. If you'd like a wash, there's hot water in the kitchen."

They didn't want a wash. They wanted to go back to sleep, as who could blame them? Funny ladies, Madoc thought; they hadn't shown much interest in what had happened to Lucy Shadd. Perhaps they hadn't really believed him; maybe they were still so traumatized by their own near-miss from being killed on the plane that a failed attempt at a murder down the hall seemed trivial by comparison. It might simply be that they felt Lucy Shadd as staff didn't merit the same concern that she would have if she were still principal horn player.

Or maybe Helene and Corliss just didn't like Lucy Shadd. Maybe her officiousness annoyed everybody else the way it had got under Madoc's own skin last night. That was one more thing to think about. He went next door and tried another experimental rap.

Nobody was home. A beautiful dark blue suit with an ever so faint pinstripe was hung with great care over the back of the one wooden chair, a black cashmere overcoat across two hooks on the wall. An initialed calfskin carryall stood beside the chair, an expensive shaving kit and a black homburg hat reposed on the stained and battered dresser top. The bed had been neatly made up, but nobody was lying in it. Madoc cocked an eyebrow and continued his explorations.

The neighboring room was empty of inhabitants but far from unused. Both beds were a mess of rumpled blankets and shed garments. The floor and dresser were strewn with objects ranging from an empty vodka bottle to an old-fashioned shaving brush and mug to a toy wind-up mouse that was a pretty good imitation of the real thing except, of course, for the key in its backside. Madoc didn't need the two open instrument cases to inform him that this had to be where the trumpeter and the trombonist had set up housekeeping. But where were they?

They weren't in the room occupied by the sleeping Lucy Shadd and the wide-awake Frieda Loye. Madoc met the flautist's horrified stare with a reassuring nod.

"Just checking," he murmured, and backed out, closing the door with exaggerated care, not that he supposed it mattered much.

In the room beyond, he discovered the missing concertmaster, slumbering peacefully in a double bed beside the opulent Madame Bellini. Both Monsieur Houdon and his lady were wearing flannel pajamas, silk eyeshades, and fuzzy white earplugs. *L'amour, toujours l'amour.*

So by the process of elimination, Delicia Fawn must be at the far end of the hall. And so she was, looking ravishing in her sleep. And so was Steve MacVittie, looking ravished. And so were Cedric Rintoul and Jason Jasper, wearing surgical masks and tiger-striped pajamas with feet in them, standing one on either side of the bed with their instruments raised to the approximate presumed location of their lips.

"Rehearsing a matinatta, gentlemen?" said Madoc politely.

The sound of his voice woke Delicia, and she began to speak. What she said was not nice. It was not genteel, it was not *comme il faut,* and it was just as well her next-door neighbors had their earplugs in. But she got her point across. Boiled down, it amounted to, "You unspeakable persons, get out of here."

Madoc raised his hand to stem the flow. "Before we leave, Miss Fawn, I should perhaps explain that I'm here in my professional capacity as a detective inspector of the RCMP. My duty at the moment is to investigate a murderous assault which was made a short time ago upon Lucy Shadd, who is occupying the room two doors away from yours. May I ask how long you and Mr. MacVittie have been in one another's company?"

Steve MacVittie was slowly coming to life. "Assault, huh?" he grunted through a jaw-cracking yawn. "Is that what all the yelling was about down the hall a while back? Yeah, I've been here ever since I won the toss. I haven't had strength enough to leave. But these guys weren't."

"We were so, eh," Rintoul protested. "You just couldn't see us. We were hiding."

"Where, for instance?"

MacVittie's question was a good one. There wasn't even a closet, just a few hooks screwed into an unpainted board on the wall opposite the bed.

"We were under the bed," said Jason Jasper.

Madoc stooped and checked. "You were not, Mr. Jasper. This is an old-fashioned coil spring and it sags in the middle. Mr. MacVittie is a big man and Miss Fawn is not puny, either; therefore it sags a good deal. You and Mr. Rintoul are no lightweights yourselves, I may point out. The combined weight of the occupants is pushing the mattress and spring down so low that neither one of you would have been able to crawl underneath, much less the pair of you together. Added to that, the dust under the bed has not been disturbed. Come on, Mr. Jasper, what else have you and your pal been up to? Did you also think it would be a jolly jape to scare Lucy Shadd within an inch of her life?"

"God, no! Why'd we do a thing like that?"

"Perhaps for the same reason that Mr. Rintoul amused himself by tickling Frieda Loye's neck with a piece of violin string taped to his trombone all through last evening's concert, knowing full well that Mrs. Loye was subject to screaming nightmares as a result of previous teasing, and would probably wake up everybody tonight with another one."

With the exception of Monsieur Houdon and Madame Bellini, who'd have been wearing their earplugs, but Madoc saw no reason to go into that. "It was in fact a piece of violin string, was it not, Mr. Rintoul?"

"What's the big deal about a piece of violin string?" Rintoul was trying to be truculent, but he'd forgotten he still had the surgical mask over his mouth, so he missed his effect. He snatched off the mask and snarled at Madoc.

"And how come this crap about being a Mountie? I thought you were Sir Emlyn's son."

"The two are not mutually exclusive, Mr. Rintoul."

"Lady Rhys told me you worked for the Canadian government." Jason Jasper sounded like a petulant four-year-old. "In research."

"That is quite correct, Mr. Jasper. On behalf of the law enforcement branch of the Canadian government, I am at present researching you. Getting back to my question, Mr. Rintoul, was it in fact a piece of violin string you were using to torture Mrs. Loye?"

"I resent the use of the word *torture*."

Madoc didn't respond to his resentment, merely stood and waited. Delicia Fawn was in no mood for passivity.

"Cedric, don't be such a jackass. So what about it, Madoc? Or do we have to call you Inspector now? What's so important about a hunk of violin string?"

"Call me what you please. What's important about a

violin string is that a piece of one was used by somebody trying to strangle Lucy Shadd. Where did you get your string, Mr. Rintoul?"

"I'm not saying I had one."

"If you don't, one of your colleagues will," Madoc pointed out. "It's not possible that none of the other members of the orchestra noticed what you were up to. My mother and I could see it quite plainly from where we were sitting. You'll be hearing from my father on the subject of unprofessional behavior, I expect, but we're not concerned with that just now. Talk, Mr. Rintoul."

Chapter 7

The trombonist did a bit of snorting and snuffling, then shrugged his heavy shoulders. "Oh, all right. What the hell, guys like you couldn't see a joke if it waltzed up and jumped on their corns. It was a hunk of violin string I found on the floor of the rehearsal room, that's all."

"Where is it now?" asked Madoc.

"How the hell do I know? I threw it away."

"No you didn't, Ceddie," Jason Jasper contradicted eagerly. "It's still in your case. I noticed when you put your instrument away."

"Thanks, pal."

"Go and get it, will you please, Mr. Jasper?" Madoc could perfectly well have gone himself, but he felt like staying here and making Rintoul sweat a little more.

Rintoul was shuffling his tiger-striped feet, looking silly and no doubt feeling even sillier. "What's the big deal?" he mumbled. "I just thought it would be a handy thing to tickle somebody with."

"The somebody being, of course, Frieda Loye."

"Sure, because she was the one who happened to be sitting in front of me last night. Big deal! If it hadn't been Frieda, it would have been somebody else."

"Who, for instance? A man wouldn't have felt the tickling through his shirt collar. There weren't all that many women in the orchestra, and not all their gowns were identically cut. Mrs. Loye wore one that was perfectly designed for tickling, though I don't suppose she thought of that when she chose it."

Jasper was back with the trombone case only a few seconds after he'd gone. He must be anxious to make points with the law. Rintoul obviously wasn't. As for MacVittie and Miss Fawn, Madoc couldn't tell whether they were even still awake. It must have been quite an audition, but that was none of his business.

"Open the case, please, Mr. Rintoul."

Grunting something scurrilous under his breath, the musician obeyed. There lay his trombone, gleaming like a horn of gold, still sporting that wisp of whisker at the nethermost curve of its slide. Madoc could see now that it was a stiffish piece of what still looked to him like wire, about four inches long, wound around with darkish blue thread.

"Is this all the string you found, Mr. Rintoul, or did you cut it from a longer piece?"

"I shortened it. What the hell, I only needed a little bit."

"Just enough to reach from your slide to Mrs. Loye's collarbone. What did you shorten it with?"

"A little Mickey Mouse jackknife I had in my pocket," he mumbled. "I always carry it."

"Along with your exploding cigars and your whoopee cushion, no doubt. And what did you do with the rest of the string?"

"How the hell do I know? I most likely dropped it where I'd found it. Or else I stuck it in the pocket of my tailcoat, in which case it's still there and you can see it for yourself once we catch up with the wardrobe trunks, if we ever do. So get off my back before I report you to the Musicians' Union."

"I don't come under the jurisdiction of the Musicians' Union, Mr. Rintoul. Now, since you and Mr. Jasper here were in fact not hiding under Miss Fawn's bed, when Mrs. Loye and Mrs. Shadd began to scream, where were you?"

"Oh, for God's sake! We were trying to get a rise out of Delicia, that's all. Actually, we were in our own room across the hall when we heard the yelling. We thought it was just Frieda having another nightmare."

"As a result of your harmless little prank last night?"

"Jeez, you never let up on a guy, do you? We were sort of wondering if we ought to get up and do something to quiet her down. Then we heard Lady Rhys coming down the hall so we thought we'd better not butt in. Then you came along."

"How do you know I did?" asked Madoc. "Were you watching through the keyhole?"

"Cripes, we didn't have to. The door in our room has a crack in it big enough to put your fist through," Jasper put in.

"Yeah." Rintoul mightn't have wanted to talk, but he wasn't about to let Jasper take the floor. "So anyway, once we were up it didn't seem worth going back to bed, so we waited till things had quieted down and you and your mother had gone back up the hall. Then we thought what the hell, we'd drop in and play reveille for Delicia and her new boyfriend. Kind of cheer things up a little, you know. We saw you sneaking into Helene and Corliss's room and we were going to serenade you next. Only I guess we sort of misjudged what you were going for, eh?"

Madoc was not amused. Rintoul, at last, was abashed.

"What the hell, Inspector, I'm sorry. You think we got a little bit out of line, eh?"

"Tell me something, Mr. Rintoul, do you wear contact lenses?"

Whatever the trombonist had been expecting, this clearly wasn't it. "Huh? Hell, no. Why should I?"

"I was just curious," Madoc replied.

Actually, he'd been thinking back to that scene in the other bedroom. Even now, it wasn't quite full daylight. When he'd responded to the two women's cries, the room had been barely light enough to see one's way around. Lucy Shadd and Frieda Loye were both on the thin side, neither of them young. Both wore their graying hair in the neat, short cut that was favored by the majority of professional women. Lucy was a few inches taller than the diminutive Frieda, but that difference wouldn't show up in bed. In a poor light it mightn't have been difficult to mix them up. Was it possible that the strangler had left his task unfinished not because Frieda screamed, but because he'd caught on just in time that he was trying to kill the wrong woman?

Madoc knew he had a fat chance of getting either of this pair to admit anything that might conceivably involve them in so totally unfunny a caper. They must realize they'd already set themselves up as prime suspects.

"All right, you two comedians," he told them. "I suggest you apologize to Miss Fawn and Mr. MacVittie. Then you either go back to your room and stay there or else come downstairs where I can keep an eye on you."

"What's downstairs?" said Jasper. "Any chance of something to eat?"

"There should be hot water to wash in, at any rate." The fires must not have gone out; otherwise the upstairs would be colder than it was. "And I expect we can scare up some sort of breakfast. Can any of you four cook?"

They all not only insisted they couldn't, they seemed proud of their inability. Madoc sighed and went downstairs.

He could have asked to borrow Rintoul's or Jasper's razor, he supposed. On the other hand, anything belonging to either of that pair would no doubt have either produced rude noises or else squirted cheap perfume up his nose. Give him a rogue instead of a fool any day in the week.

There was no bread in the kitchen, but there was flour. There were powdered eggs and powdered milk. There was baking powder, there was salt, there was cooking oil. There were cans of Spam and jugs of syrup. Madoc tried to think what Janet would do in a case like this, and did it.

The batter bore a reasonable resemblance to Janet's. At least it was worth a try; he suddenly realized that he was totally ravenous. He sliced himself a frying pan full of Spam. He greased a griddle and poured out two neat,

round blobs for flapjacks. They bubbled up nicely; he
turned them over. They were browned just the way he liked
them. He was about to fill himself a plate when Steve
MacVittie entered the kitchen, limping slightly.

"God, Madoc, that smells like the breath of angels. Any
chance of a bite for a man who'd done a hard night's work?"

"Sure thing, Mac." What else could Madoc say? "Here,
take these. I'll fix myself some more."

He sliced up the rest of the Spam and greased the griddle anew. He fried four pancakes this time because Steve
was making awfully quick work of those first two. Apparently he'd guessed right on the recipe. Janet would be
proud of him, if he ever got to tell her. He used some of his
hot water to make a big pot of tea, and set out sugar and
dried milk.

There were restaurant-size cans of peaches, the old
sourdough's staple, on the kitchen shelves. Madoc thought
some of those might be a welcome addition to the feast he
was still hoping to get some of. Before he could take down
a can, much less get it open, Ed Naxton was on deck looking hopeful. Smiling on the outside and growling on the
inside, Madoc gave Ed the second breakfast he'd fixed for
himself, mixed another bowlful of batter, and opened two
more cans of Spam.

It was as well he'd done so. Perhaps it would have been
better if he'd never started this breadline in the first place.
Rintoul and Jasper appeared, unabashed and wearing false
noses with mustaches attached. The mustaches were red-
dish and droopy, much like the one Madoc himself had
shaved off when it began to get in the way of his relationship with Janet. He wished to God Janet were here. She
could cook and he could eat. He cut more Spam and kept
on frying.

Helene Dufresne and Corliss Blair came down with Joe
Ragovsky and the still silent David Gabriel, then Carlos
Pitney, who offered to open the peaches if Madoc would
show him how to work the can opener. Madoc said sorry,
he didn't have time. Helene did know how, or so she

claimed, but she didn't dare make the attempt and risk cutting her finger. Uncut fingers were, she explained, vital to a cellist's ability to perform; it was not herself but the orchestra she was thinking of. Madoc took a short break from flapjack flipping and opened the peaches.

He was just thinking he might snatch a bite for himself when Ainsworth Kight swam into view, reeking of charm and throat spray and clamoring for honey to put in his tea. There was no honey. Helene suggested pancake syrup, which seemed to work just as well. Naturally, however, Ainsworth then demanded pancakes to go with his syrup. Madoc opened all the Spam he could find and mixed a great deal more batter.

For the first time since they'd been grounded, the atmosphere among the company had become downright bonhomous. Nobody was in any hurry to leave the warmth of the stove and the geniality of his fellows. They did get cramped for space around the table; in fact the entire kitchen got pretty congested as people kept coming and dragging in more chairs. Madoc had barely space enough to mix batter, open cans, replenish the teapot, cook the food, and add more wood to the stove.

As for getting anything to eat for himself, he'd more or less given up on that notion. He fried on and on, gaining what satisfaction he could from the odors of flapjack and Spam and the sounds of munching jaws. Madame Bellini alone kept him busy for quite a while, nor was Monsieur Houdon backward in coming forward with his plate, even though he did express a wistful preference for *jambon à moutarde de Dijon* over Spam. Both he and Madame Bellini looked quite understandably rested and refreshed. They'd entered the room a decorous ten minutes apart, each expressing a courteous hope that the other had slept well. Both had replied in the affirmative. Madoc was not surprised.

Lady Rhys came down in her gorgeous housecoat to get a pitcher of hot water for Sir Emlyn to shave with. She cast a reproving look at her son's dark-shadowed cheeks as her pitcher was being passed from hand to hand over the heads of the assembled multitudes so that Madoc could fill it from the boiler on the stove. She took the water and went back upstairs.

A little while later, she arrived with Sir Emlyn, both of them scrubbed and shiny and properly garbed for a morning in the country in well-worn tweeds. Helene Dufresne offered to set a small table in the lobby for them, but they said not to bother, they'd just join the party in the kitchen.

It became apparent, however, that the party wasn't going to join them. People began remembering they still needed to wash and dress. Pitchers were brought, water was taken, the tumult and the shouting died, and in the firebox sank the fire. Madoc shoved in another stick or two, scraped the last of the batter from the bowl, and made himself one extra-large pancake.

"Good heavens, Madoc," his mother expostulated, "you're not planning to sit at the table in front of your father with whiskers all over your face?"

"Yes, Mother, I am," he told her. "I'm just the hired man around here, don't forget. I'll borrow your razor after a while if you don't mind, Tad. Mine's somewhere in the bowels of the plane."

Lady Rhys sniffed at the deliberate indelicacy of *bowels,* but went on eating her pancakes and peaches. Sir Emlyn smiled shyly at this interesting young chap he so inexplicably had sired, and helped himself to another slice of Spam.

"Haven't had any of this since 1944," he remarked. "Tastes about the same, don't you think, Sillie?"

For some reason Madoc doubted he'd ever understand, Lady Rhys wiped her lips on one of the paper napkins Madoc had unearthed from the supply closet, and gave her husband a fond and emphatic kiss right in front of Frieda Loye, who was at last putting in an apologetic appearance with her empty enamel pitcher. The flautist stepped back in considerable embarrassment.

"Oh, I beg your pardon. I didn't mean to interrupt a family breakfast."

"You haven't." Madoc got up and pulled out a chair for her. "We're just the tag-end of the throng. Can we interest you in some peaches and Spam? I'm afraid the pancake batter's all used up, but I can easily throw together another batch."

"Please don't bother on my account. I couldn't eat a thing, honestly."

"Then you must at least have a cup of tea," said Lady Rhys.

Frieda Loye replied faintly that tea would be lovely, but Lucy was awake and wanted to wash.

"She'll have dozed off again by now, I expect," Lady Rhys insisted. "That's how those pills always work with me. Sit down here and drink this tea."

Frieda could hardly do anything then except obey. She made a decent pretense of drinking the mugful Lady Rhys had poured out for her, and managed half a slice of peach at her ladyship's earnest hest that she needed something to keep her strength up. However, this was clearly a struggle. As soon as she could manage without being positively rude, she made her escape with her pitcherful of hot water. All three Rhyses looked after her with real concern.

"There's something more wrong with that woman than getting tickled with a violin string," Sir Emlyn observed as he chased the last bite of Spam around his otherwise empty plate.

"I'm wondering whether she may be afraid the strangler picked the wrong bed," said Madoc.

"Madoc, that's really penetrating of you. More tea, anyone?" Lady Rhys peered into the depleted pot, shook her head sadly, and set it down on the plate that had been pressed into service as a trivet. "I must say I've been wondering the same thing. Lucy Shadd seems such an unlikely victim. Not that I haven't felt like strangling her myself once or twice, and you may make of that what you please."

"But how could we replace her on such short notice?"

Sir Emlyn pointed out. "And who'd do the work if she weren't around?"

"I know, dear. Lucy's frightfully efficient, one has to admit. And that's what's so scary, don't you think? It's a shocking thing for me to say, I know, but I'd be easier in my mind if it had been Frieda. She's a born victim, you see, whereas Lucy's just the opposite. And that must mean a totally undiscriminating murderer, wouldn't you say? A psychopath, I believe they're called? They used to be just loonies when I was a girl, but I understand nowadays that's not considered quite nice. Some crazed desert rat, perhaps, who just happened to wander by in a bad mood."

"We're not in the desert, Sillie," her husband pointed out.

"A frustrated prospector, then. It's got to be someone, Emmy."

"Someone other than ourselves, you mean. I understand your feelings, Sillie, but we mustn't jump to conclusions. What do the others say, Madoc?"

"I'm not sure they all know, Tad. Helene Dufresne and Corliss Blair do. They caught me breaking into their room when I was checking around to see who was where, and I had to explain my way out. Those two jokers from the brass section know, also. I caught them with Steve Mac-Vittie, the pilot, in Delicia Fawn's room."

"Good heffens, was she running an orgy?"

"Not quite." Madoc described the unedifying but hardly orgiastic circumstances in which he'd found the four of them. "Anyway, nobody said anything about the incident at breakfast. I don't know whether they were waiting for me to speak first, which I didn't have time to do; whether they were trying to pretend it hadn't happened; or whether the word simply hadn't gotten around."

"Orchestras are hotbeds of gossip usually," Lady Rhys observed. "Helene and Corliss have struck me as being decent sorts, though; they may have kept their mouths shut on principle. And I doubt whether Delicia Fawn has ever had a thought that didn't directly concern herself."

"Good point, Mother," said Madoc. "Steve MacVittie would no doubt have been embarrassed to bring the subject up, considering how he'd learned the news. As for Rintoul and Jasper, they had every reason to stay off it. Right now, they've set themselves up quite neatly as prime suspects."

"That's a bit of all right as far as I'm concerned," said Lady Rhys. "The less said, the less panic, don't you think? Now I expect I'd better take something up to poor Lucy. The rest of those peaches ought to slip down easily. Too bad there's no pretty sauce dish to put them in. These thick little bowls make me think of Aunt Oldrys bathing her canary. Ah well, what can't be cured must be endured with equanimity. And tea, of course. Is there a speck of hot water left, Madoc?"

"Just about."

"Then you'd better heat some more for the washing up, hadn't you? Thanks, dear."

Lady Rhys blew a kiss in the general direction of her son's right ear and went off with Lucy's breakfast, such as it was, on a tray. Madoc and his father exchanged shrugs, picked up a bucket apiece, and went over to the pump.

Chapter 8

"Why don't we simply bung all the dishes into the copper and let the water boil up around them?"

Sir Emlyn appeared to be quite taken with himself in the role of scullery boy. "And shouldn't soap come into it somewhere? It seems to me there used to be a little wire cage one swished through the washing-up water. One put the leftover bits of soap in it, if one had any. One didn't always, in wartime. I believe there was also ground-up soap in a box one shook some out of."

"Nowadays one usually has a plastic bottle that squirts," said Madoc. "I'll tend to the dishes. Why don't you rinse out the tins so they won't draw varmints? Use one of the buckets, and dump the water out on the ground. If we let it go down the sink, it will probably freeze there and bust the pipes, and we're fairly well into the depredations already."

"I'll squash them flat." Sir Emlyn was really warming up to his new job. "That will thwart the varmints good and proper. By the way, son, not to be indelicate but what are we going to do about what my old nanny used to call the vahses?"

"We let everybody cope with his or her own," said Madoc firmly. "I hadn't given it much thought, Tad; what would you suggest? Have people holler 'gardy loo' and chuck it out the upstairs window in the Edinburgh tradition? Or dig a decent-sized hole to empty them into and throw earth on top?"

"The latter course seems the less objectionable. Very well, son, though I may not be much of a hand at digging. It wouldn't do for me to sprain a shoulder on the way to the festival, assuming we ever get there."

"Oh, we will. Our plane must have been reported overdue by now. I expect there's a search on already."

"But how will the searchers know where to look? We didn't go the route we were intended to, you know."

Madoc didn't have to be reminded. "If we had, we'd have been found already, though possibly not in the best of shape. This way, it will simply take a bit longer."

"Of course, son. We must count our blessings. Here, I can do that. Why don't you nip on upstairs and get yourself shaved? We have to maintain the dignity of my position, you know."

Sir Emlyn permitted himself a sly chuckle as he tied a tea towel around his waist for an apron and began to scrape the plates. Madoc smiled back, took the tea kettle in lieu of a pitcher, and went upstairs.

His mother was not in the parental bedroom. She must be down the hall comforting the afflicted. It was as well she was not in the kitchen having a fainting fit at the sight of her distinguished husband in his present occupation. Actually, Sir Emlyn was showing his usual expert leadership, Madoc realized. Once it got about that the maestro himself was pitching in with the dog work, there might be less of the cut finger routine and more shoulders to the wheel.

And a damned good thing, too. Madoc had no inclination to remain the lone skivvy for whatever the duration of their stay might be. He was lathering his chin with his father's shaving cream when Lady Rhys came back.

"Madoc, whatever are you doing here?"

"Shaving, Mother. We have Tad's position to think of, you know."

"But what about the washing-up? And where is your father?"

"Washing dishes. How's your patient?"

"Much better, thank goodness. Her throat's not so sore. She has it wrapped up in a scarf and says the warmth is doing some good. Lucy's taking it wonderfully well, I have to say. Some women would be totally shattered. Madoc, what did you say your father was doing?"

"The washing-up, Mother. As soon as he finishes that, we're going to dig a latrine out back to dump the slops into."

"Madoc, dear, I realize it's incumbent upon all of us to keep our spirits up during this difficult time, but I must tell you that I find your attempts at humor a trifle coarse for my personal taste. Is your father planning to call a rehearsal?"

"He didn't say. He was busy squashing tins so the varmints won't get them. Listen, Mother, do you hear that?"

Actually, there was a great deal to hear since most of the party were still in their bedrooms: splashing and swearing as they tried to take baths in the tin basins; lamenting the lack of electricity for their razors, scalp massagers, garment steamers, curling irons, and mechanical toothbrushes; running through their scales; or, as in Ainsworth Kight's case, spraying their throats. From far over the hubbub, however, came the unmistakable drone of an airplane engine.

And from the interior of the hotel came a mass pounding of feet as the castaways abandoned whatever they were doing and raced pell-mell down the stairs, and out into the road. Still plying his father's razor, Madoc watched from the front window as they waved their arms, musical instruments, throat sprayers, and in one case a ruffled crimson pettiskirt. That was Delicia Fawn, standing there in an off-the-shoulder Carmen-style blouse and practically nothing else. If she didn't fetch that plane down, nothing would.

"Look at that idiot woman! She'll catch a cold and be hoarse as a frog for the festival," fumed Lady Rhys. "Here, Madoc, for goodness' sake take this blanket down to her before she freezes her protuberances."

Madoc scraped off what he hoped was the final inch of

whiskers, splashed in the basin to dissolve any clinging smears of lather, rubbed his face dry on the first towel he could lay hands on, and ran downstairs to join the welcoming committee.

He was just in time to witness the landing, which was a remarkably bad one. The plane bucked and bounced and seesawed like a kid's teeter-totter, and almost smacked into the grounded Grumman before it finally joggled to a safe stop.

"My God, who's that? The Wright brothers?"

That was Ed Naxton, and his question was a valid one. Not many of those present had ever laid eyes on an open-cockpit triplane, or any kind of triplane, for that matter. That anybody could be flying such an antiquated crate among the treacherous downdrafts of this mountainous area was a matter for wonderment. None of the watchers was at all surprised when the pilot climbed out over the left lower wing wearing jodhpurs with big patches on the seat and knees, a peeling sheepskin jacket, a Lucky Lindy helmet with the chinstraps dangling, cracked and blurred goggles, and a once-white scarf wound four or five times around his neck and still having plenty of frayed ends left to trail in the approved manner. This magnificent man in his flying machine did in fact appear to be male, and he was alone.

Madoc's first thought was that this must be one of the turns they put on for the tourists at the ghost town. The pilot was gazing over the assemblage: Delicia, now cocooned in Lady Rhys's blanket, accepting a squirt of throat spray from Ainsworth Kight; Jason Jasper and Cedric Rintoul with their respective trumpet and trombone to their lips, tooting a snatch of "Come, Josephine, in My Flying Machine"; Madame Bellini and Jacques-Marie Houdon dignified and impassive; Joe Ragovsky and all the rest bouncing with excitement, except for David Gabriel, who remained totally blank.

The newcomer took off his helmet, presumably so that he could scratch his head. Then he put it back on, shoved his goggles up on top, leaned over to check out the tussocky ground, and finally sat on the wing with his legs dangling. His apparent intention was to let himself down, but it was easy to see why he was hesitating. The drop was maybe five feet, no jump at all for a young man; but this chap was seventy if he was a day. Ed and Steve had already caught on to his dilemma and were on their way to lend him a hand, so Madoc stayed with the waiters.

As the triplane's pilot approached, hobbling between Ed and Steve, Madoc judged seventy to have been a conservative estimate. This gaffer couldn't be one of the Wright brothers, but he might conceivably have patronized their bicycle shop in his youth. He could even have bought the parts for his flying machine there, from what Madoc could see of it.

At least he wasn't bashful. He walked straight up to the group in front of the Miners' Rest, tilted back his head, and roared, "You the bunch that got kilt in the plane crash?"

Sir Emlyn was with them now. He'd forgotten to take the dish towel from around his waist and Madoc hadn't seen fit to remind him. Lady Rhys, last to appear (except of course for Lucy Shadd, who hadn't come at all), whisked the thing out of sight and gave her son one of those exasperated looks he'd been hoping he'd seen the last of. The towel wouldn't have made any difference; Sir Emlyn was Sir Emlyn no matter what. He stepped forward and addressed the inquirer.

"How do you do, sir? I am Emlyn Rhys, and these are members of the Wagstaffe Symphony Orchestra. We are on our way to the Fraser River Music Festival; our plane had to make a forced landing here last night. Are we fortunate enough to discover that you have come looking for us?"

"You sure as shootin' are, pardner. Ace Bulligan's my name an' flyin's my game. Any casualties?"

"None whatever, thanks to the skill of Mr. MacVittie here. However, we are without power to continue our journey and also with no means of communication, so we're most grateful to you for coming to our rescue. How did you know where to find us?"

"Smart flyin' or dumb luck, dependin' on how you look at it. Ol' *Moxie Mabel* had a little juice in 'er so I thought I might's well go up an' take a look around, but she won't climb too good so all's I could do was comb the flatlands, of which there ain't none to speak of around here, 'cept Lodestone Flat, which is where you're standin' now in case you didn't know. I smelt your smoke an' knowed the Miners' Rest was bunged up tight shut for the winter so when I seen your plane settin' down in front of 'er, I figured I must o' found the missin' murderers."

"Murderers? I fail to understand you, sir. As I said before, we are musicians."

"You don't have to tell me twice, mister. I ain't deaf. Not that deaf, anyhow. You're the buggers who done in some other poor son of a bitch that played the coronet."

"Do you mean cornet? What cornet? The cornet is primarily a band instrument. We don't use them all that much in orchestral music."

"You couldn't prove it by me, mister. Maybe it was a kazoo or a bugle. Like them things them two buzzards over there is carryin'. You ain't kiddin' me none for all your hifalutin' talk. You didn't even shoot 'im down like a white man. You bunged 'im full o' some kind o' fancy rat pizen an' left 'im to drown in his own puke while you made your darin' escape in that there flyin' saloon over there. I heard it on the six o'clock news this mornin'."

"Just a minute, Mr. Bulligan." Madoc thought he might as well horn in here, since his father was looking decidedly out of his element. "This cornet player you're talking about, was he in fact a French-horn player, and was his name Wilhelm Ochs?"

"Yeah, that's him. Dead as a strung-up rustler in front o' three million people."

"Three million?"

"Well, three thousand. Three hundred. Three somethin'. What difference does it make? Dead's dead, ain't it? You look like kind of a sneaky little cuss to me. You the one that slipped 'im the pizen?"

No, but I'm the cuss who's going to pinch you for flying an unregistered plane, Madoc thought of replying. It was inconceivable that such an agglomeration of baling wire and wishful thinking could have passed any sort of inspection within the past thirty years. However, Ace Bulligan was at the moment their only hope of a linkup with the outside world, and all they could do was humor him along.

"Wilhelm Ochs was a member of the orchestra which Sir Emlyn Rhys here is conducting," he explained in as unsneaky a manner as he could manage. "He became ill during last night's performance, collapsed backstage after the concert was over, and died just before the ambulance arrived to take him to the hospital. He'd been having serious problems with his stomach for quite some time and it was assumed at the time we left that he'd died of natural causes. Otherwise, we shouldn't have been allowed to leave. If you have definite information that Mr. Ochs was poisoned, we naturally want to know the details. Can you remember exactly what was said on the radio?"

"Who's askin'?"

"Oh, sorry. My name is Madoc Rhys. Sir Emlyn is my father and Lady Rhys over there in the tweed coat and skirt is my mother."

"Lady Rhys, huh? Howdy, ma'am." Ace Bulligan raised his goggles and then his helmet by way of courtesy. "Used to be a Lady Lil worked at the Miners' Rest. She wore black silk stockings an' pink satin bloomers. Seen much o' the Queen lately?"

"Not since shortly after Christmas," Lady Rhys answered quite matter-of-factly. "Her Majesty was in excellent health and spirits at that time, I may say."

"Well, next time you run into 'Er Majesty, tell 'er Ace Bulligan says hello. What's a titled lady like you doin' with a bunch o' sidewinders like these here, if you don't mind my askin'?"

"They are not sidewinders, Mr. Bulligan, and I can assure you that Her Majesty would take an extremely dim view of your calling them rude names."

Lady Rhys had flipped open her lorgnette to give him a reproving glare, but she thought better of it just in time and switched to an ingratiating smile. "Now, would you please answer my son's question? We are all deeply grieved over the death of Mr. Ochs and I personally find it most disturbing to learn that he may have been the victim of foul play."

"No maybe about it, ma'am. Accordin' to what I heard on the news, somebody fed 'im castor oil."

"Castor oil wouldn't have killed him! It would have"— Lady Rhys paused momentarily—"produced somewhat different symptoms from those he evinced last night."

"Well, it wasn't just castor oil. It was something like castor oil. With rice in it. Seems to me it was the rice that done 'im in."

"Ricin," said Madoc. "Of course. Ricin is what kills children who chew on the beans from the castor oil plant. They have a delayed reaction, sometimes several hours, sometimes a day or more. Ochs wasn't a health food freak, by any chance?"

"Hell, no," said Joe Ragovsky. "He was a food freak, period. Bill liked his grub. What does this ricin taste like?"

"I have no idea and am not too eager to find out," said Madoc, "but I can't imagine it's too awful if kids eat the beans. You have to chew them to get the poisoning effect, otherwise they just slip through the digestive system intact. If you were to run a few through a food mill and mix the resulting mash with something spicy, I suppose you could get your intended victim to ingest a dose that would do the job. The kicker would be, you see, that he wouldn't know he'd had any. He wouldn't relate his symptoms to what he'd eaten because so much time had passed. By the time he began to feel sick, he'd already be in serious trouble, as Ochs plainly was for quite some time before he managed to get offstage."

"I ought to have noticed," mourned Sir Emlyn.

"I doubt whether your noticing would have made any difference, Tad. Ochs was clearly determined to tough it out. And he did, poor chap. Mr. Bulligan, you don't by any chance have a two-way radio in your plane?"

"You kiddin'? I ain't even sure I got an engine."

"Then how about a battery that we might borrow in the hope it would operate the hotel's radio?"

"Huh. Mister, the only radio I own's one o' them weeny pocket transistor kind an' the batteries is about the size o' my little finger. An' it's in my shack about fifty miles from here an' I don't even know if I got juice enough in my tank to get home, never mind bring the dang thing back here."

"We could siphon some fuel out of our emergency tank for you," Steve MacVittie offered. "Though I'm afraid it might not—" His gaze drifted over to the tattered wreck parked too near the Grumman, and his voice faltered into stillness.

"Might not? You can bet your last two bits it might not, brother. You know what'd happen if I went an' poured one little slug o' them high-voltage atom squeezin's you burn into my ol' *Moxie Mabel?* She'd go straight into orbit an' come down about a teaspoonful o' rust an' sawdust, that's what."

"Then what do you run her on? Just regular gasoline, like a lawn tractor?"

"I do when I can get it. Mostly I run 'er on homemade alcohol. I got a little what you might call a—"

"Still?" Madoc suggested.

"I was going to say processin' plant. Anyways, that's what she's used to an' she don't seem to mind it none."

"There's liquor on the plane," said Ed Naxton. "I doubt if it's as powerful as the stuff you make, but we could try."

A smile of wonderful radiance overspread the old flyer's grizzled features. "Never can tell, pardner. You just trot 'er out, an' we'll give 'er a go."

Chapter 9

They'd made a terrible mistake. Madoc had realized that as soon as the old aviator reacted to that magic word, *liquor*. It was too late now; Ace Bulligan was testing.

"I got to find out whether this hooch is compatible with the stuff I been usin', ain't I? And there's only one way to do that."

The two-liter bottle was large, but Bulligan's thirst must be larger still. He was glugging down genuine Russian vodka straight from the bottle's mouth, barely stopping to swallow. It was downright scary to watch.

"Mr. Bulligan." Madoc thought he'd better try to find out all he could while the old soak was still conscious. "Have you a map in the plane?"

"Map?" Bulligan took the neck of the bottle out of his mouth long enough to catch his breath and consider the question. "What the hell would I want a map for? Us old-timers fly by the seat of our pants. Can't you tell by lookin' at mine? Here, have a slug on me."

Madoc shook his head. "Not just now, thanks. I'd like to know where we are."

"I told you where you are. You're here, damn it."

"Yes, but I'd like to make the location a bit more precise. Where are we in relation, say, to Calgary or Edmonton?"

"You ain't noplace near either one of 'em. Try me on Bickerdike."

"All right then, what about Bickerdike?"

"You ain't noplace near there, neither. I just like the name."

"Then what town are we near? In other words, Mr. Bulligan, where might one reasonably hope to find a telephone or a two-way radio by means of which we can call for somebody to come and get us out of here?"

"What the hell do you want to leave for? You just got here. Let 'em know where you are and they'll slap you in jail. This ain't a bad place to hide out, an' I don't mind havin' a little company for a change. Gets kind of quiet up here alone in the wintertime. I hibernate, mostly."

"But you must need to get in supplies now and then," Madoc persisted. "Where do you buy your food?"

"None o' your goddamned business. I ain't givin' out no information to no smartass murderer that's too goddamned stuck up to take a drink with me. Git out o' my sight, you mangy coyote, or I'll bean you with this bottle. Come on, you other two ornery sidewinders, I'll take on the whole goddamned kit an' boiling of you. Put up your dukes!"

"Not to be inhospitable, old-timer," drawled Ed Naxton, "but that's our vodka you're drinking."

"Then I better quick drink some more before you snatch it back, eh."

And that was that. Before Ed could snatch the bottle away, Bulligan had taken one last, mighty gulp and gone out like a light.

Steve MacVittie snorted. "Fat lot of help he turned out to be. Now what do we do?"

"Wait for somebody sober to come along, I suppose," Madoc told him. "Is there any hope of your finding out what's wrong with the Grumman?"

"Not a hell of a lot, but we can try. See, those old-time crates like Bulligan's were so simply constructed that you didn't need to be any great mechanic to repair whatever needed fixing. Though old Ace here must be either a wizard or else the biggest damned fool going to have kept that mess of rags and rot in the air all this time," Steve conceded.

"But the planes we fly nowadays are so damned complicated that you have to be a trained mechanic even to make any sense out of how they're put together. I don't know, Madoc. Ed and I will do what we can, but I'm not making you any promises. And I'll tell you another thing; I'm not going up in that crate of Bulligan's, and neither is Ed."

"I shouldn't dream of asking you to. There'd be no sense to it, anyway, since we haven't the faintest notion of which way you ought to go or how soon you'd run out of fuel. Steve, can you at least get your luggage compartment open?"

"That we can do."

"Then why don't we tell people they can have access to their suitcases if they want? That may buck them up a little. I wouldn't mind a clean shirt, myself."

"Sure, let 'em come. What are we going to do about Ace here?"

"Tuck him up and let him enjoy his nap, don't you think? It's not that cold out here now." In fact, it must have been well past noon of a bright, mild day, and the interior of the Grumman was warming up nicely now that they had the door open. "Is there a rubber sheet or something we could slide under him, just in case?"

"A couple of those plastic bags we use for the garbage would do the trick." Steve lowered one of the reclining chairs. "Here, he might as well ride in style. He's a gutsy old bugger, you have to say that for him. Pretty crazy, though, don't you think?"

"Has to be to fly that wreck on faith and alcohol fumes," Ed agreed. "Here's a blanket and pillow."

Together the three men made a comfortable bed on the luxurious recliner and lifted Ace into it. He didn't weigh much.

"I wonder what he eats and where he gets it," said Steve. "I wonder what I'm going to eat, if it comes to that. Any chance of some lunch, Madoc?"

"Don't worry, you won't starve for a while yet. We'll scrape something together. Speaking of which, is there anything left from last night that might as well get used up?"

"See for yourself, it'll be in the food locker here."

There wasn't a great deal: mostly sweet cakes and the bottom layer of that huge box of chocolates, plus some cheese and fruit and about half a tin apiece of regular and decaffeinated coffee. Coffee was one thing Madoc hadn't been able to find at the hotel. With soup and crackers, these gleanings would make quite a decent meal.

Madoc didn't feel particularly hungry himself; he didn't see why anybody else should, after the way they'd pigged out at breakfast. Maybe it was the mountain air. Or the fact that Ed and Steve had been first to get fed this morning while he himself had been the last. He bundled the viands into a big white cardboard box that had probably held sandwiches and carried them over to where most of the onlookers were still standing, discussing the appalling news about Wilhelm Ochs and their chances of being rescued soon.

Joe Ragovsky detached himself from the group. "Need any help, Madoc?"

"Thank you, Joe. Would you mind carrying this stuff into the kitchen and checking the fire? It probably needs more wood."

"Sure thing. What's happening out there? Is that old guy going to get help for us?"

"I hope so. Unfortunately, though, he's taken a bit of a turn and will have to rest for a while before he can set off." It wouldn't help morale any to explain that Bulligan had in fact got sloshed and passed out.

"Then I may as well call a rehearsal," said Sir Emlyn. "Come along, ladies and gentlemen."

"Sir Emlyn, I don't have my instrument," said Helene Dufresne. "It's on the train."

"Along with our music," Cedric Rintoul pointed out. "So I guess we can't play, eh, maestro?"

"Ah, but we can," said the concertmaster. "We 'ave on the plane the scores for the new piece. It is possible to get them, yes?"

"Yes," said Madoc. "You can all get your suitcases, if you like."

"We'll have to rehearse in the lobby," said Sir Emlyn. "That's the only room big enough to hold us all."

The Fraser River Cantata had been composed especially for the upcoming occasion by a young Canadian with whose work both Sir Emlyn and Monsieur Houdon were favorably impressed. The singers liked it too, because he'd written them all parts that were showy but not too demanding. At the prospect of something to do, the whole group perked up.

Since the chairs were still in the kitchen, it was decided that they might as well eat lunch before moving them out to what had now become the rehearsal room. Sir Emlyn, who had done a really splendid job of cleaning up the kitchen considering his lack of experience, looked rather downcast at the thought of having it dirtied up again, but bowed to the will of the majority.

Opening cans of soup and heating up their contents was no great chore compared to flipping flapjacks. Madoc set out the cheese and fruit with some biscuits to keep the pack occupied while he resumed what was by now generally considered his official role as company chef.

He wondered whether he ought to have a bonfire going outside, now that they knew the search for them was on. But there was the smoke from the chimneys where no smoke ought to be, and he was loath to burn up the hotel's entire supply of firewood on the off chance that some circling plane would spot the blaze.

Besides, the two downed planes were in sight, or rather one downed plane and one downed pilot. The ancient triplane was a distress signal in itself. Madoc hoped Ace Bulligan would come out of his stupor in a more chastened and rational frame of mind, but he wasn't about to bet any money on the probability.

Needless to say, the cheese and fruit disappeared before Madoc could get any. He did manage to snaffle himself a bowlful of soup and a handful of crackers. His thought had been to sit at the table with the rest, but there was no chair left for him to sit on. He'd never considered himself a big eater, but he was beginning to feel himself a damnably frustrated one.

He took his soup out to the lobby to eat it at the counter for lack of a better place. Even here there was no peace for him. As he was approaching his destination, giving serious thought to the enjoyment of that first hot, savoury spoonful, Lady Rhys came down the stairs.

"Oh, good, you're taking soup to Lucy. But dear, couldn't you have set the bowl on a tray?"

"Mother, I am not taking this soup to Lucy," he replied with some asperity. "I'm going to eat it myself. After I've done that, I'm quite willing to take Lucy some soup on a tray or a broomstick or whatever you fancy. If you want any for yourself, I strongly recommend that you get it now. That's no orchestra we're feeding, it's a flock of vultures."

"And do you feel that their appetites excuse your rudeness in not being willing to sit at the table with them, even though your own father is one of the party?"

"I'm not sitting with them because they didn't leave me any place to sit. For you, I expect somebody will have the courtesy to get up. Or the timidity. I suppose you know they're all terrified of you."

"I should hope so, indeed! Very well, then, get on with your soup. I can serve myself."

"I'm sure you can, Mother. *Bon appetit.*"

"Madoc, you grow more like your father every day of your life."

With this totally astonishing remark, Lady Rhys took herself kitchenward. Stunned, Madoc ate his soup.

The soup wasn't all that great, but Madoc enjoyed it. When his bowl was empty, he carried it back to the kitchen and made sure there was washing-up water heating on the stove. Mindful of his mother's critical eye, he spread a paper napkin on a tray, added a couple of pink petits fours for a touch of color, and loaded it with a fresh bowl of soup, another napkin, a spoon, a cup of pre-milked and sugared tea, and a few crackers on a little plate. Lucy could crumble them into the soup if her throat was still too sore to eat them dry. He carried the trayful upstairs and tapped at Lucy's door.

"Feel like a bit of lunch?"

"Is that you, Madoc? Come on in. What sort of lunch?"

"Soup and crackers and a cup of tea. I hope you take milk and sugar."

"Yes, thanks. Actually, I feel quite hungry. I must be getting better. How's the pantry holding out?"

"We can manage another day or two if we have to, but I don't expect we shall. The news is out that we're missing, so I expect someone will be along to rescue us before long. Did my mother tell you we already have one visitor?"

"The crazy old man in the toy airplane? Fat lot of good he'll do us. Oh well, maybe the next one will be a Boeing. This smells good."

Lucy applied herself to her soup. When Madoc had come in with the tray, she'd been sitting propped up against a couple of pillows, reading a paperback thriller. At least he assumed it must be a thriller; the cover showed a voluptuous redhead in a few wisps of black lace, sprawled over the side of a barber's chair. A straight-backed razor lay in a deepish pool of blood just below her slashed throat.

She must have been the manicurist, Madoc thought, or perhaps the girl who did the shampooing. That would explain the skimpiness of her attire; she must have reasoned that she'd be far less apt to get her clothes wet if she wasn't wearing any to speak of. If that was supposed to be her blood on the floor, however, the artist had made her far too rosy-looking a corpse to convince a policeman. Rather than sit staring at Lucy eating her soup, Madoc picked up the book and started to read:

> *Hunk crumpled the empty Coors can in his hairy, sweaty paw and flung it into the fireplace. There was no fire in the fireplace, merely a messy heap of crumpled Coors cans and dirty shirts he'd been meaning to take to the laundry for the past month or so. The stench of stale beer and unwashed shirts was perhaps a trifle on the overpowering side, but to Hunk it meant home sweet home.*
>
> *That broad who'd phoned him last night begging him to protect her from some guy who was trying to make her give him back the deed to his barbershop had sounded like a nubile redhead. She'd be twenty-three years old; his redheads were always twenty-three years old. He sometimes wondered what they saw in a sixty-seven-year-old cop who'd turned private eye not for the glamour of it but because there wasn't much else for a cop to do after he'd been kicked off the force for chronic alcoholism and unclean habits. Whatever he had, they sure wanted it. It was tough on his hemorrhoids, but what the hell?*
>
> *Hunk hurled the now empty beer can after its predecessor and went to answer the door, at which somebody had by now been thumping frantically for the past ten minutes or so. Was it the redhead with the deed to the barbershop? Was it the landlord optimistically hoping to collect the rent? Was it a hood with a tommy gun and a contract on Hunk Murgatroyd's life?*

Hoping it was the hood with the tommy gun, Madoc laid the book back on the bed and went back to watching Lucy finish her soup.

Chapter 10

Lucy Shadd looked almost as rosy as the corpse in the barber chair. The rest must be doing her good despite the way she'd earned her right to take a day off. The silk scarf she'd wound around her neck prevented Madoc from seeing whether the red line had faded any. However, it couldn't be bothering her too much; he made his Holmesian deduction from the fact that she was eating the crackers dry instead of dunking them in the soup.

She cleaned up everything he'd brought, including the two pink petits fours. "Thanks, Madoc, that tasted really great. I must have been hungrier than I realized. But please don't go spreading the word around that I'm feeling better. This is the first day off I've had in ages. It's a tradition in orchestral touring that the head of operations never sleeps. And, believe me, we never do. What's happening downstairs?"

Madoc filled her in on the morning's developments, adding that suitcases were now accessible and that he'd bring hers up if she wanted it.

"I don't, actually. If I could get at my clothes, I'd begin to feel guilty about not putting them on. Once I'm dressed, my holiday will be over. So that old man heard on the news that our plane had turned up missing? Was there anything about Wilhelm, did he say?"

If Lucy Shadd was resilient enough to beguile her re-

89

covery from a near-strangling by reading about a nubile redhead getting her throat slashed, Madoc decided she probably had the stomach to be told now what she'd have to learn sooner or later anyway. "Yes, there was. I don't know how much stock to put in anything Bulligan told us, but from what I could piece together out of his ramblings, Ochs has been found to have died from ricin poisoning."

"Ricin? What's that? I've never heard of it."

"As it happens, I have. We had a case back in Fredericton last year. Ricin is one of the potentially lethal vegetable alkaloids like taxine and digitalin. The only source for it I can think of offhand is the castor bean."

"And what's a castor bean? I only know castor sugar and casters on furniture legs."

"Well, surely you've heard of castor oil?"

"Ugh, did you have to remind me? God, that stuff is awful. Does castor oil come from castor beans?"

"Yes, it does. They in turn come from a rather handsome plant that's often grown as an ornamental in people's gardens."

"Whatever for? That sounds like an awfully stupid thing to do, but then, I've never been much of a gardener. Wilhelm was, though. At least he used to buy little potted plants to take with him when we went on long bus tours. I should think he'd have known better than to swallow a castor bean."

"Mere swallowing wouldn't have killed him. The beans would have simply passed through his digestive tract. They must have been ground up and mixed in with his food or something of the sort. I'm told Ochs was a fairly enthusiastic trencherman."

"Lord, yes. Poor Wilhelm ate like a pig, even though he had all kinds of ghastly stomach problems. Didn't anybody tell you that?"

Madoc nodded. "I've heard."

"From Frieda, I'll bet. She always hated Wilhelm's guts. Oh, God! I didn't mean that the way it came out. I just meant she hated having to cope with his stomach. You can imagine what it's like to be jammed up in close quarters with somebody who's always belching or breaking wind. And of course it's been worse since Sir Emlyn took over as guest conductor."

"Good Lord, why? Was he allergic to my father?"

"No, but it means we're doing all those choral pieces. You can't fit a chorus onstage without squeezing the musicians closer together than usual. Frieda's prissy in some ways, and Wilhelm did have a pretty gross sense of humor."

"You and he were good friends, though, I'm told. Wasn't it you who got him promoted to first chair?"

"After I couldn't blow my own horn anymore, sure. Actually I like what I'm doing now a lot better, but that's beside the point. Yes, I did put in a good word for him, which was about all I could do. It's not the musicians who carry the clout, as any of them will be only too willing to tell you. Wilhelm would have been the logical choice anyway. He'd been with the orchestra almost as long as I had, he was a really fine player, and he knew the Wagstaffe sound."

"Your sound?"

"Every major orchestra—minor ones too, I suppose—has a distinctive way of playing. Some go for a big, grand noise; others are crisper, lighter. It's hard to explain to somebody with a tin ear; your father could probably tell you better than I. Anyway, if you've got somebody in the orchestra who's capable of playing first position, it makes sense to protect him rather than bring in somebody new who'll need time to play himself in. Not that it wouldn't be the fair thing to do anyway, but fairness isn't always a conductor's primary consideration."

"Surely you can't call my father unfair?"

"He wouldn't have any say in the matter unless he was the permanent music director. Guest conductors usually make the best of what they get except for choosing the big star soloists who aren't normally members of any orchestra. We knew Sir Emlyn would be bringing his own singers

with him, but who cares about singers? They're not interested in us, they're just along for the laughs, as you may
have gathered. Naming no names, you understand."

Lucy picked up the empty tray to set it aside. Madoc
leaped up from the windowsill where he'd been perching
and took it from her.

"Did Ochs complain to you about not feeling well either
yesterday or the day before?"

"Wilhelm was always complaining about not feeling
well. I can't say I remember particularly. But why the day
before?" Lucy was sharp, no doubt about that.

"Apparently ricin can take quite a while to act after it's
been ingested."

"Surely not a whole two days?"

"What about late evening of the previous day?" Madoc
pointed out. "That would be only a twenty-four hour span,
perhaps even less. Don't the orchestra members ever go
out for a late supper after a concert?"

"Oh yes, often, particularly the horns and the winds.
We—they, I suppose I ought to say—tend to eat lightly
beforehand. And playing a full symphony concert is des-
perately hard work, in case you didn't know, so one's often
starving by the time it's over. Wilhelm was always hungry
anyway. He claimed he ate to quiet his ulcers down which
no doubt would have happened if he'd chosen his food
sensibly, but he never did."

"What sort of food was Ochs likely to have ordered?"

"Chili dogs, curries, fried fish, fried potatoes, fried
steak, fried chicken, fried anything. Mexican food when he
could get it, Chinese food, Italian food—he loved that.
Giant hamburgers with lots of raw onion. You know,
macho he-man stuff, though he'd even eat quiche in a
pinch. And douse it with ketchup, no doubt. He was great
for Worcestershire sauce, piccalilli, mustard, all that stuff."

"Did he drink much?"

"Liquor, you mean? A fair amount of beer and wine if it
was on the table, but seldom anything stronger. Wilhelm
was basically an eater, not a drinker. If he was in fact

poisoned on purpose and not by accident, I expect you're right about its having been put in his food. It wouldn't be hard to fool him. He'd order shrimp cocktail, for instance, and doctor the sauce up with so much tabasco and horseradish that he couldn't possibly have tasted anything else unless it was strong enough even to overcome the horseradish. Wilhelm would eat horseradish by the spoonful."

"So what you're saying, Lucy, is that he must have pretty well paralyzed his taste buds long ago."

"I should think so, yes. But why would anybody want to murder poor old Bill?"

"Why should anybody want to murder you, for that matter? I'm sorry to bring it up again, Lucy, but when an attempt is made on somebody's life, it's usually for a reason, even if the reason is a totally insane one. Can you think why anybody connected with the orchestra might have wanted to kill either of you?"

The middle-aged woman in the shabby twin bed stared up at Madoc for a long moment, then shook her well-groomed gray head. "God, Madoc, what a question! I suppose I get under a few people's skins now and then. I'm the one who has to keep nagging them after all, about things like not stuffing their personal junk in the wardrobe trunks and being on time to make connections. And paying their hotel charges before they leave. I'm sure everybody thinks I'm a pain in the neck, but I find it hard to believe I've managed to make anyone mad enough to kill me."

She shifted her position, as though the sagging mattress had grown too uncomfortable to tolerate any longer. "As for Wilhelm, the only reason I can think of is that one of the other horn players might want his chair. But there's no guarantee they'd get it even if they did bump him off. Surely any player must realize that. I'll grant you it would have been physically possible for one of the musicians who went on the train to have slipped him the poison either at supper the night before or any time yesterday. Maybe even in a candy bar or something. Would that work?"

"I suppose so," Madoc replied, "if you were clever

enough to pull it off. Invite him to a movie, perhaps, and sprinkle ground-up castor beans on his caramel corn in the dark."

"Or take him for a walk and buy him a hot dog, and mix the poison in with the piccalilli and chopped onion. Wilhelm always ordered raw onion when he could get it. He used to say that was the only way he could bear hanging out with Cedric Rintoul. Cedric eats onions by the bucketful. Ugh, this is scary to think about! You don't suppose there's any chance somebody dumped ricin into that soup I just ate?"

"If they did, we'll go together," Madoc reassured her. "I ate soup from that same kettle and so did everybody else in the company. I shouldn't worry about the soup, Lucy. It came out of tins which I opened myself, and my father was right there helping to stir it."

"Sir Emlyn was working in the kitchen?" Lucy was gaping at Madoc as if he'd all of a sudden sprouted antlers. "Madoc, you can't be serious!"

"Why not? Tad washed the breakfast dishes."

"Don't bother talking nonsense to me, Madoc. I have no sense of humor to speak of, and I never appreciate stupid jokes. Sir Emlyn did no such thing."

"Oh yes he did, and quite capably, too. Why shouldn't he?"

"Because it's highly inappropriate. Conductors just don't act like that. I'd better get up."

"Whatever for? We're managing perfectly well without you."

That was unkind, but she had no business calling Sir Emlyn inappropriate. "Lucy, you can't honestly believe my father would behave in an unseemly manner under any circumstances. We're in a highly unusual situation. For however long we're stuck here, everybody's going to have to pitch in and help out. My father is setting an example which I sincerely hope the rest of the crowd are going to emulate, because I'm not finding it all that appropriate for me to get stuck with the dog work every time."

"Oh well, that puts a different face on the matter." Lucy pulled back the foot she'd stuck outside the blankets and resettled herself on the pillows. "I just hope they understand why he's doing it."

"If they don't, I'm sure my mother will be glad to explain. Now let's get back to the important stuff. Tell me about Cedric Rintoul."

"What do you mean, tell you about him? What do you want me to say?"

"I shan't know that till I've heard it, shall I? My work consists largely of gathering information that's not going to do me any good, but I have to keep on asking silly questions because sooner or later somebody will give me the right answer. Since we have nothing else to go on, Lucy, we may as well act for the time being on the premise that the person who fed ricin to Wilhelm Ochs is quite likely the same one who tried to strangle you."

"But suppose it isn't?"

"Look at the facts, Lucy. It's generally known among the orchestra members, is it not, that you and Wilhelm Ochs were old friends as well as close colleagues?"

"Oh yes."

"It's also common knowledge that you have a special advantage in being both an ex-player and the present director of operations. If anybody is in a position to have inside information or opinions about why or by whom Ochs was poisoned, you're a likelier person than anyone else. Isn't that what they'd think?"

"But I don't."

"But you might, Lucy. You see, the poisoner couldn't very well come up to you and ask."

"All right, Madoc, you've made your point."

"So that rather whittles things down, wouldn't you say? It has to be one of the people here with us now who put that violin string around your neck."

"Yes, of course. I'm not altogether stupid. And they all knew Wilhelm and as far as I know, they all had plenty of opportunity to kill him. And you think it was Cedric who did it."

"No, Lucy, I do not. At this stage, I have to suspect everybody alike, except myself because I have an airtight alibi. Ricin is a slow-acting poison, so Ochs must have got it quite some time before it began to work, as we've already discussed. I was working at my desk in the Fredericton RCMP headquarters until late afternoon day before yesterday. My wife drove me to the airport. My plane was late arriving in Wagstaffe, and I didn't get to the concert until the orchestra was onstage tuning up. By that time, Ochs was already heading for the last roundup."

"But the rest of us are all suspects. Even me, I suppose. What about your parents?"

"I can't rule them out, can I? I will say they're not likely suspects because they're only temporarily connected with the orchestra, don't have any guilty secrets, didn't know Ochs well enough to hate him, and in any case, wouldn't have had to kill him to get rid of him. I expect we can eliminate both the pilots because they had no connection with the orchestra and never even got to meet Ochs. Unless it turns out one of them is his long-lost cousin who'll step into the family fortune now that Ochs is no longer in the way. You see, we mustn't overlook any possibilities."

"No, I suppose not. Okay, Madoc, I'll play."

"Good. So tell me about Rintoul. Have you known him long? Was there any friction between him and Ochs? Does he get on well with the rest of the orchestra? What about his personal life? As to why I happened to mention Rintoul first, don't go getting any ideas. It's just that he rather tends to thrust himself forward."

"That's a tactful way of putting it, I must say. I like Cedric well enough, but he can be an awful pest sometimes. So can his buddy, Jason."

"We'll get to Jason later." Madoc pulled out his notebook and waited.

Lucy rubbed her chin fretfully. "I'm on, eh? Oh gosh,

let's see. Well, Cedric joined the Wagstaffe about ten years ago, I believe it was. He came from one of the provincial symphonies, I can't remember which but it'll be in the personnel files. He'd known Wilhelm long before that, so they got to be great buddies. Wilhelm thought Cedric was a riot and egged him on, which of course Cedric loved. He's not a particularly happy man underneath, if you want my personal opinion. It's the old Pagliacci act. You know, laughing on the outside, crying on the inside."

"Why should Rintoul be unhappy? Does he feel threatened in his job?"

"No reason why he should. Cedric's about as good as they come on trombone. But he's pretty much of a washout otherwise. Especially with women."

"Any particular woman?"

"No, just women in general. He always comes on strong to any new woman in the ensemble. Corliss Blair, for instance; he made a big play for her, but she wasn't playing. Cedric's problem is, he doesn't know how to act. He's like a kid in school, thinking he can get a girl's attention by teasing her with a dead mouse or something."

"Has he ever waved a dead mouse your way?"

"Getting personal, aren't you? No, you see it was different with me. I was just one of the boys in the brass section. We'd go out and grab a bite together, that sort of thing, but that was as far as it ever went."

"You haven't been doing that nowadays?"

"Once in a while. Now that I'm director of operations, I never have time to eat. Besides, I'm not one of the gang any longer."

Lucy put her hand up to her neck. "Is your throat bothering you?" Madoc was constrained to ask. "Would you rather not go on with this just now?"

"No, I'm all right. I could use another cup of tea, when you get around to it. I did want to say about Cedric that he's really not a bad guy, even though he does drive people nuts sometimes. He's generous, for one thing. Too generous for his own good, sometimes."

"What do you mean by that?"

"Well, he lends money and doesn't get paid back."

"To whom does he lend it? People in the orchestra?"

"Well sure. Those are the only people he knows. The only ones he associates with, anyway."

"Can you think of anybody who's heavily in debt to him at the moment?"

"Look, I think you'd better ask Cedric himself that. I don't see what it has to do with this business of my getting strangled."

"Nor do I," Madoc admitted cheerfully. "By the way, you're not—"

"I'm not in hock to Cedric, no, nor to anybody else. And I don't lend, either. My money belongs to me, and I hang on to it. Next question?"

Chapter 11

Lucy had said all she was going to say about Cedric Rintoul, that was clear. Madoc was too experienced an interrogator to force the issue. "Then what about Rintoul's pal, Jasper?"

Lucy shrugged. "You needn't try to borrow any money from him, either. Jason's always broke. He has five kids to support, two of them in college, not to mention a wife and a mortgage. I believe the wife's gone back to work, though, to help foot the college bills. She was a trained nurse before they started having kids."

"So he's a real family man?"

"God, yes. Don't let him back you into a corner, or he'll start showing you photographs. Jason hates having to leave home. I think that's why he clowns around with Cedric so much when we're on tour, to keep himself from feeling homesick. He doesn't do it when we're back in Wagstaffe."

"That's where he lives?"

"Just outside the city, in an area that used to be country and is getting to be another bedroom community. He's got quite a decent place, and he's crazy about it. We never see him in Wagstaffe except at rehearsals and concerts. The rest of the time he's lugging the kids to hockey games or puttering around his garden. He has a little greenhouse, too. He comes to rehearsal with big bags full of stuff: cu-

cumbers, cabbages, out-of-season tomatoes, you name it, and passes them out to anybody who wants them. Flowers sometimes, too, but the veggies are his big thing. He says they save a mint on the grocery bill."

"With five kids, I expect they do," said Madoc. He was thinking about castor oil plants. Jasper wouldn't have room for one in his greenhouse, but he might grow some outdoors, now that his children were evidently old enough to leave the seeds alone. "You say he's always hard up. Does he borrow from Rintoul?"

Lucy scowled. "I wouldn't know about that. Look, Madoc, I told you I don't like these questions about money. As far as I know, Jason doesn't borrow from anybody, unless you count the bank. His wife works, as I said. The kids get part-time jobs, and in a pinch they could all live on peas and carrots. He's getting by. And in case you were about to ask whether he fools around on tour, the answer is no. He's so monogamous it's pitiful."

"Does he gamble?"

"What do you mean by gamble? Jason plays cards with the bunch, but not for big stakes. Offhand, I can't think of anybody on your list who does. They can't afford to. Musicians in the Wagstaffe are decently paid, but they don't make wads of money like rock stars. On tour, the management pays for transportation, food, and lodging, but not for incidentals. It gets expensive, all those little things like paying for your laundry and having to tip somebody every time you turn around. The only thing Jason squanders money on are silly jokes like whoopee cushions and presents he can take home to the kids. He's a really simpleminded guy."

"How long has he been with the orchestra?"

"Forever, I think. He was here before I was, anyway. I'm not sure but what this is the only orchestra he's ever played with. The only major one, certainly. Jason didn't get to be principal trumpet until about five years ago, though. He rose from the ranks, like Wilhelm. I ought to be downstairs talking with Sir Emlyn about lining up another horn player."

"There'll be time enough for that when you get to where you can hire one," said Madoc. "Anyway, you can't talk to my father now. He's called a rehearsal."

"Then why aren't they rehearsing? I don't hear anything."

"Come to think of it, neither do I. Maybe he hasn't finished washing the dishes yet. I hope he's also seeing about that pit for the latrine. It slipped my mind entirely."

"Latrine pit? Remind me to compliment Lady Rhys on what a classy conversationalist she's got for a son. And don't tell me Sir Emlyn's doing the digging himself, I already told you I don't like sick jokes."

"No, my father's afraid of straining his shoulder before the festival. I expect my mother's doing it for him. So that's all you have to tell me about Jason Jasper?"

"That's all I can think of. Unless you'd like to know his kids' names, ages, and the brand of toothpaste they prefer."

"Later perhaps. Let's see how well we can do on Frieda Loye. Did you offer to share with her last night because you're friends or because you consider it part of your job to cope with her nightmares?"

"Wrong both times. I like Frieda well enough but wouldn't call her a close friend. We have, however, been roommates lots of times, simply because for quite a while we were the only two women in the orchestra. She doesn't snore, she doesn't invite guys into the room, she's neat in her habits, and she doesn't always have nightmares. Why shouldn't I room with her? Next question?"

"Is she married?"

"No, the Mrs. is sort of a courtesy title. She had what they call nowadays a significant other, but he died."

"How long ago was this?"

"Oh, ages. I don't believe there's been anybody since, certainly nobody from the orchestra. She has a little apartment in Wagstaffe. It's nice."

She meant it wasn't. Madoc wondered what sort of living quarters Lucy herself had, and what kind of reaction he'd get from Frieda if he asked.

"What does she do with her spare time?"

"She needlepoints. She's got needlepoint pillows on her couch, needlepoint seats on her chairs, needlepoint pictures on her walls, a brick covered with needlepoint that she uses for a doorstop. I couldn't stand doing that artsy-craftsy stuff myself, but Frieda says it calms her nerves."

"Frieda's nerves seem to be giving her a great deal of trouble these days," Madoc ventured. "Was she always like this?"

"Like what?"

"About two jitters from a nervous collapse."

"Well, my God, what do you expect? How'd you like to wake up and find your roommate getting strangled?"

"I shouldn't like it at all, but I don't think that's her problem. She was the same way last night at the concert. And I can't say your friend Rintoul was helping her out of it. What does he have against her?"

"What do you mean, against her? Nothing that I know of. I told you Cedric makes a pest of himself because he wants to be noticed. He was trying to get a rise out of her, that's all. Frieda's such a damned stoic that she just toughs it out instead of turning around and telling him to stuff himself, so he tries all the harder. If you're trying to hold me responsible for his pulling that trick with the violin string during the performance, I'm here to tell you I didn't know anything about it. If I had, I'd have taken the fool thing away from him during intermission, not that it would have been my job to do so. As it happened, I had the wardrobe trunks to cope with, the buses to organize, and about seventy million other things on my mind. And then there was Wilhelm. Damn it, I liked Wilhelm! Why don't you get off my back for a while, eh? My throat hurts."

"I'll get you that cup of tea. Oh, just one more thing. You said back in Wagstaffe that Ochs had a brother. Was that his only family? He never married?"

Lucy jerked her body straight up to a sitting position, her hand still pressing the scarf to her throat. "Madoc, why didn't I think of that before? Sure, Wilhelm was married for a while, to a young singer he met somewhere in the provinces. That was ages ago, too. She's not so young any more. Her real name was Norma Belschi but of course she changed it."

"Ah so. Am I correct in inferring from your information that Madame Bellini hasn't always been Madame Bellini?"

"You are. And she wouldn't stand a chance of being Madame Houdon, either, if Jacques-Marie ever found out about her and Wilhelm. Jacques looks like a nice, quiet, gentlemanly guy, but don't let that fool you. He's jealous as hell and has the temper of a fiend once he gets wound up. Madoc, could I please have my tea now?"

"Sorry. I'll get it right away."

For the past couple of minutes, Madoc had been hearing tentative tweets and hoots, from which he'd deduced that the rehearsers were finally getting down to business. As he went downstairs into the lobby, he saw them grouped around his father in the chairs they'd dragged back from the kitchen. Lady Rhys and Helene Dufresne were there, too, either to lend moral support or for want of other entertainment. Helene was sitting with her knees apart and her hands making tune-up motions that suggested she was all set to rehearse even without her instrument.

Cedric Rintoul was sitting on the opposite side of the circle from Frieda Loye, Madoc noticed. Sir Emlyn wasn't taking any chances this time. However, he'd reckoned without the tricky trombonist's infinite resources. As Frieda raised her flute to her lips and glanced down at the score she was having to hold in her lap for want of a music stand, something small and furry whizzed across the floor, straight at her feet.

Madoc recognized the thing at once; it was the wind-up mouse he'd seen in Rintoul's room. Frieda recognized it, too. After one shrill yip, she laid down her flute, bounded across the room, and started belaboring Rintoul with her fists, screaming like a banshee all the while.

"Damn you to hell, leave me alone! Leave me alone!"

Her screams degenerated into inchoate shrieks; she went totally out of control. Sir Emlyn stuck his baton in his pocket, stepped over to Frieda, and gave her a pretty hard slap in the face. For the second time in his conducting career, Sir Emlyn raised his voice.

"This is unprofessional behavior, and I will not have it! Mrs. Loye, you had better go to your room. Lady Rhys will go with you. Rintoul, I have no authority to fire you but you are out of this orchestra for as long as I am conducting it."

"What?" The huge trombonist stared up at the furious little Welshman as if he could not believe what he was hearing. "But I was only trying to—"

"You were making an ass of yourself and you were deliberately disrupting my rehearsal. You have behaved abominably during every performance I have conducted thus far on this tour. I will not have you playing under me again. Please go away. Now."

As if he were sleepwalking, Rintoul took his trombone and his mouse, and lumbered off into the kitchen. Sir Emlyn turned back to the circle. "Ladies and gentlemen, I apologize for having lost my temper. I do not feel myself sufficiently collected to go on with this rehearsal. I ask your pardon for having taken up your time to no avail. This has never happened before, and it will not happen again. I am going out for a walk."

He laid his baton on top of the score they'd never got to work on, made his usual diffident half bow, and walked out the front door. Those left behind turned to Madoc.

"I have to make a cup of tea for Lucy Shadd," he told them. "Why don't you all go out for a walk?"

They started shuffling their chairs, putting their instruments in their cases, murmuring and shrugging to one another. Madoc walked into the kitchen. Rintoul was there with his trombone, almost in tears.

"I didn't know he could be like that. I was only trying to liven things up a little."

"You appear to have succeeded beyond your expectations." Madoc pulled the simmering tea kettle to the front of the stove to make it boil. "What is it you have against Frieda Loye, Rintoul?"

"I don't have anything against her!"

"You just like to hear her scream, eh? You're not deliberately trying to drive her round the bend?"

"Of course not! What do you take me for?"

"Either a fool or a liar or both. Is it possible you honestly had no idea that your so-called jokes are raising hell with Frieda's nervous system?"

"Look, I haven't the foggiest notion what you're talking about."

The kettle was bubbling now. Madoc found a clean teapot, threw in what he thought was probably an adequate amount of tea, and set it to steep on a tray. Remembering that his mother and Frieda would probably be upstairs with the invalid by now, he added three mugs, three spoons, and little bowls of sugar and powdered milk. He often carried tea up to Janet at home; he wished to God he were doing so this time. She'd also have heard the radio reports about the missing plane by now; she must be frantic.

Why the bloody hell didn't somebody come searching? He'd have to go see whether Bulligan had slept off the vodka yet, and try to bribe or threaten him into taking that old crate to wherever it was possible to get out word that they hadn't crashed. This time, Madoc would pour the liquor into the gas tank himself if necessary. Which wouldn't be any guarantee against the old bugger's trying to siphon it out. He knocked at the door of the bedroom he'd so recently left. Lady Rhys met him at the door and took the tray.

"Thank you, dear. I've given Frieda another tablet. Where's your father?"

"Gone for a walk. You know, this is the first time in my life I've seen Tad lose his temper."

"It doesn't happen often. What's happened to Cedric?"

"I left him in the kitchen, looking stricken."

"As well he might. Beastly fellow! We'd been hoping he'd straighten out as the tour went on, but he's gotten worse. I don't know whether he got the idea your father's a pushover. People don't make that mistake, as a rule. It's odd, you know; one expects a certain amount of horseplay and tolerates it within reason, but this out-and-out sadism is something quite new in our experience. Has he always been such a monster, Lucy?"

"I've already talked to your son about Cedric, Lady Rhys. If you don't mind, my throat's really bothering me."

"Of course, Lucy. We'll discuss it later, Madoc."

Thus dismissed, Madoc wandered back downstairs. Rather, he tried to wander. Left with nothing to do, the musicians and singers must have come to a group decision that they weren't going to be rescued today and might as well get their luggage out of the plane before it got too dark. Since they were limited to one suitcase and one carry-on bag apiece, the suitcases tended to be on the large side. Getting down that narrow wooden staircase through a minefield of Samsonite was a good deal like trying to go down the up escalator at Toronto airport during rush hour, Madoc found. Being slim and agile, he made it unscathed, but it took time. Joe Ragovsky was waiting for him in the lobby.

"I dug us a hole out back."

"Oh good," Madoc replied. "Do people know what to do about it?"

"Yeah, I spread the word."

"Thank you, Joe. I'd meant to tend to it earlier, but one way and another, this has been a busy day. I'd like to chat with you a bit when you have a minute."

"No time like the present," the viola player replied. "Let's go to the kitchen and make ourselves a cuppa."

Madoc was about to object in case Rintoul was still there, then he shrugged. They could always take their mugs outside if the atmosphere got too sticky. However, the deposed trombonist was not to be seen. Perhaps Rintoul had gone to waylay Sir Emlyn in the surely vain hope of getting him to change his mind. More likely, he was upstairs rewinding his mechanical mouse and trying to elicit sympathy from his colleagues.

While Joe got down the mugs, Madoc pumped a kettleful of fresh water, took off a stove lid, and set the kettle directly over the hole to get the full benefit from the handsome bed of shimmering red coals that had collected over the day.

"This shouldn't take long to boil," he remarked. "I wish we had a piece of my wife's pie to go with the tea."

"Your wife does her own baking?" Joe sounded surprised. "I figured you'd have a bunch of maids in the house."

"On a policeman's salary? Figure again, Joe. We have a cleaner in once a week and a neighbor's kid to water the plants and feed the cat when we go away, which we don't do all that often, except for overnight visits to her brother's farm. How about you?"

"About the same. My wife's a schoolteacher, so it's next to impossible for us to go anywhere together except during the school vacations. With three kids, it's too damned expensive anyway. My mother-in-law lives with us, which takes some of the load off. She's a good egg. But a terrible cook. I get most of the meals when I'm around. I like to cook."

"Damn your eyes, why didn't you tell me sooner?"

"What? And miss being able to say I've had my pancakes flipped by the guy who captured Mad Carew?"

Madoc scowled. "Oh, you know about that?"

"Sure, I caught on right away to who you were, but I haven't told anybody. I thought you might be traveling incognito."

"Hold the thought, Joe. I'm sick of hearing about Carew, and my mother thinks the whole business was dis-

gustingly uncouth. Tell me something." Madoc fished out
the short pieces of violin string he'd taken from Rintoul's
trombone and the longer one he'd picked up from Lucy
Shadd's bedroom floor. "Could these possibly be from the
same string?"

Joe took the two bits of wire and held them up to the
fast-fading light. "Could be. This is a D-string with one
end cut off, and this little bit here looks like the end."

"It's wrapped in a different color thread from the other
end," Madoc objected.

"I know, that's how they come."

"The string wouldn't have been yours, by any chance?"

"Nope, this one's from a violin. I play viola. Our D-
strings are thicker and longer. You wouldn't notice the difference, but it's perfectly obvious to me."

"How do you suppose the cut was made? Could you do
it with a small pocket knife?"

"Hell, no. This string was made to withstand up to
ninety pounds pressure; it's chrome steel wire wound
around a gut core. The sensible thing would be to use a
wire cutter."

"And where would you get one of those in a hurry?"

"From Dave Gabriel, I'd say offhand. Oboe and bassoon players spend about half their time playing their instruments and the other half making new reeds for them.
That's what those mouthpieces are, you know, just hollow
reeds like you'd pick out of a swamp. Only this is a special
kind of reed that only grows in France or somewhere. The
guys have kits with knives and stuff they use to cut and
shape the reeds, and string and wire to bind them with.
Bassoon reeds have to be wired, then wrapped with string
over the wire. Dave coaches a woodwind ensemble, so he
carries a great big kit with every kind of tool known to
man, pretty much. He's sure to have wire cutters."

"Would the cutters be easy to steal?"

"I guess so, if you were mean enough. What the guys
usually do is slip their tools inside the canvas covers of

their instrument cases. You could sneak a cutter out and stick it back again easily enough without getting caught, but why go to the bother? Couldn't you just ask to borrow it for a second?"

"Certainly you could," said Madoc, "provided you weren't planning to use the string to strangle somebody."

Chapter 12

"God, what minds you cops must have!"

Joe Ragovsky actually backed away from the strings Madoc was holding out to him. "What the hell possessed you to say that?"

"I found this longer piece on the floor beside Lucy Shadd's bed after that screaming incident early this morning. She claimed she'd been attacked by a masked intruder, and had a red line around her throat that suggested an attempt at strangulation."

"My God! I didn't know that."

"Not many of this crowd do, and I'd as soon you didn't spread the word around. We don't want mass panic. This smaller piece I took off Cedric Rintoul's trombone slide. He'd been using it to tickle the back of Frieda Loye's neck during the concert last night. Perhaps you noticed?"

"No, I didn't notice. If I had, I'd have busted the son of a bitch's jaw for him. Cedric's been tormenting Frieda lately every chance he gets, and it makes me sick. What the hell, I don't mind a little clowning around. I do it myself sometimes. But picking on a middle-aged woman who's halfway round the bend to start with—I'm damned glad your father gave him the shove, if you want the truth. Cedric ought to have had his ears pinned back long before this."

Joe simmered down from irate to bothered. "Only thing

that worries me is what's going to happen with our brass section at the festival. It'll be tough having to play with two new guys."

"I'm sure my father will be able to cope," Madoc reassured him. "He's got out of worse messes than this. But why do you say Frieda Loye's a mental case? On account of those nightmares she's been having the last few weeks?"

"No, not that. It's more that she's been so—I don't quite know how to put it. Funny. Jumpy, snappish, tight as a G-string. I get the impression she's scared all the time and trying not to let on. I didn't mean to imply that Frieda's really gone nuts. She's just—different, I guess. Maybe it's her time of life. My mother-in-law went through a spell a while back. She'd wake up in the middle of the night worried sick about some damned little thing without knowing why. She was turning herself into a nervous wreck for no good reason. The doctor gave her some pills and she straightened out okay. Probably Frieda ought to be taking something."

"Are you sure she's not already taking something?"

"Huh? Oh, you mean drugs? No, you get that stuff in the pop bands sometimes, but symphony players don't go for it as a rule. Specially not Frieda, she's big on vitamins and long walks to keep her wind in shape. But that's terrible, what you said about Lucy. I don't know why the heck anybody'd try to strangle her. Say, you don't suppose Cedric was trying to get another rise out of Frieda and picked the wrong bed, by any chance? It would be a hell of a stupid thing to do, of course."

"Criminal would be a more apt word than stupid. Do you honestly think Rintoul would go that far?"

"Gosh, Madoc, I'd hate to say. Cedric's pulled some pretty crazy stunts, but faking a murder, I don't know. Did Lucy really get hurt? Is that why she's stayed upstairs all day?"

"She says her throat's still bothering her. I can't say whether that's from the choking or from all the yelling she did when she was attacked. Anyway, she's decided it made a reasonable excuse for her to take a day's rest for a change, which she apparently deserves. One gathers she's kept hopping pretty much of the time when the orchestra's on tour."

"Oh yeah, we have a tradition in this business that the head of operations never gets a chance to sleep. It's not a job for weaklings, that's for sure, but Lucy took to it like a duck to water. At least it keeps her with the orchestra. I suppose you know Lucy used to be first chair horn?"

"So I've been told." Madoc couldn't recall how many times by now. "Were you with the orchestra then, Joe?"

"Not really. She switched just a couple of weeks after I got taken on. They claim Lucy used to be first-rate, but you sure couldn't have proven it by the way she was playing then. There's no way they could have let her stay on in the brasses and she must have known. Being shifted out must have been an awful blow to her but she took it like a soldier, I have to say. I'll bet she's toughing out the strangling, too, eh. Christ, women are rugged. I don't know many men, myself included, who'd have the nerve to stay up there by themselves all day after having a thing like that happen to them."

"My mother's been with Lucy a good part of the time."

Joe grinned. "No wonder she feels safe, then. It'd take a pretty damned determined strangler to try again with Lady Rhys around. No offense to your mother, Madoc. We all think she's a great lady."

"Mother's not a bad sort, once you get to know her."

Afraid Joe might think he sounded overenthusiastic about his own parent, Madoc reverted quickly to the main topic at hand. "You could be right, you know, about the alleged strangler's being Cedric Rintoul trying to get another rise out of Frieda Loye. In that case, Lucy would certainly have recognized him, but wouldn't want to say so for fear of getting him in serious trouble. She and Rintoul have always got on pretty well, haven't they?"

"Far as I know. He's the one she hangs out with when she gets the chance, he and Jason Jasper and poor old Wilhelm Ochs. She's going to miss Wilhelm, they played together for so long. That's how it is in an orchestra, you know, we tend to club in with our own section. You're right: if Lucy knows it was Cedric, she won't rat on him, you can bet your bottom dollar on that. She'll wait till she gets the bugger alone and tear him to pieces with her own hands."

"If he's still around," said Madoc. "You don't think Rintoul will be fired on account of my father's kicking him out today?"

"Nah, the guys will back him up with the director. Some of them, anyway. Cedric will promise to behave and sober down for a while, then gradually start working his way back into the old routine. We all know it won't take long. Cedric's beginning to flat his high notes a little. You wouldn't notice it yet, I don't suppose, but I'll bet your father has. Our director's known for a while. He's a good egg, he'll go easy till he has to make a move."

"I see. Rintoul will go back and claim my father was one of those Brit bullies who can't adjust to our informal Canadian ways."

"Yeah, that's right, a real Captain Bligh." Joe was having a lovely time now. "But you don't act like a Brit."

"Not I. I was born on this side and never wanted to leave. My wife's a New Brunswicker. We live in Fredericton."

"That's a nice city. I bet you wish you were back there right now."

"You can say that again, Joe. Were you planning to cook supper tonight?"

"If it's a case of cook or get pinched, sure. What are we having?"

"Your guess is as good as mine. What is there to have?"

"I'll scout around the kitchen and see what I can scare up. Say, Madoc, do you think maybe we ought to start going easy on the grub in case we get stuck here for a while?"

"I don't know what to think. We can't be too far off the

beaten track if this place is able to function as a tourist trap, and Ace Bulligan knew about us from this morning's early news broadcast. It doesn't seem possible he's the only one to come searching. I think I'll go see if I can't persuade the old buzzard to talk a little sense for a change."

Madoc left Joe to research the food situation and walked out toward the plane. He'd have to take up the matter of the violin string with Houdon, when he could get him into a corner. There was also La Bellini to tackle. What a turn-up that she'd once been married to the lubberly Ochs. Could either of his parents have known? If so, why couldn't they have told him? Was it possible his father and Madame Bellini—no, it was not possible.

Somewhere around the closed-up ghost town MacVittie and Naxton had found a couple of not very safe-looking wooden ladders. They'd propped them up against the side of the Grumman and got part of the cowling off. Now they were standing side by side, brooding with bewilderment over the innards thus exposed.

"Any luck?" Madoc called up to them.

Ed Naxton scrambled down and beckoned him over. "Be my guest. Steve can show you better than I."

Since the ladder hadn't crashed under Ed, Madoc decided there was the off chance it wouldn't break under him, either. He went up, testing each rung before he put his weight on it, and peered into the technological tangle with no hope of comprehension. Steve wasn't much help.

"See, it's pretty clear what happened. This clyde here must have joggled loose when we took that big drop and started to bounce. The clyde hit that thing there and tore out this other thing, which in turn dislodged the thing underneath it and knocked hell out of the whole damned business. See what I'm saying?"

"Frankly, no," Madoc admitted. "I do see that things appear to be in a good bit of mess there. Is there anything you can do about it?"

"Without tools, spare parts, or any idea which end is

up, not a hell of a lot. We figured we'd try faith healing, but we're not sure how well it works on airplane engines."

"Well, keep at it. One never knows. How's our sleeping beauty?"

"A picture no artist could paint. Have a look."

Willingly, Madoc climbed back down the shaky wooden ladder and back up the short metal one into the body of the plane. Ace Bulligan was still stretched out on the plushy club chair, making horrible noises through his sunburnt nose. Sparse, long strands of gray-white hair framed a face that wore an expression of bliss beyond measure. He'd feel a damned sight less euphoric, the old pirate, when he woke up and tried to move his head. Though Madoc was not a vindictive man by nature, he took some satisfaction in the prospect.

Maybe the ancient aeronaut's senses had been sharpened by his life in the backlands. Anyway, he must have realized that somebody was standing over him, for he opened one eye in a tentative and experimental manner.

"Who the hell are you?"

"Detective Inspector Rhys of the RCMP. We've met before, remember?"

"No. Pretty damned fancy jail you got here."

"You're not in jail this time around. You're in a private airplane that came down last night in Lodestone Flat with members of the Wagstaffe Symphony Orchestra aboard."

"You don't say! What'd you pinch them for?"

"Disturbing the peace. Mr. Bulligan, do you mean to say you don't remember flying in here this morning? You told us you'd heard a radio broadcast about a missing plane, and had come to find it."

"Wait a minute. Hold your horses. It's beginnin' to come back to me. You're the sneaky bugger that pizened the other bugger."

"No, no. You've got it all wrong. I'm the nice fellow who gave you the drink."

"Drink?" Bulligan sat up and flung aside the blanket. "Did I leave any in the bottle?"

"No, you drank it all." It was a lie in a good cause, Madoc easily managed to convince himself. "However, I might be able to get some more. It would depend on how willing you are to help us out of here."

"Huh. I knowed you was a sneaky bugger. Cripes, my mouth's full o' fuzz. What'd I do, swaller the blanket?"

"Would you like a mug of tea? Or some black coffee?"

"Hell, no, not if I can get anything better. What about that hooch you was goin' to get hold of?"

"I'd have to call somebody up and tell them to bring it," Madoc replied guilefully. "Who's got the nearest telephone or radio hookup around these parts?"

"Right over there at the hotel."

"Then you do remember where you are. You might also remember that I told you this morning they hadn't left any spare batteries."

"Goddamnedest, meanest set o' stingy buggers I ever run into. Got sore when I borried a couple first winter they'd been up here an' ain't left none since. You sure that bugger you're goin' to call up will bring the whiskey?"

"Cross my heart and hope to die, Mr. Bulligan. You ought to know a Mountie's as good as his word. It says so right in *Renfrew of the Mounted*."

"I dunno, you still look like a sneaky little bugger to me. Last time I saw any Mounties, it was down in Calgary. They was all wearin' them Stetson hats an' red coats an' ridin' horses."

"Yes, I know. We do that sometimes. But you see, the pilot wouldn't let me bring my horse on the plane. As a flyer yourself, you must surely see that it wouldn't have done. And if I didn't have the horse, I wouldn't be needing my red coat and Stetson hat, so I didn't bring them, either. It's just the same as your not needing to wear your goggles and helmet when you're not flying your plane."

"The hell I don't. I'd o' wore 'em to sleep in, only some bugger took 'em an' hid 'em on me."

"They're right here on the floor beside your chair, Mr. Bulligan. Why don't you come over to the hotel and get some coffee into you, then we'll decide what to do about making that telephone call."

"I ain't budgin' from this seat till I get the reward."

"What reward is that?"

"The reward for findin' the murderer."

"What makes you think there's one being offered? Did they say so on the radio?"

"No, but they got to, ain't they?"

"Like hell they do." Madoc decided he'd better talk a language Bulligan could understand. "Those stingy buggers down there aren't going to give you a plugged nickel. They're a bunch of rotten skinflints. The only reward you're going to get is the whiskey you'll get from us, and we can't give you that till we get hold of the chap who's going to bring it in. Have you got that straight? Look, if you don't feel up to walking as far as the hotel, why don't I go get some coffee and bring it out to you? In the meantime, you'd better be thinking over what I've said."

If Bulligan was still capable of thought. As Madoc left the plane, he began to see what would have to be done. It was going to be dark in another hour or so. There'd been no sign of a rescue plane yet and there might not be one tomorrow. The search must be taking place in the area over which they were supposed to have been flying, and that could be a very long way from where they actually were. Janet couldn't know there was quite possibly a murderer among them; even so, she must be frantic. The festival staff must be frantic. Even Sir Emlyn must be close to the edge of panic, though he hadn't yet shown much sign of it. Here he came now, back from his walk and looking much like his usual self. Madoc walked out to meet him.

"Hello, Tad. What's out there?"

"A great deal of nothing I care to see again, son. There is a road, but it doesn't look as if it went anywhere. Are they making any progress on the plane?"

"They seem to have discovered the problem, but they say there's nothing much they can do about it without tools and parts. How desperate is the situation with the festival?"

"If we're not there by tomorrow night, I shall have no chance to rehearse and get hold of replacements for my brass section. If we don't make it by Wednesday for the opening, we shall have forfeited our contract and quite possibly ruined the festival, or at the very least caused its producers a good deal of bother having to get substitutes at such short notice, should that be possible. I suppose there's some kind of insurance; nevertheless, it would cost both the orchestra and the sponsors a great deal of money."

Sir Emlyn was letting the bitterness show, as who could blame him? "I've never missed an engagement before, Madoc, even during the Blitz of London. The prospect of having to do so now is bitter to me, I have to confess, though I ought to be ashamed of so paltry a feeling in view of what so many other people, including our dear Janet, must be going through; not knowing whether we're alive or dead. Is there no way out of this, Madoc?"

"I hope so, Tad. I'm working on a plan right now."

"Can I help in any way?"

"Yes. Get hold of Mother and keep her occupied for the next fifteen minutes or so. Come on in with me, I was about to get Ace Bulligan a cup of coffee."

"You still have hopes of him, then?"

"I think he can be made to see reason. It's just a matter of getting him back into flying condition."

"But where does your mother come in?"

"That's just the point, Tad. My plan's more likely to come off if Mother doesn't come into it at all. Bulligan isn't used to women of her sort, and Mother does tend to be helpful."

"Yes, I know, bless her heart. Very well, my boy, no sacrifice is too great. I shall come down with a sudden attack of gastritis and let her doctor me. You wouldn't mind if I attribute my indisposition to your pancakes and Spam? It's got to be something I can recover from quickly, you know. Actually I found them quite good."

"No problem at all. Joe Ragovsky's going to cook supper, by the way."

"What a pity he didn't do lunch. Then I could lay the blame on him instead of you."

"Not on your life! I'd much prefer that you have a miraculous recovery as a result of tasting his superb cuisine. Even if my plan should work, there's not much chance of our leaving here tonight. That means somebody will still have to cook breakfast in the morning. I'd much rather let Joe do the work and reap the glory."

Chapter 13

When Madoc went back out to the plane with Ace Bulligan's coffee, he was also carrying Joe Ragovsky's coat. This was a down-filled parka with a fur-edged hood and a pair of buckskin mittens in the pocket. The garment was a bit heavy for a concert tour at this time of year; Joe said he'd brought it along mainly for company. However, the parka was ideal for what Madoc had in mind; much too big for him, but that was all to the good. It would cover his thighs, even his knees. As for his feet, he could swipe a blanket from the Grumman to wrap them in.

While Ace drank the hot coffee and ate some crackers and peanut butter out of Ed Naxton's private store, Madoc nipped out to the *Moxie Mabel* and measured her gas tank with a dipstick. As he'd suspected, she had more fuel in her than Bulligan had led him to believe. The old pirate must actually have meant to sit tight until he'd pressured somebody into turning over that mythical reward. Well, let him earn it instead.

Madoc was gambling on the premise that early airplanes, especially beat-up crates like this one, didn't have much lifting power. When he'd watched Bulligan come in for his landing, the *Moxie Mabel* had been cruising at a leisurely rate not more than fifteen or twenty feet off the ground. With an extra hundred and sixty pounds of passenger aboard, it might not even be able to get that high, which meant there wouldn't be far to fall if the engine dropped out or the wings came off. Of course there was also the possibility that the plane wouldn't get off the ground at all, but he'd worry about that when it happened.

While the coffee was brewing, Madoc had shoved a box of biscuits and a tin of corned beef hash into one of Joe's pockets, and filled a plastic jug of water. These and a bottle of whiskey, borrowed from MacVittie and Naxton, he stashed in the rear cockpit and hid under the parka. He didn't intend to starve in the foothills while waiting for a rescue. Ace couldn't have come far on so little juice. Now to get that scoundrel back into his cockpit.

That was the hard part. If Bulligan hadn't been a man with a thirst, Madoc might never have managed. The aeronaut was greatly disposed at the moment to loll back in his comfortable chair, nurse his hangover, drink his coffee, and regale his captive audience with lies about his flying prowess and scurrilous tales of buggers he had known.

Trying not to fret about the dimming daylight and the unnerving possibility of his mother's leaving Sir Emlyn to that chimerical tummy ache and coming out to offer a helpful suggestion, Madoc managed to sort out from Ace's ramblings that there did exist a ranger's station not far away, that the ranger had a two-way radio, and that he and his family were well-disposed toward Ace for reasons that Madoc could not even conjecture.

"Splendid, Mr. Bulligan!" he cried. "The very person we want to see. He'll help us get that whiskey to you in jig-time. Have you any preference as to the brand? How do you want it? Jugs, barrels, or small bottles you can carry with you at all times?"

Babbling and cajoling, he succeeded in prying Ace loose from the chair and getting him over to the plane. Steve and Ed trailed along behind, wondering what the hell was going on. When they actually saw Madoc put on Joe Ragovsky's parka and climb into the rear cockpit, they were aghast.

"Jesus, Madoc, are you stark, raving crazy? You're not going up in that bag of bolts?"

"That remains to be seen. Would you be good enough to twirl the propeller and see if the engine starts? I believe that's how it's done. Isn't it, Mr. Bulligan?"

"Yeah, what the hell. Give 'er a whirl. Maybe somethin' will happen. Where do you want to go, Mountie?"

"Straight to the ranger station."

"What ranger station?"

Madoc tried not to groan. What, he asked himself, would Sergeant Renfrew have done in a case like this? "The one you were just telling us about," he replied through clenched teeth. "Where your friend Ranger Rick lives. The chap with the radio."

"Oh, him? Why in hell didn't you say so? Sure, I know Rick. Only what if he ain't home?"

"Then we'll simply go in and use his radio. Rick won't mind. He's a pal of yours, remember?"

"Is he? Glad to hear it. Okay, boys, let 'er rip. Off we go, into the wild blue yonder!"

Being tone-deaf was probably an advantage, Madoc thought, as far as Ace Bulligan's singing was concerned. Anyway, he didn't get to hear much of it. Steve MacVittie gave the hand-carved propeller a few heaves in a spirit of aeronautical research and, wonder of wonders, the engine started. The old plane crawled forward, bumped across the ground at a snail's pace, gradually picked up a little speed, and to the astonishment of all present, left the ground.

Madoc remembered too late that he'd forgotten to bring that blanket, but it didn't look as if high-altitude chill was going to cause him any real problem. *Moxie Mabel* wasn't rising much higher than a pan of baking-powder biscuits. That was fine with him until they got over among the rocks, where sudden updrafts and downdrafts added a stimulus he hadn't counted on.

Ace Bulligan appeared to find them great fun. Madoc did wish the crazy chap wouldn't turn around and yell "Whee!" at every lurch and joggle. He wished the wheels wouldn't skim quite so close to the peaks, and he wished those three sets of wings wouldn't flap so much. He wished it weren't getting dark so fast. He tried to take a detached sightseer's interest in the scenery so very close below, but those jagged spears of rock failed to appeal.

Then he noticed something off to his right, something that looked like a great snake twisting and winding among the humps and jags. A road! And a house! And a radio tower! He leaned forward and patted Ace Bulligan on the back.

Ace turned around, showing all seven of his brown snags in a grin of triumph. "There she be. Don't look like there's anybody home, eh. I wonder if they took their batteries with 'em."

"Oh Jesus!"

Madoc was not a profane man. His outcry was more in the nature of a supplication, and it worked. A light flashed on over the back door of the house. Two children ran out waving their arms and screaming. He never in his life had seen more appealing moppets. Now if only Ace Bulligan didn't squash them on the way down.

No, Ace wouldn't squash them. A young woman in blue jeans and a green jersey was rounding them up, herding them back toward the house. Now they were all three standing on the doorstep, waving at the plane. Madoc waved back. Ace, he was relieved to note, kept his hands on the joystick and his eyes on the space that had been cleared for a landing strip. At the far end sat a small single-engine plane painted a businesslike forest-green.

And here came the man who must be Ranger Rick, swooping the smaller child up to his shoulders, taking the larger one by the hand, walking out to meet them. The triplane settled itself on the ground, well away from the monoplane, and taxied to a halt. Madoc could have sworn he heard the aged vehicle give a sigh of relief as its engines shut off, but the sigh might quite possibly have been his own. He leaped to the ground—it was only a long step, really—and held out his hand.

"Ranger Rick, I assume? I'm Madoc Rhys."

"Madoc Rhys? Hey, you're not by any chance the Mountie who captured Mad Carew, the Murdering Maniac of the Miramichi, single-handed, all by yourself?"

"Sneaky-lookin' little bugger, ain't he?" Ace Bulligan put in sociably. "I brung 'im down from Lodestone Flat. He's goin' to get me some whiskey."

Madoc cocked an eyebrow at the ranger. Rick shrugged and nodded. Madoc reached back into the rear cockpit and pulled out the bottle.

"There it is, Mr. Bulligan, and thanks for the ride. Why don't I let Ranger Rick here hold it for you till you've had some supper?"

"Sure, glad to." Rick grabbed the whiskey before Bulligan could get his hands on it. "Come on in the house, Ace. Ellen will fix you a plate of stew. We were just getting ready to sit down. This is my wife, Inspector. Brian here's our oldest and Annie's the runt of the litter."

"So far." Ellen was noticeably on the way toward a third. "It's a thrill to meet you, Inspector Rhys. What brings you out here, if it's all right to ask? And how in the world did you get up nerve enough to ride with Ace? I'd rather face Mad Carew than risk my neck in *Moxie Mabel* any day."

"I didn't have any choice, actually. Bulligan's the only one who showed up. I don't know if you've heard on the news today that a private plane carrying Sir Emlyn and Lady Rhys and a group of singers and members of the Wagstaffe Orchestra was missing?"

"Oh yes, isn't it terrible? We've been catching reports on the radio all day. There was another plane crashed down around Calgary, and a car blown right off the road into a cornfield. They're saying now that the Rhys plane must have crashed with no survivors. My gosh, they're not relatives of yours?"

"My parents. And I was traveling with them."

"But what are you doing way up here?" said the ranger.

"They're looking for you down around Montana and Idaho."

"That's what we've been afraid of. Apparently the flight plan didn't get corrected. You see, our pilot elected to go above instead of below that freak windstorm or whatever it was, but it caught up with us. We took quite a tossing around, which knocked out our entire electrical system."

"My God! Did you crash? How many are left alive?"

"All of us, I'm glad to say. The pilot pulled off a miracle, gliding in to an almost perfect landing in the dark without any lights, right smack in front of the Miners' Rest Hotel."

"I can't believe it!" cried Ellen.

"Neither could we. Nobody was injured and the plane's intact except for the fact that it can't start until it's repaired and we have no way to fix it. I have to get us some help and call my wife. Bulligan says you have a radio hookup."

"We sure do, and you're welcome to use it all you want. How about a bit of supper first?"

"Thank you but why don't you just go ahead and feed the children?"

"An' me," said Ace Bulligan. "But I'm goin' to have a slug o' my whiskey first an' there ain't no damned Mountie goin' to stop me."

"All right, but you've got to drink it out of a tumbler instead of the bottle," said Ellen. "I'm not having you teach my children bad manners."

Leaving her to cope, which she was obviously quite capable of doing, Rick led Madoc into his office, where there was a setup similar to the hotel's but complete with batteries that worked. "Here we are. We're on a relay. What you do, Madoc, is just speak your piece into the microphone here. The chap at the next station will pass the word to headquarters. They'll telephone your messages anywhere you want. Where's your home?"

"Fredericton, New Brunswick."

"They'll get hold of your wife, never you fear. Just give

Frank, that's the guy at the next station, your home phone number."

Rick was already at the controls, fiddling switches and twiddling dials. "Frank? Come in, Frank. Hi, Frank, guess who I've got here, eh. Nope. It's the Mountie who captured Mad Carew. He was on that missing plane they've been looking for. It's down on Lodestone Flat. He's got to get the word out. Here, I'll put him on." Rick got up and motioned to the chair. "Go ahead, Inspector."

"Hello, Frank? Madoc Rhys here. Yes, that's right. No, he didn't give any trouble. The whole affair got blown out of proportion." Madoc wished by now that he'd never laid eyes on Mad Carew. "Look, I have to get some messages out right away. Do you have a pencil handy?"

Frank had a pencil. Madoc got down to business. "First, you'd better let them know at the board of aeronautics that everyone on the plane carrying the Wagstaffe Orchestra group is alive and well, but the plane itself is disabled and we need transport. Do you know Lodestone Flat yourself? Can you give the precise location and the landing situation? No, it would be impossible for a jet. They'll have to come in with a small plane or a big helicopter."

Frank tried to get in another question about Mad Carew. Madoc relentlessly kept to the main subject. "We've moved into the Miners' Rest Hotel. The owners ought to be notified of what's happening if there's any way of reaching them. No, we weren't able to turn on the water or the electricity. We're using a hand pump in the kitchen and depending on wood fires and oil lamps. Yes, there's enough to get by on for the moment. Canned foods, dried milk and eggs, flour and so forth. I'm afraid there won't be much left of their stores by the time we leave. They'll be recompensed, of course. I'm not sure how that will be handled, but tell them not to worry."

Now for the important part. "You'll need to get in touch with the office of the Wagstaffe Symphony Orchestra and explain the situation to them. They must have the addresses of all the musicians and, I hope, the singers who were aboard, and can notify their families." He ran through the names. "And I have to get a call through to my wife, Janet Rhys, as well. She won't be on their list because I'm not a member. Yes, as a matter of fact, he's my father. My mother's with us, too. No, you needn't do that, my wife will take care of the other relatives."

Madoc gave his home telephone number and made Frank read it back so there couldn't be any mistake. "Tell Janet—just have them tell her not to worry. I'll be in touch as soon as I can get to a telephone. Yes, we must have a good chat about Mad Carew one of these days. Right now I have to get off the air so you can get cracking on those messages. Maybe you'd better have them get hold of my wife first, if you don't mind."

But Frank had one more question, and it was a good one. "No," Madoc had to tell him, "we can't manage signal fires tonight. We've already burned up far too much of the hotel's firewood. First thing in the morning, then? Absolutely crack of dawn? Thanks so much, that's wonderful of you. Good night."

Neither Rick nor Frank had said anything to him about Wilhelm Ochs. They probably thought he was on the case and couldn't talk about it. Sensible fellows. As he cut off and stood up, Madoc realized he was sweating like a pig. Was that nerves, or the fact that he was still wearing Joe Ragovsky's parka? He slipped off the heavy coat and left it on the chair.

"Thanks very much, Rick. That's a great load off my mind."

"I can imagine. How about a jolt of that rye you brought, and something to eat? Ellen's made hunter's stew and dumplings. Stay the night, if you want to."

"Sounds awfully good but I ought to be getting back. Does that road of yours run up to Lodestone Flat, and is there any sort of vehicle I might borrow? The people up there will be anxious to know what's happening."

"Won't hurt 'em to wonder another hour or so, will it? Yes, the road'll take us there. It's only about twenty miles.

I'll run you back myself in the wagon after we eat. I expect you've had just about enough flying for a while."

"How right you are. Right then, let's have stew and dumplings. I expect it's canned peas and lamentations up at the hotel. Thank you, Ellen, this is awfully kind of you," he added as the ranger's wife handed him a tumbler of rye and water with genuine ice cubes in it.

"It's our pleasure, believe me," she told him. "We don't get to see many new faces around here once Lodestone Flat closes for the season. We don't see all that many while it's open, as far as that goes. They don't get a lot of tourists willing to make so long a drive for what little there is to do. It's mostly sales conferences and conservation groups, things like that. They fly the parties in and out."

She chatted on, making the most of their unexpected guest while she dished out the food and started the children and Ace, who rather seemed to count as another youngster, eating their supper. Madoc enjoyed his drink and let himself unwind. After a bit of coaxing and as a courtesy to his rescuers, he related the story of how he'd tracked the deranged lumberjack through the wilds until a wiggly caterpillar down Carew's back had tickled the mass murderer into surrendering.

For an encore, he told some stories about his parents and the orchestra, which interested Ellen quite a lot, Rick a little, and the children not at all. Then they chatted on about things in general while they ate up an apple pie that was almost but not quite as good as Janet's.

Afterward, he offered to help with the dishes, a gesture that struck all the Ricks as hilarious. Finally Ranger Rick heaved himself out of his chair.

"Well, Madoc, if you really want to get back to Lodestone Flat tonight, I guess we'd better get started."

Chapter 14

Ace Bulligan wasn't coming with them. After supper, the old man had retired with his bottle to a cot in the shed that the Ricks kept set up for him. He was planning to drink himself into oblivion, though he didn't phrase his intentions in quite those words. Madoc had a few qualms of conscience about having provided Ace with the means to do so, but Rick told him to forget it.

"Ace manages to get fried one way or another whenever he feels the urge. He's got a still out behind that shack of his where he boils down anything he can get his hands on."

"Yes, he told us about the still. He claims that's what he flies his plane on."

"And so he does, when he can't wheedle me out of a few gallons of gasoline. How the hell he keeps that cussed old thing in the air is beyond me. Black magic, I guess."

"I just hope he doesn't try to fly it blind drunk." Madoc was still feeling a trifle guilty.

"Don't fret yourself. He'll sleep off the whiskey and Ellen will get a decent breakfast into him before he takes off again. We feed him up two or three times a week."

"Good Lord! Is that all he lives on?"

"Oh no. He gets the Old Age Security Pension and Supplement, and makes a few dollars in the summertime up at the flat, charging tourists to get their pictures taken with him and *Moxie Mabel*. He'd like to give rides, but the hotel folks won't let him. Don't want their front yard cluttered with mangled corpses, and I can't say I blame 'em. I don't know who'd be damned fool enough to go up with him, anyway."

Rick glanced sideways at Madoc and grinned. "Sorry, Inspector. Guess I put my foot in it that time."

"Believe me," Madoc assured him, "if I'd known you were only twenty miles away, I'd much rather have hoofed it. The trouble was, I couldn't get any sense out of Bulligan about where the road led to and how far I'd have to go to find a radio. Is he really as crazy as he makes himself out to be?"

"Ace is crazy, all right, but he's foxy, too. I gave up trying to figure him out long ago. Somehow or other, Ace always seems to land on his own feet. Wearing somebody else's shoes, like as not. Say, I didn't like to mention it in front of the kids, but what about that guy who got poisoned on stage in the middle of the concert?"

"Actually he didn't," Madoc replied. "You heard it was ricin, I assume. Ace said they'd mentioned it on the news."

"Yes, that's right, ricin. Comes from castor oil beans, doesn't it?"

"So I understand. We had a case some time back. Ricin is slow-acting as a good many of those vegetable poisons are. That means Wilhelm Ochs, the chap who died, must have ingested it quite a while before the concert, probably mixed in with something he ate. He was a real glutton, from what the other musicians tell me. I never got to meet him, myself."

Madoc saw no harm in giving Rick a brief rundown on the various orchestra members. They'd be written up in the papers anyway, no doubt. Loyalty to his parents, not to mention his calling, demanded of course that he keep certain information to himself, such as Delicia Fawn's auditions and the fact that Madame Bellini was once Mrs. Wilhelm Ochs. Was the concertmaster actually intending to marry Bellini and had she ever been divorced from Ochs? Houdon was such a meticulous-appearing chap, it was hard to picture a man like that doing anything not wholly *en règle*. He ought to have talked to the pair before this, Madoc thought. But he'd been too busy in the kitchen.

The road wasn't great, but they had it all to themselves. They made the distance in a little over half an hour. The ride up in Rick's wagon had been a lot more pleasant than his peak-skimming trip down; still, Madoc was relieved to spy the oil lamps in the front windows of the Miners' Rest. This must have been how they welcomed weary prospectors coming in from their claims with their pokes of dust, or sacks of ore, or whatever it was they'd mined for around here. It occurred to him that he hadn't got around to asking, and that right now he didn't give a rap.

Ed and Steve must have spread the word about his having gone off with Ace Bulligan. He got a full-dress reception from the entire company, including Lucy Shadd in a Black Watch tartan bathrobe, with a dark blue scarf wound twice around her neck.

"By the way," Madoc had to murmur when it came time for introductions, starting of course with Lady Rhys. "Is Rick your first name or your last?"

"Both; it's Richard Rick. Don't ask me what my parents were thinking of at the time. How do you do, ma'am? This is a real honor for me."

"The honor is ours, I assure you." Lady Rhys hadn't put on her black gown and diamonds, but she could be just as impressive without them. "We are delighted to see you. Tell me, Mr. Rick, have you been able to let people know where we are?"

"Oh yes, we got the word out. To the next relay station, anyway. They'll pass the word along, never you fear. There won't be a plane in here tonight. Trying to land in the dark would be too dangerous, so you all might as well go on to bed. I guess you didn't get much sleep last night, eh? Don't worry, you'll have plenty of company come morning."

Most of the group were concerned as to whether their families had been notified, but Lucy Shadd wanted more.

"What time in the morning? What sort of plane? Or will it be a bus? Who's supposed to provide breakfast? Are they bringing milk and eggs?"

"We don't know anything about anything yet," Madoc had to keep replying. "Ranger Rick has explained to you that his radio is on a relay. The only person we got to talk to was the ranger at the next station along the line. He promised to pass on our messages so they could be telephoned to the right people."

"For God's sake, Madoc, how stupid can you be? Couldn't you have waited for the answers?"

"And leave us wondering whether our son had crashed in the mountains, risking his neck with that crazy old man?" Lady Rhys did not lose her temper, but it was a near-miss. "Lucy, you forget yourself. You know as well as I that it's going to take time for arrangements to be made."

"But we have to find out what they are."

"We'll find out when the time comes. There's not a blessed thing we can do about them anyway. I suggest you nip on back to bed and save your fretting until you've something to fret about. Mr. Rick, Sir Emlyn and I are immensely grateful for your efforts on behalf of us all, and particularly for your kindness to our son. Would you care to come into the hotel? Our hospitality is limited, but we'd be happy to offer you a cup of tea. Or perhaps a drink?"

"Thanks, Lady Rhys, but we just got up from the supper table. I expect likely I ought to get back home and find out what's happening on the radio. I wish I'd had an extra battery to bring so you could get the one up here going, but it just so happens I had to lend out my spare and haven't had a chance to replace it yet. I'll most likely be up in the morning if something important comes along. Anything else you can think of before I go that you'd like to have transmitted?"

Lucy Shadd thought of several things. However, it turned out Madoc and Rick had thought of them, too. Frustrated, she picked up the skirt of her long robe so she wouldn't trip over it and went back into the hotel.

Most of the others, especially the Rhyses, stayed to see Rick off. By the time no glow from his headlights was visible, they were all yawning. As soon as they got inside, just about everybody headed for the stairs.

Jacques-Marie Houdon was a barely discreet four steps behind Norma Bellini, Madoc noted with no great feeling of disappointment. That projected conversation would have to wait till morning. Too bad. He was damnably tired himself. In fact, his father was making a gentle suggestion that Madoc get to bed before he undermined the family's dignity by falling on his face.

That was as good an excuse as any. Going through the lobby, Madoc noticed that Cedric Rintoul was seated over in a corner by the window with David Gabriel, another orchestra member Madoc hadn't yet got around to chatting with. Gabriel had the lamp at his shoulder and his hands busy with some finicky task. Making another reed for his oboe, no doubt. Madoc still hadn't checked on those wire cutters, but they probably didn't matter.

Rintoul had one of the hotel's thick tumblers balanced on his knee. Whiskey or brandy, Madoc supposed, to make him sleep. He or Gabriel, as the last ones, would no doubt bring that lamp along to light their way upstairs. The stove was dampered down for the night. Joe Ragovsky had probably seen to that. They wouldn't have to be thinking about such tasks this time tomorrow. Madoc went into the bedroom where Ed Naxton was already peeling off clothes and getting into pajamas, and followed Ed's sterling example.

Nobody screamed, nobody thumped around the hallway. Madoc slept straight through till the watch he'd adjusted by the Ricks' kitchen clock said six o'clock. He got up, splashed his face and brushed his teeth with cold water from the pitcher he'd brought up last night, got into his last clean shirt in anticipation of the rescuers who, God willing, would be arriving before long, and went downstairs.

It was cold again, colder than yesterday morning. They'd be getting away from here none too soon. He fed the lobby stove and opened the damper to make the fire

burn hotter, went out to the kitchen, and fell over Cedric
Rintoul.

Passed out, the bloody soak. Couldn't he have picked a
less awkward place to sleep it off instead of lying down in
front of the stove like a damned great Saint Bernard?
Madoc gave the gross body a none too gentle nudge with
his toe.

"Rintoul, wake up."

He kept his voice down because he didn't want to wake
anybody else. Evidently he didn't speak loudly enough to
do any good. Rintoul didn't stir. Madoc leaned over to give
the trombone player a shake, and found out why. It was a
waste of time trying to wake somebody who had an icepick
rammed into the back of his neck.

"Oh my God, another one!"

That wasn't much of an epitaph, and Madoc was
slightly relieved there'd been nobody around to hear him
say it. Now what to do?

First, he must make doubly sure Rintoul was indeed
beyond the veil. There could be no doubt about that; one
touch told him the body was cold as an iceberg and stiff as
a boot. Death must have been virtually instantaneous, he
thought; one quick stab straight into the base of the brain.
Bold, resolute, but not bloody. Hardly a trickle showing, as
far as Madoc could see in the none too good light. There'd
have been more, no doubt, had the icepick been with-
drawn.

Somebody had known enough not to do that, and also
had been clever enough not to leave any fingerprints on the
handle, most likely. Still, Madoc wasn't going to touch the
icepick itself, just in case. He'd have to find a camera;
surely there must be at least one shutterbug in the party.
Rintoul must not be moved until photographs had been
taken of the body in its present position.

That meant not being able to get at the stove, which in
turn meant no hot water and no tea, until Madoc remembered his mother's trick with the fancy stove in the lobby.
He hooked the kettle toward him with a long toasting fork,

regretted the fact that whatever water had been in it last night was now simmered away, and filled it fresh at the pump. He was lifting the curlicues off the lobby stove when his father came downstairs in the scruffy brown Jaeger robe Madoc had known since his knee-perching days.

"Ah, son, good morning. I was hoping to fetch myself some shaving water before things start to pop around here."

"Sorry, Tad, but they've already started. We have a problem in the kitchen."

"Not the water pump?"

"No, Rintoul. He's dead."

"Madoc, no! God help me, if I've driven the man to suicide—"

"Tad, he's got an icepick jabbed into the back of his neck."

Sir Emlyn stood perfectly still while Madoc got the kettle on the stove, then raised his right hand in the decisive upward flick he used when he was about to give the downbeat. "I'll have a look."

He walked ahead of Madoc into the kitchen and stood over the huddle on the floor. "Poor, poor fellow. No, I agree with you, Rintoul would not have found this an amusing joke to play on himself. What now, son?"

"You didn't happen to bring a camera with you?"

"No. There are always too many people around taking pictures. Your mother and I got sick of cameras long ago. Carlos Pitney has one, I know. Photography is quite a hobby of his. Shall I wake him up and ask if we may borrow it?"

"I'll go if you like."

"I'd rather go myself, son. Carlos and I are old friends, and murder before breakfast is not a pleasant thing to be wakened for."

"I'll have your shaving water ready for you." It was the best that Madoc could do.

"Thank you, Madoc. I suppose you know the press will

be here before anyone else. Will you have to tell them?"

Madoc sighed. He also had had experience with the zealous folk of the media. News of the downed plane would have reached them last night; they were probably on their way already.

"Here's the drill, Tad. It's any citizen's duty to report a murder to whatever law enforcement officer is most readily available. That's myself, in this case, so consider it reported. As soon as Rick shows up, I'll find out from him who has jurisdiction over the area and ask him to get a message through as quickly as possible. It's the local man's job to release the information about Rintoul's death, not mine. In the meantime, I'll have to proceed with the investigation, which I'll do as expeditiously and as discreetly as I can."

"That's better than I'd have dared to hope. This is going to be terrible publicity, you know. First Ochs, then Shadd, now Rintoul. People will be coming not to hear our music but to see who's going to get murdered next. It is a hateful thing to think of."

"Let's not worry about Shadd, anyway. I expect Lucy herself would rather we kept that incident quiet as long as we can. As soon as we've got our photographs and checked for whatever evidence there may be, we'd better move Rintoul's body out to the woodshed and lock the door. It may not be possible to keep his death a secret from the rest of the party until after the media people have come and gone, but we can try."

"Somebody already knows, Madoc."

"Oh yes, no doubt about that. It's quite possible two or three others know, too. Anyone who happened to come down to the kitchen last night for a late snack or a drink or whatever could hardly have failed to discover the body."

"And not said anything because they saw no point in disturbing our rest when there was nothing to be done, you think?"

"And not said anything for fear of getting hit with a murder charge themselves, more likely. I should say from the look of him that Rintoul's been there for quite a while. He's still dressed as he was last night. He may have been killed not long after I myself saw him last."

"That would have been around the time your mother and I went to bed?"

"Pretty close. You were among the last to go. Rintoul and Gabriel were the only two left in the lobby when I went. The pair of them were sitting over there in the corner by the window, as you may recall. There was a lamp on the sill."

"Yes, your mother put it there to light her wandering boy back home. We were worried about you, Madoc."

"That's all right, Tad. I was worried about me, too. Anyway, Gabriel was working at something or other under the light. One of his eternal reeds, I suppose. Rintoul was nursing a drink. Not his first, I'd say offhand. They seemed content enough at the time, but the stove had been banked for the night and it wouldn't have been long before they began to find the room uncomfortably chilly."

"Couldn't they have opened the damper and put on more wood?"

"Yes, but I doubt if they did. I expect Gabriel's going to tell us he finished what he was doing and went upstairs leaving Rintoul by himself, which may quite possibly be the truth. Rintoul may have said something about fixing himself another drink. Anyway, the odds are that's what he went to the kitchen for. Somebody grabbed the chance and stuck the icepick into his neck."

"Dreadful!" Sir Emlyn shook his head. "But simple enough. The icepick would be the one that was in that rack next to the sink, I suppose. I saw it yesterday when I was washing dishes."

"Yes, and I noticed it was gone from the rack this morning. You'd better get that camera, Tad, before somebody else wakes up and comes looking for breakfast. You can tell Pitney you want to photograph the first press plane coming in."

"I would not lie to my friend. Furthermore, I am hoping

Carlos will come himself to work the camera. He's quite expert, and his discretion is impeccable."

Softly, in his old-fashioned felt slippers, Sir Emlyn padded upstairs. Madoc went back to the kitchen, took out the flashlight he'd stashed in the kitchen cupboard against emergencies, and used it to take a closer look at the ungainly sprawl that had been Cedric Rintoul.

The
Curtis would come himself to read the sentence. He's capti
appears, and his discretion to impose s...
world, or the old-fashioned... If necessary, Sir Harry and
finally...

Chapter 15

Without moving the body, he couldn't see much. Rintoul had fallen face down with his hands doubled under him. Madoc did find the tumbler he'd been drinking from; it had rolled under the stove. The indication was that he'd dropped it when he fell. Since Rintoul hadn't lifted a hand yesterday to tidy up after himself, it was unlikely he was bringing the tumbler back to be washed. More probably, he'd been meaning to get himself another drink, and that was interesting. He couldn't have been worried about getting murdered.

Yesterday morning Rintoul, along with everybody else, had heard Ace Bulligan talking about that early news bulletin. Last night, he'd heard Madoc and Rick confirm the report that Wilhelm Ochs had been poisoned. Maybe he'd thought he knew who'd murdered Ochs, and that the culprit was among those who'd gone by train. Maybe he knew the real killer was here at the Miners' Rest, and had been stabbed because he couldn't be trusted not to tell. Maybe he himself had killed Ochs, and had been murdered out of revenge. Had Norma Bellini née Belschi, late Ochs, felt it her duty to avenge the death of her former husband? Would she have chosen an icepick to do the job?

Why not? Icepicks made excellent weapons because their points were so sharp and their shafts so slender. A woman with plenty of weight behind her could drive one in easily enough, assuming she knew just where to set the point. Maybe La Bellini hadn't been bent on vengeance, merely anxious to shut Rintoul's ever-flapping mouth before he told her current lover about her having been married to Ochs.

Or maybe this had nothing at all to do with Ochs. Maybe Frieda Loye had finally decided she'd had as much of Rintoul as she was going to take. Maybe Corliss Blair had killed him for breathing garlic fumes at her during rehearsals. Maybe Jason Jasper had got tired of being second banana.

Among all the maybes, Madoc could sort out one incontrovertible fact which he hadn't had the heart to mention to his father. If the question of who'd stabbed the prankish trombonist was not resolved before their rescue plane, bus, truck, or mule team came along, the local law officer would have every right to keep them here in Lodestone Flat until it was. He was somewhat relieved when his father came back with Carlos Pitney and an impressive-looking Nikon in tow.

Pitney allowed himself one quick, "God help us, what a thing to happen!" then got down to business. He took a quick reading on his exposure meter, then began to snap. He knew about angles. His flash worked every time. Madoc had no doubt whatever that the photographs would be excellent.

In about five minutes' time, Pitney had finished his job. Madoc wrapped a clean cup towel around his hand, took a careful grip on the icepick down by the base of the shaft, and pulled it out. Pitney took a couple more shots of Madoc performing the operation so that there'd be no doubt that it was he who'd done so. Madoc then laid the weapon, wrapped loosely in the towel, inside a long candle box he'd found in the pantry, and put the cover on the box.

"Thanks a lot. Here, Tad, hold this. Now if you and I, Carlos, can lift Rintoul very carefully away from the stove and lay him on this blanket you so intelligently brought down with you, we'll get him out to the shed."

Madoc had no great hope of learning anything from the state of the floor. It was nothing but rough wooden planks with a few squares of linoleum at strategic areas, all of them by now hopelessly tracked up. The urgent task right now was to get Rintoul out of sight. Already a few creaks from overhead told them that some of the people upstairs were beginning to stir.

Madoc didn't want his father to help with the carrying. They'd manage without him. He himself was a good deal stronger than he looked and while Rintoul had been big, Carlos Pitney was even bigger. The two of them got the body wrapped in the blanket and safely stowed in the shed while Sir Emlyn, with great presence of mind, fetched the now boiling kettle off the lobby stove, restored the iron curlicue to its proper place, and made a pot of tea. By the time the self-appointed pallbearers came back, he was setting out mugs and powdered milk in the coziest manner possible.

Madoc had brought back an armload of firewood, with which he quickly stoked the big kitchen range. Carlos Pitney was snapping a photo of the father and son sipping their tea by the time Joe Ragovsky came downstairs already dressed for the day.

"Hey, what's this, a pajama party? I thought I was going to be the first one down."

"Ah, you Canadian wheat farmers are no match for us Welsh sheep herders," Sir Emlyn replied as complacently as though he hadn't just been an accomplice in a clandestine concealment of a murdered man. "I had intended to fetch myself some shaving water so that I could uphold my well-known dignity among you by appearing clean and unwhiskered, but as you can see, I got sidetracked. Sit down, Ragovsky. Have we anything left to eat, I wonder?"

"Not a heck of a lot," Joe replied. "There's flour and baking powder and canned shortening. And jam. I thought I might whomp us up some hot biscuits to tide us over till the relief plane gets here. They'd be better than nothing, anyway."

"A good deal better, I have no doubt," said Pitney in that deep organ tone even Madoc could appreciate. "Let me pour you a mug of tea first. Sir Emlyn made it. I never knew you were so handy around the kitchen, Em."

As Joe was throwing dry ingredients together and cutting in the shortening, Pitney lolled back till his chair creaked, appearing perfectly at ease in a sumptuous maroon cashmere bathrobe with gold piping. "You know, I wouldn't mind coming back here sometime, with you fellows to cook for me. And the plumbing hooked up."

And no bodies in the woodshed. Madoc admired the basso's aplomb; Pitney'd been looking a trifle unnerved back there watching Madoc go through Rintoul's pockets. Madoc still hadn't had a chance to decide whether he'd come across something important. From the sounds he was catching now, he wouldn't get much opportunity for cogitation any time soon.

"Tad," he said, "you'd better grab that kettle and slide back to your room. I think I hear a plane."

That might, of course, be only Ranger Rick in his little puddle-jumper. It might, God forbid, be Ace Bulligan coming back for more booze. Leaving Joe to finish the biscuits, Madoc went outside to check. No, this was a bigger plane than Rick's, though not a great deal bigger. Press, for sure. He went back inside to report.

Pitney was gone. The kitchen was crammed with pitcher-carriers, all of them clamoring for hot water and not getting any. Nobody had thought to fill the reservoir in the stove or the wash boiler that had served so well the night before. Ainsworth Kight was taking the oversight as a personal affront. Nobody else was paying any attention to him. Jason Jasper was trying to work the pump and not having much luck. Joe Ragovsky was still cutting biscuits.

Joe's curly golden beard made an agreeable contrast to the unshaven cheeks around him. Madoc felt his own ill-shaven chin and wished he'd kept the mustache he'd sacrificed during his courting days. Janet had complained that it prickled when he kissed her; but Janet, alas, was not here to be kissed. He took the pump handle from Jasper and got down to business.

The sound of the plane could be heard now even over the creaking and splashing of the pump and the gabble of the pitcher-bearers. Sir Emlyn and Lady Rhys came downstairs, he now clean-shaven, she morning fresh with not a hair out of place. Both were in their British tweeds, ready to do credit to Sir Emlyn's position, thereby to the Wagstaffe Symphony Orchestra, thence to the festival. They bore their heavy responsibilities well, Madoc thought with pride.

By the time he'd got all the pitchers filled, the plane was circling over Lodestone Flat. Going outside again, this time with his parents, Madoc could easily read the lettering on its side. BUED, in red and orange with a green line around the edges. A television crew, beyond a doubt. Madoc endured his mother's scrutiny, held up his chin as she tried to straighten his collar, then ducked back into the hotel. His aim was to maintain the lowest profile possible and try to get some work done.

He'd found a key in the woodshed door. It wasn't much of one, merely the old iron sort that would probably fit any of the doors in the hotel, but it was better than nothing. He'd turned it in the lock and slipped it into his pocket. Now he nipped back into the kitchen and offered to keep an eye on the biscuits so Joe Ragovsky could go out to watch the plane land. As soon as Joe was gone, Madoc unlocked the door again and slipped into the cold woodshed.

He and Pitney had laid Rintoul on the floor, over at the right-hand side of the shed where there wasn't much of anything except a few chairs and nightstands the hotel keepers were perhaps intending to repaint before their season began next spring. A couple of these with a tarpaulin draped over them had made an adequate screen to conceal the trombone player's remains from anybody who might happen to catch a glimpse inside. Madoc ducked under the improvised tent and knelt beside the body.

After another, more painstaking examination, he decided he'd been right the first time. There was not one blessed thing about the body that even suggested a clue as to who'd wielded the icepick. This had been either a very skillful or a very lucky killing. He'd better get back and check on those biscuits.

And a good thing he did. The stove was burning really hot now. Another couple of minutes and the biscuits would have been burning, too. Madoc reached in with a potholder and pulled out a huge roasting pan filled with puffy, well-browned, good-smelling humps. Joe was without question a sound man on biscuits. To confirm his appraisal, Madoc extracted one of them from the pan, split it, anointed the halves with dabs of regrettably sweet marmalade which was the best the larder had to offer, and ran a consumer test.

Yes, Joe knew his biscuits. Madoc only wished he could be sure of what else Joe knew. Had Ragovsky meant to be first in the kitchen only out of the goodness of his heart, or because he'd remembered there was a cadaver to be tidied away before the biscuits could be baked?

The plane was landing. The people from upstairs who'd been frantically making themselves presentable for this moment streamed down the stairs. Ed Naxton was the only one who didn't head straight for the front door.

"Hi, Madoc. Any coffee going?"

"It seems to have got all used up yesterday. There's tea, if you don't mind it slightly stewed."

"Hell, no. I've been stewed a few times, myself. Caffeine's caffeine, isn't it?" Ed picked up the big brown teapot that had been left to keep warm on the back of the stove, and poured himself a mugful. "How come you're not outside getting your picture taken with the rest of the bigwigs?"

"I had to stay around and watch the biscuits. Would you care for one? So it's a television crew, eh? I thought it must be when I saw the plane circling just now. My father predicted they'd be the first to show up."

"Yeah, just our luck. Steve and I were hoping for a mechanic, or at least some word from Mr. Zlubert."

"He's the man who owns the Grumman?"

"No, he's the owner's right-hand man. Private secretary, I guess they call him. The owner's off to Paris on the Concorde this week, which is how come he was bighearted enough to lend his plane to the orchestra, though they probably don't know that. Anyway, whatever they do for the rest of you, I expect Steve and I will be stuck here till the plane's repaired and we can fly her out. Steve's going to be one lonesome guy when Delicia leaves. Say, these aren't bad biscuits. Be better if we had something besides jam to put on 'em, though. Not to complain about the grub we've been having, but I'll sure be one happy man when I can sit down to a great big steak and fried potatoes. Come on, let's go take a look."

"Why not?" Ed would think it strange if he didn't, Madoc supposed. "Just let me set a pan of water on the stove first, in case somebody else wants tea. Tea and biscuits are all we have for breakfast, I'm afraid."

"Better than nothing." Ed took another one as they left the kitchen. "You make these yourself?"

"No, Joe Ragovsky did."

"Oh yeah, the big guy with the yellow beard. You know, it's funny to think of Joe playing a fiddle for his living. He looks as if he ought to be out driving a tractor or something."

"I expect Joe's driven one plenty of times. He grew up on a wheat farm, he tells me. Well, well, we seem to be just in time for the main event."

Delicia Fawn was beating them out the door. She'd got herself up in what could perhaps best be described as a sports outfit, and it left no doubt as to what her favorite sport must be. The green and beige plaid skirt stopped short of her knees and was slit up the back for further freedom of action. The tan silk shirt had been bought a size too small and left unbuttoned a good way below the point of discretion. She'd thrown a bulky knit green cardigan over her shoulders, arranging it so as to conceal nothing of importance. Her hair was an artful tumble, her lips a crimson pout of welcome.

Once he'd spied Delicia, the cameraman lost any interest in the downed plane, the stranded orchestra, the distinguished conductor, and even the conductor's impressive wife. The effervescent chap with the microphone almost trampled poor little Frieda Loye underfoot in his rush to get at this delectable new goodie. Madoc realized he need not have worried about becoming a center of attention. These people didn't even know he was here.

"Good work," said the announcer after he and the cameraman had explored the possibilities as far as limitations would permit. "Now how about some indoor shots? You orchestra chaps get your instruments and make believe you're rehearsing, eh. Delicia baby, how about if you belt us out a little song?"

"Miss Fawn is not the only singer present," Ainsworth Kight observed in a lofty and disapproving tone.

"Oh yeah? Who else?"

Sir Emlyn was having a hard time, Madoc could tell. This brash exploitation must be disgusting to him, yet he couldn't afford to antagonize the media on account of the orchestra's already precarious position with regard to public relations. He turned to his wife, who sailed forward in her grandest dame manner.

"Perhaps you haven't yet realized, sir, that we have with us not only several first chair musicians of the Wagstaffe Symphony Orchestra but also four of Canada's most distinguished classical singers. Allow me to present Ainsworth Kight, whom we're privileged to have as our tenor soloist on our festival tour. Madame Norma Bellini, whom you will of course remember from her superb solo recital last month in Stratford, is our contralto, and the great Carlos Pitney is our bass."

"Super! They can all sing."

Lady Rhys gave the announcer a forgiving smile. "I'm sorry, it is simply not possible for singers of their caliber to belt out a little song on the spur of the moment. Their voices are both precious and delicate instruments. Just to get them warmed up would take a good deal more time than I expect you want to spend here. Might I suggest instead that we take the camera indoors and show you how we've been camping out in this quaint old hotel since our plane was forced down? You know how viewers love these little behind-the-scenes glimpses of famous people."

The publicity might also soften the hotel owners into taking a more lenient view of the company's depredations. Lady Rhys was naturally too intelligent to say so.

"That is an idea to which we cheerfully subscribe, Lady Rhys," boomed Carlos Pitney. "If these gentlemen want, we could even duplicate the scene after our heroic Mr. MacVittie had brought us safely to the ground, all of us huddled around that picturesque old stove in the lobby, drinking tea in a state of shock."

"Hey, terrific!" cried the announcer. "Delicia can be passing around the cups. And Madame Bellini pouring the tea," he added out of the kindness of his heart.

Madame Bellini was not going to play. "It is for head of operations to pour tea," she growled. "I do not make public display of myself in such manner. Excuse, please, I go back to my room. This cold air is not good for my throat."

Chapter 16

All the time she'd been standing out there, Madame Bellini had been keeping a lacy black woolen stole wound around her head and across her face like a yashmak. She tucked its folds more securely around her mouth and nose, and stalked back into the hotel. Madoc was not a bit surprised. To be acclaimed on the concert stage as the incomparable Norma Bellini was one thing. To appear on television screens all over Canada and risk getting herself recognized by some former landlord or postman as the ex-wife of the suddenly deceased Wilhelm Ochs would be quite another kettle of fish.

Thanks to Delicia Fawn's voluptuous distractions, the announcer had not yet thought to mention the French horn player's mysterious death. He'd get around to it, no doubt, over the tea and biscuits. Madoc could only be thankful Carlos Pitney had suggested the lobby instead of the kitchen. The farther everybody could be kept away from that woodshed door, the better.

As for himself, it was easy enough to fade quietly out of the crowd and into the kitchen. He filled the kettle, which his father had been thoughtful enough to bring back downstairs, and was putting mugs on a tray to take to the lobby when Lucy Shadd bustled in, reeking with efficiency after her day's layoff. She was dressed in her trim gray suit, not a wrinkle in it. Except for the scarf—a flowered silk one today—wound high around her neck, nobody would have had a clue to what had befallen her yesterday. Even that wasn't any real clue. Any woman could wear a scarf for no reason in particular, and no doubt Lucy often did.

"What are you bothering with a tray for? Why don't you just set the mugs on the table?" was her cheery greeting.

"Because they're going to have breakfast around the stove in the lobby for the benefit of the cameraman," Madoc replied with what patience he could muster.

"That's a stupid idea. Why not here, where they can eat in some kind of comfort?"

"We wouldn't be able to fit everybody around the table."

"You did yesterday."

"No, we didn't. People had to eat in relays. You weren't here," Madoc had to remind her, "so you wouldn't have known. If we did squeeze them all into the kitchen, there'd be no room left for the cameraman. Anyway, we've nothing to eat this morning except tea and biscuits. They can manage those easily enough on their laps."

"Well, I still think it's a stupid arrangement," Lucy grumbled. "They'll need plates for their biscuits, and that's two dishes to juggle."

"They could set their mugs on their plates if we were planning to give them plates, which I see no reason to do."

"Then how do you expect them to manage the jam?"

"Lucy, these are not puling infants. They're grown men and women."

"That's what you think. They'll spill the jam on their clothes and I'll get stuck with taking the stuff to the cleaner's in Vancouver because everything will be in a last-minute flurry by the time we get to the festival. Don't you know yet when the relief plane's coming?"

"I have no more idea than I did the last time you asked me. Those chaps out there haven't a clue and show no sign of caring. All they want is to get their story and be off."

"Huh. I'd better go see if I can get any sense out of them."

"Lucy, you'd better do nothing of the sort. It's my father's place to deal with the media, and he's edgy enough already. Here, let me carry that trayful of mugs for you."

"I'm not helpless. Bring the teapot and the bloody damned biscuits."

Madoc would have preferred to pour the tea over her head, but this was hardly the time to provoke another scene. He gathered his own trayful of spoons, knives, and jam, along with bowls of sugar and the powdered milk they were all so sick of by now, took them to the lobby, set them on the counter, and went back for the teapot and the big platter of biscuits.

Lucy began pouring out mugs of tea and handing them around. Delicia followed with the biscuits. She'd discarded the heavy sweater so that the camera could get the full benefit of her bendings and twitchings. Madoc still couldn't work up any amorous yearnings but he was most humbly and fervently grateful for her diversionary abilities.

He'd gone out to cast another furtive glance at the woodshed door and fetch more boiling water for the teapot when he heard the drone of a second airplane. Hoping it might be somebody useful, he went to take a look, but it was just another television crew from a different network. Its pilot just managed to skin his plane in between the previous arrival and the grounded Grumman. Lodestone Flat was beginning to look like a parking lot. All they needed now was Ace Bulligan in *Moxie Mabel*. Please God, they wouldn't get him.

They wouldn't be able to get anybody else, either, until one of these TV crews pulled out. Already a third plane was buzzing angrily around the inadequate landing field, circling wide to inspect the rocky dirt road over which Madoc had driven last night with Ranger Rick, wisely thinking better of trying to land there, and going off. Madoc walked out to the two parked planes, whose respective pilots were now amicably engaged in shoptalk.

"Did either of you chaps happen to catch a radio signal

from that plane?" he asked. "Did they mention who they were?"

"No," said the first arrival, "they just asked how soon we were going to get the hell out of here so they could come down. I told 'em we shouldn't be much longer. We'll need to get the films and tapes back in time to be processed for the late morning news. They'll be back, don't you worry."

"I certainly hope so. There's always the off chance they've thought to bring a bag of hamburgers with them."

"Pickings getting a bit slim in there, are they?"

"More than a bit, I'm afraid."

Madoc stayed and made desultory conversation with the two pilots until the first television crew came out, with Delicia waving bye-bye from the hotel steps. No sooner was their plane airborne than the third one was winging back in heading for its space. This time it was a gaggle of newspaper reporters and yet another cameraman. But no hamburgers.

Before the second crew was ready to leave, there were two more circling. Madoc stuck his head in the cockpit of the one on the ground and heard the two overhead pilots sputtering at each other about which had priority to land.

"Break in and tell them we want the one that isn't press," he begged his new acquaintance. "All this picture-taking isn't going to do the orchestra any good unless we get out of here."

The pilot grinned. "What makes you think they want you out of here? You're a damned good story and there's nothing else on the wire this morning. Cheer up, brother, there are lots more cameras where these came from."

Yet another airplane appeared over the ridge, a small green one that Madoc recognized. He said a word of which his mother would not have approved and grabbed the microphone. "Look here, fellows, that plane up there is from the local ranger station with some important radio messages for us. For God's sake, let him in here."

But they weren't about to yield. When the second cam-

era crew came out, the silver plane had already asserted its
precedence over both the red one and the green one, and
was on its way down. Ranger Rick dipped his wings in
resignation and headed back across the peak. Gone to get
his car, Madoc hoped. No sense in trying to fight a losing
battle. Now who was this new affliction?

A dapper middle-aged man with a bald head and a
briefcase was stepping out of the silver plane. He lost not a
second in getting down to business. "Where are MacVittie
and Naxton?"

"Mr. Zlubert?" said Madoc.

That stopped him for a second. "Why yes. How did you
know?"

"Wishful thinking, I suppose. Ed Naxton was just saying he hoped you'd turn up. Would you care to go inside
and get your picture taken for television, or shall I send
your chaps out?"

"Young man, I'm in no mood for persiflage. Go get
them. Now."

"Yes, sir."

Madoc thought about touching his forelock but decided
not to. He went in and found Ed and Steve still sitting at
the edge of the circle around the lobby stove, looking
bored. He reached over and tapped Ed, who happened to
be nearer, on the shoulder.

"You're wanted outside. Mr. Zlubert's here."

"Great!"

The two pilots raced for the door. Madoc edged his way
among the chairs to where his father was trying not to look
bored and not quite succeeding. "Sorry to interrupt, Sir
Emlyn, but could you possibly cut this short? The people
are here about the Grumman, and we have a stacking problem overhead."

"A what? Oh, you mean there are other planes wanting
to land?"

"There were three a moment ago. The ranger was here
but he couldn't find a place to park so he went away
again."

"Madoc, this is terrible! He must have had important messages to deliver."

Automatically, Sir Emlyn cast a beseeching glance at Lady Rhys. She at once stood up and began shaking hands with the dumbfounded media representatives. "We are most grateful for your interest in our plight. Thank you so much for coming. Perhaps we shall have the pleasure of seeing you again under less difficult circumstances. Madoc, will you see these kind people to their planes?"

"I'll do it!" Lucy Shadd was off and running again.

Madoc didn't try to stop her. That one biscuit he'd eaten so long ago was no more than a faint memory, and faint would be the operable word if he didn't get something more substantial inside him fairly soon. The platter was so empty it gleamed, but there must be something edible left in the kitchen.

There was also, of course, the matter of Rintoul in the woodshed. Fortunately the interviewees were drifting out onto the flat instead of back to the kitchen. Madoc collected a trayful of used mugs and carried them out to the sink. Carlos Pitney gathered up some more of the post-breakfast debris and followed him.

"What are you planning to do about our little dilemma, Madoc?" the basso murmured.

"Fume and sweat, until I can get hold of Rick and find out who's the law around here. Have people been asking for Rintoul?"

"He has not been greatly missed. The consensus appears to be that he's keeping a low profile in the hope that your father will soften enough to let him play at the festival. Cedric is variously assumed to be lurking in his bedroom or communing with nature somewhere out back. I have gently encouraged the latter view. It is, after all, closer to the truth. Is there any hope of our being taken out?"

"I couldn't say, but I expect we'll find out pretty soon. The assistant to that big shot who lent us the plane has arrived. I hope he brought a mechanic with him, but I wasn't given the time to ask. Shouldn't you be out there with the rest of the stars?"

"Oh, I expect Ainsworth can do enough starring for both of us. He eats that stuff up, he and Dellie Baby."

"Madame Bellini doesn't go for it much, would you say?"

"Not a bit. Norma's a lady in the old-fashioned sense. I suppose you know what's going on, Madoc, but, you mustn't be misled by appearances. She and Jacques-Marie are a respectable married couple in all but the legal sense. The hitch is that they're both staunch Catholics."

"Ah." Madoc wished he'd known sooner. "Is Houdon a married man?"

"A widower of many years' standing. He's older than Norma, as you may have gathered."

"So Ochs was the only fly in the ointment?"

Carlos Pitney's eyebrows shot all the way up to his silvery hairline. "Do you know, Madoc, that hadn't once entered my head. If it had," he admitted, "I'd probably have kept my mouth shut. How did you find out Norma was married to Ochs?"

"Lucy Shadd told me. She and Ochs had been friends from way back. She seems to be under the impression that the marriage had been dissolved some time ago, but I assume what you're saying is that Mrs. Ochs's religious scruples didn't allow the divorce. Rintoul was such a pal of Ochs that he may well have known they were still married. It begins to look as if Houdon's the only one who's still in the dark. Have you any information on the matter? I'm sure I needn't remind you that, while loyalty to friends and colleagues is an admirable quality, it's out of place in a murder investigation."

"Yes, I understand that. To the best of my knowledge, Madoc, Houdon does not know. That is, he's been aware there was a husband somewhere. I suspect Norma may have spun him a romantic tale of a hopeless invalid in a mental hospital or something of the sort. The truth would hardly have appealed to Houdon's aesthetic sensibilities, from what I saw of Ochs during our brief acquaintance. And of course it would have been extremely awkward for Houdon, being in the same orchestra with that buffoon."

"What happened when Bellini showed up with my father and the rest? Did Ochs show any sign of recognizing her as his wife?"

"If he did, I wasn't aware of it. But then, I wouldn't be. Orchestra members look on visiting singers as mere temporary nuisances, you know. With a few obvious exceptions."

Pitney smiled a trifle sadly. "Norma wasn't acting particularly worried, if that's what you're getting at. Theirs had not been a bitter separation, she told me one night in Paris after we'd split a bottle of wine and were both feeling sad and sentimental. It had been more a realization after the initial euphoria dried up that Wilhelm was not the shining white knight of Norma's dreams and that Norma was not the strudel-baking hausfrau whom Wilhelm hoped he'd married."

"But didn't Ochs understand that his wife had her own career in music?"

"I don't believe the career amounted to much at that stage. Norma was only a youngster then, still singing 'Oh Promise Me' at church weddings. Naturally a voice like hers couldn't be kept under wraps, though. She began getting invitations, and accepted the ones that took her farthest away from Wilhelm. He was doing well himself by then, on tour a great deal of the time and all that. Better marriages than theirs have fallen apart under that kind of strain. But it was a marriage in law and in church. Norma couldn't bring herself to apply for a divorce and Wilhelm, I gather, didn't want to be bothered. So there they were, up a gum tree and stuck there."

It was an oddly childish expression for a man of Pitney's presence to use. Madoc smiled a little. "Where does she live now?"

"In Montreal, when she gets the chance. She and Jacques-Marie keep an apartment there, though since he's been with the Wagstaffe, I doubt whether he gets to spend much time in it. He's bought himself a small house not far from Wagstaffe. I expect she visits him but they're pretty cozy about their relationship, as you must have gathered."

Thinking of those two black silk sleeping masks and the two pairs of fuzzy earplugs, Madoc refrained from comment except to ask, "Does Houdon have a garden at his house?"

"I expect so. He likes to think of himself as a *bon bourgeois*. Wait a minute, Madoc. You're not trying to imply—"

"I'm not implying anything. I'm just fishing around. What else can you tell me?"

"Not much. You must remember that I don't really know Houdon, except professionally and not much of that. He's a tremendous musician, one of the best. From what Norma's told me, he's also a fine person. Please don't get the impression that I'm any great confidant of hers; it's just that we sing together a lot and a certain camaraderie is bound to develop, particularly on tour in unfamiliar places. Ainsworth's a dear chap in his way but he's not much company, and Delicia has other interests." Pitney's chuckle was low and mellow. "Norma and I tend to hang together when there's nobody else around to chum with. She's an interesting woman, and I enjoy her company. Within the bounds of decorum, needless to say."

"Needless, indeed," said Madoc. "I think I'll pop up myself and get to know her better."

"I thought you were hungry."

"I am, but I don't feel particularly tempted by anything I see here. I daresay Ranger Rick can find us some food if the situation turns desperate. That's assuming we get a chance to let him know we need it," Madoc added bitterly.

Yet another press conference was going on in the lobby, he noted as he went upstairs. Sir Emlyn was looking definitely fed up. Even Delicia Fawn appeared to be losing her zest for exposure. He'd like to find out what, if anything, was going on with Mr. Zlubert and the airplane, but first things first.

Madoc was a trifle nonplussed as to which room he ought to look for Madame Bellini in. He plumped for the one in which he'd seen her sleeping, and was right. She answered his discreet rap with alacrity, but recoiled when she saw whom she'd got.

"I'm sorry to disturb you, Madame Bellini," Madoc apologized, "but we have to talk."

"So? Then come in and close the door. Is it still a zoo down there? And is the monkey still capering? What is all this planes buzzing around?"

"It's still a zoo," he affirmed. "The monkey's getting tired of the game, as I'm sure we all are. Unfortunately, the news planes have been keeping others from landing. There isn't much space out there, and our plane is right in the middle of it. Madame, I do not come here to talk about airplanes. You are a woman of discretion, may I confide in you?"

"Is this an affair of the heart?"

"My heart is safely with my wife in Fredericton. This is an affair of the police, whom I represent, in case you hadn't heard."

"Yes, you are Mad Carew. It is known. Seat yourself. Confiding is easier so."

She herself perched on the edge of the bed and nodded toward the only chair in the room. Obediently, Madoc sat.

"You must have heard by now, Madame, that Wilhelm Ochs is assumed to have been deliberately poisoned."

"And you know, is it not, that Wilhelm Ochs was my 'usband? I am not fool, Inspector Rhys, I expected this. Why came you not earlier?"

Chapter 17

Madoc hadn't expected to have to apologize again so soon. "I beg your pardon, Madame. It was not through lack of respect, just that something else always seemed to need doing first. You and Mr. Ochs had been separated for many years, is that not so?"

"That is so. We would never have married had he been less handsome then and I more fluent in English. When I thought he was talking love to me, he was talking instead love about food. Norma Bellini could not remain forever playing second fiddle to a double cheeseburger! If what you wish to confide is a warrant for my arrest, I tell you frankly you are wasting your time. I did not poison Wilhelm. I have not the temperament to murder him or anybody. Besides, there was still a small fondness, as for an old friend from whom one has grown away. Also, I would have not known this ricin. Of gardens I know only that red roses grow on different bushes from white roses and of even that I am not quite certain. Is it not so?"

"It is at any rate logical. I have no warrant for your arrest, Madame Bellini. What I wished to confide to you is that Cedric Rintoul has last night been murdered, also."

Her fine dark eyes met his without blinking. "That is regrettable but not surprising. Why do you tell me?"

"Because I've been given to understand that Rintoul was a longtime friend of your late husband."

"That is true. Cedric was one of the reasons I found life with Wilhelm insupportable. That first whoopee cushion he put in my chair opened my eyes, I can tell you. Wilhelm thought me insensitive and prudish not to laugh. I knew from that moment that I would have to live for my art alone. Was Cedric also poisoned with ricin?"

"No, he was stabbed late last night with an icepick."

"Indeed? An unimaginative but efficient weapon, one assumes. I know little of such things. He would have preferred I think to be blown up by an exploding cigar. For Cedric always the big boom. Could this not have been suicide, in view of his having been dismissed from the orchestra in disgrace yesterday afternoon?"

Madoc shook his head. "I grant you it might be technically possible to stab oneself in the back of the neck, but it's not a method generally favored by people committing suicide."

"And it is not something one does for the laugh," Madame agreed. "Unless by chance Cedric thought this was a collapsing icepick? He had once a trick dagger. He tried to stab me with it. I was not amused."

This was an angle Madoc hadn't thought of. Nor did he think much of it now. "I believe we can safely reject that theory, Madame Bellini. Rintoul appears to have been about to make himself a drink."

"That is likely. He was drinking last night, one observed. And the icepick? He did not have that, I think?"

"No, it had been in the kitchen, where I found his body. I'd noticed it earlier, an old-fashioned one with a solid wood handle and a strong steel rod, pointed at the end."

"Then a tool for serious business. You are quite right, Cedric would have not have done that to himself. Possibly to somebody else. I sensed always in those practical jokes an element of malice, of cruelty. To annoy, to frighten, to humiliate is not the act of a generous temperament, do you think? Even the ricin Cedric could have administered, thinking perhaps not to kill but only to make Wilhelm sick on stage. But the icepick, who?"

"I was hoping you might have some ideas. Obviously you knew Rintoul well enough while you were still living with your husband."

"I knew him too well. They were big buddies. It was impossible to be with Wilhelm and not with Cedric. But not for long, you understand. When I got my first invitation to sing in Ottawa, I jumped for joy and never went back, at least not to stay. I do not say it was Cedric alone who broke up my marriage. It was perhaps more that Cedric made me realize Wilhelm was a lout. Already in one year after the wedding Wilhelm had begun to get fat and lose his looks. I am sensitive to a good appearance in a man."

The opulent brunette could smile exactly like the Mona Lisa, Madoc noticed. "But Wilhelm was a superb French-horn player and I regret his loss, not at all for myself but for the world of music, you understand. I am being open with you. Even Cedric I have to regret a little although he had begun to flat his upper register and it would not have been long anyway. He had not the temperament for a good teacher or even to be staff like the fussy-budget Shadd. Perhaps it was better the icepick. Who knows? It is for God to decide."

She crossed herself. "But if you ask me who stabbed Cedric, I cannot say. It was a long time ago, you realize, and not at the Wagstaffe but in Quebec where I met Wilhelm and thus inevitably Cedric. I was a young girl out of convent school, singing in churches and taking lessons from the great and wonderful Adrienne Desjardins, to whom I owe my career and my happiness."

"Madame Desjardins is perhaps an aunt of Monsieur Houdon?" Madoc asked with an air of sublime innocence.

That was when he learned Madame Bellini also had a dimple in her left cheek. "So? It seems reasonable to you that a handsome and distinguished artist like Houdon would be attracted to fat old Bellini instead of the ravishing young Fawn?"

"Any man of taste, intelligence, and high artistic standards could have little difficulty in deciding which of you is the more truly worthy of his affections."

"Bah, you are courtier!" By George, she had dimples all over the place. "So you, too, noticed that La Fawn missed her high C at the last performance in Wagstaffe. Houdon was quite disgusted. So also your respected father. And you, no doubt."

"I found it a source of considerable discomfort," Madoc replied with at least a modicum of truth. "You knew Monsieur Houdon before you came to Wagstaffe, then?"

"Since you have taken me into your confidence, I too confide." Madame Bellini leaned toward Madoc and lowered her voice to a throaty murmur. "Madame Desjardins is only a second cousin of Jacques-Marie." She smoothed her hands over the lap of the royal-blue dress she was wearing; then in a flurry of dimples and blushes, she confessed. "Nonetheless, he has been for seven years my dearest friend."

"Monsieur Houdon has been greatly honored. And has he found the arrangement a comfortable one?"

"Do you mean has he wished, as I also, to regularize the situation? Naturally, yes. If you mean were we so desperate to do so that either of us would commit the mortal sin of murder, the answer is no."

"Did Monsieur Houdon in fact know that Wilhelm Ochs was the man to whom you were married?"

"I did not tell him that, no. He has known solely that I have a husband living from whom I have been for many years estranged. It would have made an awkwardness, you understand, had Jacques-Marie known that my husband was actually playing in the same orchestra with him. Also, Wilhelm had grown unattractively gross, and Jacques is a fastidious man. He would have been revolted to think that I could ever have—but you realize my situation. It was better for both of them not to know."

"But Cedric Rintoul knew. Weren't you afraid he'd tell?"

"Why should he? Jacques and I have been discreet, our

friendship is not known. Until this week, I had not sung ever with the Wagstaffe. I have been much in other cities, sometimes in the States, sometimes in Europe. In Italy, I can tell you, it was not La Fawn who got the big ovations! There was no reason for Cedric to speak of me to Jacques, even if it were the done thing for a trombonist to play tattletale to the concertmaster, which I assure you Jacques-Marie Houdon would not permit. In any event, Jacques is no hot-blooded young fool, to fly into a jealous rage and—"

"So!" The distinguished concertmaster hurled himself through the bedroom door and slammed it behind him. "Then, Madame, it was not your sense of what was owed to the dignity of your position, but the desire to hold a little tête-à-tête with a younger man which has impelled you to leave me alone with that pack of ghouls!"

He was talking in French; rather he was hissing French words through his clenched teeth. There was only one thing to do, and Madoc did it.

"Monsieur!" His own French was fluent enough even though, for some reason, he spoke it with a strong Welsh accent. "How dare you impugn the honor of this chaste and distinguished lady, not to mention that of the son of your illustrious conductor and his lady, and further, of my own beloved and cherished wife who descends from a founding family of Pitcherville, New Brunswick, with ancestral acres, by blue! And her brother, Bert, who has ascended to high position in the Loyal Order of Owls," Madoc appended to make it a little more impressive.

"Monsieur!" cried Houdon.

"Ah, yes, Monsieur! A hot-blooded young fool might demand satisfaction on the field of honor, but you and I, Monsieur, are men of reason. I consider to myself the agonizing strain under which you have labored. I ask of you only a full and abject apology to the deeply wronged Madame Bellini and for myself a chance to share with you the purport of our perfectly respectable and innocent discourse."

"You have wounded me, Jacques!" cried Madame Bellini, getting into the spirit of the occasion, "and wronged Monsieur l'Inspecteur, who was, after all, doing only his duty. Allow him to explain, I entreat you."

Jacques-Marie shrugged a shrug of the first magnitude. "But naturally if in the excess of my devotion I have acted upon a false impression, I am willing to render what atonement is required by my honor as a gentleman. Speak, then, and I will hear with profound attention."

"You are all that is generous and noble, my love," cried Madame Bellini. "Ah, cock not that eyebrow at me; I may now without restraint employ a term of endearment. This wise young man knows all. Let me myself reveal that which I have hitherto kept locked in my bosom, not from any reason of base deception but entirely, my dear one, to prevent an embarrassment that might even have deterred you from accepting the appointment as concertmaster of the Wagstaffe Symphony which is the crown and pinnacle of your illustrious career. It is I and no other who made the fateful decision not to tell you that my long-separated husband was none other than Wilhelm Ochs."

"Sacred blue! Wilhelm Ochs? That—that eater?"

"Yes, that eater. I feared, I confess, that you would see me through less enchanted eyes did you but know that I had long ago allied myself with so dedicated a gourmand. But reflect yourself, my Jacques, I beg you. Wilhelm was thinner then. He was attractive. He was amiable, he was generous, he was kind in his way. And he was even when younger a totally magnificent player of the French horn."

"You have right, my pigeon. What could you then have known of men, a young girl out of the convent? My cherished, I also have a confession. Adrienne Desjardins has told me all, I have known since coming to the Wagstaffe that your so mistakenly espoused was in truth Wilhelm Ochs. She thought it best that I know, you comprehend? Not to make mischief, my word, but in order to avoid any contretemps. Naturally, she relied on the strength of my attachment. It stood to reason he must once have been

thinner. I could detect in his visage the remnant of good
looks. In a way, I was reassured that he was not more
prepossessing. With such a one as he, I comforted myself,
there could have been no true union of soul and spirit."

Madame Bellini was all eagerness to agree. "Oh no,
Jacques. None whatsoever."

"Ah. I found him, I have to say, at least amiable and
diligent. And a musician *de premier rang,* after all. A decent man in spite of some thickness of the head and a
penchant for vulgar jokes. It was the temperament of the
brass player, I told myself. What could one do? Not everybody can play in the strings, or there would be no orchestra."

"Always the philosopher. I should have known I could
trust to your intelligence and compassion, my chevalier."

"Your apprehension was natural, my flower of the lily. I
myself felt some trepidation when I learned you were to
sing at the Wagstaffe, but how, I reasoned, could the emi-
nent Sir Emlyn Rhys have chosen another contralto? It is
well known that he seeks always the best, even the Fawn.
That one is a bitch in heat, no doubt, but she is a voice!
Not such a voice as you, my incomparable, and with none
of your serene beauty and dignity of manner, need it be
said? But still a voice. In any event, Ochs made no scene
but behaved himself with what grace he might command.
If he sought that which had been, I saw no sign."

"I assure you, my amorous, he did not. Wilhelm was
amiable in his greeting to me. He expressed pleasure that I
had gained a little weight; a compliment I did not much
appreciate, you understand. He invited me to lunch on the
first day, I confess, but I explained that I had experienced
enough of watching him eat during our days of cohabita-
tion. He found this a great amusement and we parted without rancor, I to a teashop and he to a Burger King. You
surely find no fault in this?"

"There is none to be found. My own, let us forgive each
other. And this young inspector of police will forgive us
both, eh?" He cast a hopeful glance at the bed on which

Madame Bellini was still sitting. She blushed, but demurred.

"But he has not yet told what you gave him permission to say. Speak, Monsieur l'Inspecteur. Of his great perspicacity, Jacques-Marie Houdon will no doubt be able to cast light on this vile deed."

So Madoc at last got to explain. The concertmaster was interested though not unduly agitated by the news that a second member of the brass section had been done away with.

"One sees it was inevitable. Rintoul was naturally from the beginning the intended victim. Ochs, poor fellow, had without a doubt eaten the poison intended for him."

Madoc turned to Norma Bellini. "Would your husband have done that? Taken food from other people's plates?"

"Oh yes, all the time. It was his favorite prank, to dart his fork across the table into some interesting tidbit on another's plate and gobble it down, laughing all the while. With his mouth open, alas. Jacques is right, without doubt. I know something of these things, I read sometimes to improve my English the Miss Marple and the Peter Shandy, you know? It has been said that murderers employ always the same methods; but I have not found this so in the books."

"That is perhaps only because the authors wish to display their ingenuity, my innocent," Houdon murmured.

"Bah, it is mere practicality. Figure yourself, Jacques. It is clear to me that, the too-cunning technique of the ground-up bean of the castor plant having proved unreliable, the murderer would then attempt what you call the hands-on method of the stabbed-in icepick. Is that not correct, my cabbage?"

"My beautiful, I have to agree with Monsieur l'Inspecteur. It is in no way correct for musicians of a respectable orchestra to be killing each other, even though I ask myself why with Rintoul, it has not happened sooner. There have been times, I admit freely, when I have felt the urge. Always I had to remind myself that here was a trombonist of the first rank who, whatever his enormities, did not ever try to imitate the swing band and put in hot licks while playing the trombone solo in the *Tuba Mirum* movement of the Mozart *Requiem,* which happened once in the States while I myself was conducting."

"My God! They are all barbarians down there, of course. Still it is incredible, the audacity," Madame Bellini remarked.

"And here is more audacity in the stabbing of Rintoul," Houdon continued. "It is therefore for us a duty to assist in bringing the malefactor to justice. Even"—he sighed and glanced once more at the bed—"when we might naturally prefer to be doing something else."

Chapter 18

"Perhaps, as a matter of form," Madoc suggested diffidently, "we might start by making sure you yourselves are eliminated from suspicion."

Madame Bellini nodded. "That is correct Sherlock Holmes procedure. One sees first that we could not have poisoned Wilhelm because, my faith, we would not have eaten with Wilhelm."

"And we could not have stabbed Rintoul," added Houdon, "because I tell you in confidence we spent all last night exchanging with one another that solace which a man and a woman can find to give in even the darkest of circumstances, you comprehend?"

"Fully," sighed Madoc. "Then what about the rest of the company? Have you any thoughts or opinions you'd like to share?"

"Opinions, yes," said Norma Bellini. "I myself am confident this murderer is none of the singers. Carlos, Ainsworth, and I have sung together many times under the direction of your excellent father, which is a privilege to be coveted. I know them well. Carlos is a brave man. He might perhaps kill if the life of one he held dear were threatened, but never by stealth, always from the front. For Wilhelm or Cedric, he had no occasion. He had not known them before, he did not wish to know them in Wagstaffe.

He is not a snob, Carlos; it is simply that singers and instrumentalists on tour do not mix."

"Yes, that's been mentioned," Madoc conceded. "And the tenor, Kight?"

"Ainsworth?" She shrugged. "Ainsworth is conscious of himself and of the audience. As there is only one Ainsworth Kight, so everyone else counts as audience except his accompanist for whom he has a fondness, you understand, but did not bring on this tour. He accepts also his fellow singers because, after all, not even the great Kight can sing *Judas Maccabaeus* all by himself. Ainsworth is a good-natured fellow, mind you. He is not unfriendly. But he regards nobody in this world of sufficient importance for him to risk his precious throat in killing."

"And what about Delicia Fawn?"

"What can I say? Except that she is more likely to become a victim than a murderess, and also to lose early both her looks and her voice if she keeps up these pretty tricks. It is all a nonsense with her, you know, but a dangerous nonsense. In effect, however, I cannot see Cedric Rintoul being mistaken for Delicia Fawn no matter how dark the night."

"Norma has a point there," said Houdon. "I believe, Monsieur l'Inspecteur, you must look among those orchestra members now with us. It was a mistake not to wait and kill Rintoul after we would be all back together at the festival; since now the field has narrowed, has it not? So we eliminate. Me, we have for the moment laid aside. Though I do not delude myself that you accept only my word, I appeal to you as a man of reason. Would I have chosen to poison Ochs with castor beans when it is known that I have in my own garden a goodly number of castor oil plants?"

"You do?" This was the most promising news Madoc had heard yet.

"But of course. I have little time for gardening, so I attempt a rich display with the least of effort. The flowers of the castor oil plant are nothing to covet, but the foliage is beyond description. One leaf may be ten inches across, I

tell you, shaped somewhat like a giant maple leaf but
creased into the most beguiling pleats like a lady's fan. The
texture is interesting and the colors most deliciously subtle
greens and bronzy shades."

"Oh," said Madoc, "are those the plants they used to
have growing in Assiniboine Park when I was a kid in
Winnipeg?"

Houdon nodded. "I too have observed them there, ten
feet tall and of a luxuriance, my word! But those were fed
on wild buffalo manure, which in Wagstaffe is not easy to
find. I have to buy that which comes dried in bags. I believe this must be only from contented cows as my plants
never grow higher than five or six feet."

"The bovine temperament would count, no doubt. Tell
me, who in the orchestra might know you have castor oil
plants in your garden?"

"Jason Jasper, for a certainty. He lives not far from me
and is also a gardener, though mostly vegetables since he
has a large family. He admires my plants and once inti-
mated he would like some seeds. I had to point out that
they are poisonous and therefore not a thing to plant around
children."

"When was this? Does he visit often?"

"Not in the sense of a visit, no. One takes the evening
stroll. If the neighbor is out in his garden, one might stop
for a moment to exchange a word. He is knowledgeable,
that Jasper, and not offensive when in his own milieu.
With his children, he has the consideration not to stop.
With his wife, he has attended a few garden parties at my
house."

"Recently?"

"The last one, yes, only three weeks ago. It was for
Norma, to meet with the orchestra and staff before the tour.
This was quite proper for me to do and gave me great
satisfaction. Ochs and Rintoul both happened to be playing
elsewhere with a brass ensemble that day," he added with a
tight little smile. "Anyway, there was much admiration of
my magnificent plants and I had to caution again to avoid

the beans. They are large, you know, and not unattractive. I had attempted to pick off and destroy the most accessible, but there were no doubt many left. I had so little time to prepare."

"You had even less time for me." Now that her cover was blown, Madame Bellini could be quite the coquette. "But this was a charming affair and enjoyed by all. Jacques is a superb host, you can imagine."

"I'm sure he is. Other than Ochs and Rintoul, were all the orchestra people there?"

"I think so, yes," replied the concertmaster. "It has been my habit since becoming again a householder to give on occasion these parties when time and scheduling permit. I hire an excellent caterer and nobody is asked to perform. I get few refusals. This is not helpful?"

"Not very, I have to say. On the strength of this, it looks as if anybody in the orchestra could have got hold of the castor beans. One more question; what can you tell me about David Gabriel, outside of the fact that he's the Wagstaffe's first chair oboist?"

"But aside from that, what is there to tell? Gabriel plays his oboe, makes reeds for his oboe, maybe on occasion he goes to bed with his oboe, who knows? Ask Ragovsky, he knows everybody. Better still, ask Gabriel."

The interview was clearly over. Madoc exchanged a few more courtesies and went downstairs. The press conference also appeared to be winding down. Most of the participants were wandering out of the lobby, some to the kitchen where Joe Ragovsky was going to make more biscuits, some out to the flat to watch the planes go off and no doubt pester the pilots for any news about a possible rescue. Only two stayed where they were. David Gabriel was in the chair by the window where he'd been sitting last night, winding wire around another reed. Sir Emlyn remained seated where he'd been most of the morning, looking as gray around the muzzle as an aged beagle. Madoc went over to him.

"Hi, Tad. Let's hope that's the last of them for a while. Where's Mum?"

"She's gone upstairs to take an aspirin and lie down. I don't blame her. Madoc, how long is this to go on?"

"I was hoping you could tell me. Hasn't Rick come back? What did Zlubert have to say?"

"To me, nothing whatever. As I understand it, Zlubert talked with MacVittie and Naxton for a short while, then took off again. I haven't had a chance to get to them myself, I've been too busy answering the same asinine questions over and over till I'm ready to go back to Wales and spend the rest of my life herding Uncle Caradoc's sheep. Sheep can be tiresome, too, but at least they don't take photographs. Rick has not come back and I can't blame him. Madoc, I am anxious, very anxious. What are we going to do about—?"

"The best we can, Tad. I've been working on it, but I need Rick. It's a rotten shame Zlubert took off so fast, I wouldn't dare ask any of these media blokes to take me down to the ranger station. You can imagine what that would lead to. Maybe Mr. Gabriel here can help us."

Gabriel didn't even look up from his reed. Sir Emlyn hiked himself out of the uncomfortable wooden chair, stiff from too much sitting, and walked over toward the window. Madoc went with him and did the talking.

"Gabriel?"

"Eh? Oh, yes. Sorry." He was even younger than Madoc had thought; he must have been some kind of child prodigy. He laid his unfinished reed carefully on the windowsill and stood up. "Good morning. Or is it afternoon?"

"Who knows? I'd like to ask you a couple of questions, if you don't mind. It's about Cedric Rintoul."

"Cedric? I don't think I've seen him this morning. Has he been around?"

"No, but he was here last night. When I went upstairs, you and he were the last ones left in the lobby."

"Were we? I thought Joe Ragovsky was still there. Joe fixed the fire, I remember that."

"The fire had already been banked when I got back from the ranger station."

"The ranger station? Was that where you went? In that crazy three-winged plane with the old chap in the funny helmet, right? You got back in one piece, eh. Good flight?"

"Gabriel, could we cut the small talk?"

"Whatever you like. I'm no good at it, anyway."

The oboist was on the gangly side, with mouse-fine light brown hair that could have stood a trimming, and baby-blue eyes that blinked a lot. No doubt he had a doting wife, mother, or sweetheart who waited on him hand and foot back in Wagstaffe; he didn't look like the sort who'd be much good at fending for himself. Right now he was casting a worried glance at his reed. "Was there something else you wanted to talk about? Because I've got this reed—"

"Gabriel, you've been making reeds the whole time you've been here."

"I know, but I have this impossible dream that one day I'll make an absolutely perfect reed. It's rather like the quest for the Holy Grail. Not quite on the same scale, I don't suppose."

"Probably not, Gabriel, but no doubt a worthy aspiration. Getting back to Rintoul, could you tell me what time you left him?"

"I don't think I left him, exactly. That is to say, if you leave somebody, it's more as if one of you were going away somewhere. All I did was go upstairs to bed, which doesn't quite count because he was going to be doing the same thing. Theoretically, anyway."

"Rintoul was, however, still in the lobby when you went to bed?"

"I assume so, if he was here before."

"But you don't know? Weren't you talking with him?"

"Not that I recall. Maybe Cedric was talking to me, and I just wasn't hearing him." David Gabriel was blushing now, a flaming crimson with flashes of scarlet. "You see— well, maybe Sir Emlyn isn't going to like this much, but

—well, what I was doing was—Sir Emlyn, do you know those Handel sonatas for two oboes and continuo?"

The elder Rhys nodded. "The six pieces Lord Polwarth discovered in Germany, which Handel is supposed to have composed as a child of ten? Yes, they are charming. Not the sort of thing I ever get to use myself, of course."

"I realize that, and I know I ought to have been thinking about the pieces we're going to be playing at Fraser River, but you see"—he really was the most spectacular blusher Madoc had ever run across—"I have this pupil."

"A young woman pupil of seemly countenance and agreeable disposition, by any chance?" For some reason Sir Emlyn was smiling. "Is it possible you were meditating on the third movement of the Number Two in D-minor?"

"Well," the young musician actually giggled, "as a matter of fact, yes."

"I can think of nothing more appropriate. You might also give some thought to the Number Six in D-major. There, you may recall, the Affetuoso is followed by the Vivace, which you may find even more effective in terms of the learning experience than the Allegro."

Madoc had only a glimmer as to what his father was talking about, but Gabriel had by now faded to a nice, rosy pink and was grinning from ear to ear. "Thank you very much, Sir Emlyn."

"Any time, my boy. And now if you could possibly turn your mind back to last night, I'm sure my son would be grateful for any recollection you might be able to dredge up about Rintoul. Perhaps it would help if you were to sit down again and get back to work on your reed? Re-create the scene, as it were."

With the reed back in his hands and his dilemma about the Handel sonatas resolved, David Gabriel was finally at ease. "Let's see. I was sitting here and Cedric was over there. You know, he did say something, I remember now. He said, 'It's getting damned cold in here.' I think he must have been talking to me, because nobody else said anything. They must all have gone to bed, as you say. Then it occurred to me that my hands were so numb I could hardly manage my fingers, so I put my reed and my wire cutters inside the cover of my instrument case and picked it up and went to bed."

"You didn't say good night to Rintoul?"

"I may have nodded or something, I'm not sure. I don't like Cedric much."

"But he was in fact still sitting here when you left the lobby?"

"Unless he got up after my back was turned. I'm quite sure he didn't come upstairs right behind me. I'm always pretty wary of letting Cedric get too close. He's too apt to do some stupid thing like pinning a sign on your back or sticking a burr in your hip pocket so you'll sit on it. I did hear somebody on the stairs after I got into my room, come to think of it, but I don't think it was Cedric. Unless he was trying awfully hard to be quiet, which isn't like him."

"It didn't occur to you to look out and see who was there?" Madoc asked.

"No, why should it?"

"Simply that you might have helped us to answer the question of who killed him."

At last Madoc had found a way to get David Gabriel's complete and undivided attention. "Oh, sweet dying Jesus!" the oboist all but shouted. "What the bloody hell's going on here, will you answer me that?"

"I hope I can, soon."

"And what happens if you can't?"

"Then I'm afraid we may find ourselves stuck here till I can. Mr. Gabriel, did you attend that garden party at Monsieur Houdon's?"

"Yes, I did."

"And did you happen to notice some rather spectacular tall plants he has in his yard?"

"With leaves like great, big fans? Yes, I—well, I'm not much good at standing around making conversation with people. I found them handy to hide behind some of the time, if you really want to know."

"That's exactly what I want to know. Did you by any chance happen to notice anyone picking beans off the plants?"

"As a matter of fact, I did. I wasn't thinking much about the beans at the time, I have to say. I was mostly hoping he wouldn't come over and start talking to me."

"He who?"

"Cedric Rintoul, naturally. But then Frieda Loye came along and told him he'd better leave those beans alone because Houdon had been warning everybody that they were deadly poison. So Cedric said, 'Then what have you been stuffing them up your nose for?' He reached over and pretended to be pulling them out. Cedric was good at magic tricks, I have to say. It honestly looked as if he was getting them out of her nose."

"And how did Frieda Loye take that?"

"Not too well, I'm afraid. She went right up in smoke."

"What did she say?"

"She said—" Gabriel swallowed and blushed. "She said, 'Honest to God, Cedric, one of these days I'm going to kill you!'"

Chapter 19

"Did she, indeed?" asked Madoc. "And what did Rintoul say to that?"

"It was rather strange. He said, 'Cool it, Frieda. You're not going to get hold of it that easily.'"

"What do you suppose he meant by 'get hold of it'?"

"Well, Cedric had such a filthy mind that I thought maybe he was telling Frieda he wouldn't—you know—have it off with her. Though I can't imagine why she'd have wanted him to. Cedric was kind of a mess. Anyway, that was just a guess. He probably didn't mean anything at all."

"And what did he do with the beans he'd picked?"

"Tossed them back among the bushes."

"All of them?"

"How could I tell? He might have palmed a few, I told you he was good at sleight-of-hand. Inspector, you're not thinking Cedric used those beans to poison Wilhelm Ochs?"

"It's fairly apparent that somebody did."

"But Cedric and Wilhelm were pals. They always hung around together."

"He could have given them to somebody else."

"Why would he do that?"

"I have no idea. We simply have to bear in mind all the possibilities."

"I suppose so. Oh look, there's a car pulling up out front!"

"It's the ranger wagon, Madoc," Sir Emlyn exclaimed, quite unnecessarily since his son was already heading for the door, feeling some sixteen pounds lighter than he had a moment ago.

Rick was out of the wagon, opening the tailgate to get at a large kettle. Ed Naxton was running over to help him. So were a number of other people. Madoc got there first.

"Ellen sent you a present." Disdaining any help, Rick was going to carry the kettle himself. "Your kitchen stove going?"

"It was the last time I looked," Madoc replied. "What have you got there?"

"Spaghetti, best she could do at such short notice. We knew from what you told us last night that the rations were getting pretty slim up here. When the message came through from Wagstaffe, Ellen got on the radio and told me I'd better get back and let her fix something for you all to eat. That was when I was up here earlier with the plane. Maybe you noticed me turn back. It didn't look as if I was going to get down any time soon, so rather than waste my gas circling the field, I went on home and waited till they quit buzzing over. You folks have had a busy morning."

"You might say that," Madoc agreed. "But what's happening, Rick? Are there any plans to get us out of here?"

"Yes, we're going to start ferrying you folks down in the wagon to the ranger station as soon as we get the word. A charter plane's coming to collect you from there and fly you on to Vancouver. They didn't want to risk landing on Lodestone Flat with the Grumman in the way. But it's going to take a while yet before they get everything organized, and we figured there was no reason why you had to go hungry in the meantime. Ellen said to tell you she's sorry she didn't have a dessert to send, but she'll have something baked by the time you get to the house. I put this kettle inside a box of straw to keep it hot on the way up, but you might want to set it on the stove a while. Better give it a stir now and then, Ellen says, so it won't catch on the bottom."

"Don't worry, this spaghetti isn't going to scorch. It won't last long enough," Joe Ragovsky assured the ranger. "Boy does this smell good! How about rustling up some plates, somebody? We'll stick 'em in the oven to take the chill off."

All was joy and bustle, everybody getting in everybody else's way and nobody giving a rap. Lady Rhys came downstairs, marvelously revived by the odor of home cooking and the prospect of getting away. Sir Emlyn kissed her right in front of the entire assemblage. It was no mere peck on the cheek, either.

Only Lucy Shadd was oddly subdued. She made no move to run the show as usual. While the others milled around making themselves more or less useful as the case might be, Lucy stayed out in the lobby, sitting next to the stove, holding the scarf high around her throat.

Since the chairs were all in the lobby anyway, it seemed silly to try to cram them back into the kitchen. The sensible thing, it was agreed by mass osmosis, would be for each person to fill a plate for himself from the spaghetti kettle and Joe's new batch of biscuits and carry his lunch into the lobby. Luckily, Ellen Rick was the kind of cook who breaks spaghetti into short pieces instead of leaving it in strings, probably because she was used to feeding small children and Ace Bulligan, so they wouldn't have much trouble managing the food buffet-style.

Steve MacVittie remembered that there were still two bottles of red wine in the plane, not much for a party of this size but enough for everyone to have a few sips in celebration of their impending rescue. Ranger Rick had already eaten, he told them; he wouldn't share the festive repast but acted as waiter and busboy instead. It was he who brought Lucy Shadd the spaghetti and wine she hadn't been able to raise gumption enough to get for herself.

Madoc noticed how quiet she was, but didn't say anything until he himself had managed to put away the double helping he felt he deserved and knew he needed. Then he asked her, "What's the matter, Lucy? Is your neck still bothering you?"

Lady Rhys and Frieda Loye were both clearly surprised that Madoc should bring up the topic which those in the know had been avoiding. So was Lucy, but she answered readily enough. "Yes, it's rather painful. I expect I did too much yesterday."

"What did you do to your neck, Lucy?" Joe Ragovsky asked.

Madoc answered for her. "Somebody wrapped a violin string around it yesterday morning. That's what all the screaming was about."

"My God!" shouted Joe, "you mean he was trying to strangle her?"

Everybody started yelling at once, but Sir Emlyn made a small gesture with his finger to his lips, and the mouths all snapped shut together. There was much to be said, Madoc thought, for a policeman's having a conductor as a father.

"That appears to have been the intention," he went on quietly. "And this morning, I must tell you, we've had a further complication. When I came down to open up the fires, I found Cedric Rintoul on the kitchen floor, stabbed to death with an icepick."

This was almost too much for them to take in. Nobody was shouting now, there was only stunned silence. Frieda Loye had her hands pressed across her mouth, perhaps to suppress a scream, perhaps because she didn't want to throw up in front of Lady Rhys. Then Corliss Blair, quite green about the lips, emitted a hysterical giggle. "So would the real murderer please raise his hand?"

"That would be extremely helpful," Madoc said in all seriousness, but nobody did. "Then, Rick, if you have a CB radio in your wagon, would you please go out right now and see whether you can get through to the sheriff or constable or whoever's in charge around here?"

"She's a sheriff."

"Good. Ask her to come as quickly as possible. I must caution you all that she will be quite within her rights not to let us leave Lodestone Flat until she finds out who's responsible for these outrages. If you hope to catch that plane, it behooves you all to cooperate as fully as possible. Now then, Lucy, do you stick to your story about that masked intruder who attacked you?"

"Why shouldn't I?" The hot food and wine had put some color into the woman's cheeks. "Did you think I was making it up?"

"I merely want to be absolutely clear as to your testimony. And it's your impression that the attacker was a man?"

"That was my impression at the time, yes."

"Could that man have been Rintoul?"

"I think I'd have recognized Cedric."

"But you said everything was blurry because you didn't have your contact lenses in."

"Frieda said that, I didn't. It wasn't completely blurred. I could see you well enough to recognize. That was why I thought the man must have had a stocking over his face."

"Thank you. Now, is there anything you'd like to add? Can you think of any way we might positively eliminate Rintoul?"

"I don't know about positively, but I'm pretty sure, yes. For one thing, Cedric never wore perfume."

"Perfume?"

"Shaving lotion. Men's cologne. You know what I mean. Like that stuff Dave Gabriel's been dousing himself in lately."

"One of the students gave it to me," the oboist mumbled. "And I don't douse myself."

"Was this in fact the same scent as Gabriel's?" Madoc persisted.

"I can't tell you. I just remember getting a whiff of some kind of fragrance when he bent over me. It wasn't awfully strong. Not like those knockout drops Delicia Fawn wears, for instance."

"Thanks, Lucy, I'll do as much for you sometime." The luscious soprano was yawning, not really interested in a dead man or a half-strangled woman. Hers could hardly be called a one-track mind, but it must certainly run on a remarkably narrow-gauge line.

"Let's keep to the subject, shall we?" Madoc pleaded. "We don't have much time left. Lucy, can you remember anything else at all about this intruder? Was he tall or short? Thin or fat?"

"I'd say he was tall. Tallish, anyway, and definitely not fat. About like Dave here." Lucy fastened her eyes on Gabriel, her face setting hard. "Quite a lot like Dave."

"And can you think of any reason why Dave Gabriel might have wanted to strangle you?"

"Only that he probably knows I saw him lurking around Jacques-Marie Houdon's castor oil plants that day at the garden party. And Dave's kind of a weirdo."

"Would you care to amplify that observation? In what way does Gabriel strike you as weird?"

"Well, he never talks to anybody, just sits there in a corner making reeds. I don't know what he thinks he's going to do with them all. Cedric snitched a few one day last month to practice one of his magic tricks with, and Dave almost killed him then and there."

"Is that true, Mr. Gabriel?" Madoc asked him.

"Yes, it's true," snarled the oboist. "That big bastard grabbed every single reed I had with me, and set fire to them. This was a Friday matinee, we were due onstage in fifteen minutes, and I was left without any way to play my instrument. One of the guys in the section offered to lend me one, but I can't play with somebody else's reed. It's like trying to chew with somebody else's teeth. Which makes me a weirdo, evidently. Anyway, I had to sit down and make myself another one, and you know what it's like when you're all upset and trying to do something finicky in a hurry. God knows what I sounded like that day. I'm sorry for swearing in front of you, Lady Rhys, but God damn it to hell, Cedric Rintoul was a bloody, rotten son of a bitch!"

"So what if he was?" Jason Jasper shouted back. "Is that any reason to go jabbing an icepick into him, eh? Does that give you an excuse to strangle Lucy, just because she happened to laugh when she saw him light the match? I laughed, too, if you want to know. I mean, here's this gink with a million reeds and not one to play with."

"A situation in which I personally fail to see the slightest vestige of humor," said Sir Emlyn. "Deliberately to render a fellow musician's instrument unplayable at any time, much less fifteen minutes before a concert, is unpardonable. Rintoul ought to have been fired on the spot. Where was your conductor? I beg your pardon, Madoc. My question is irrelevant to the matter at hand. Please go on with your interrogation."

"Thanks, Tad. Mr. Jasper, is there any other point of information you'd like to get off your chest?"

"I was just wondering whether you knew Cedric and Dave were the last two people left in the lobby after the rest of us went upstairs."

"Yes, I do know, but how did you? As I recall, my parents and I were still in the lobby when you yourself went up."

"Yes, I know, but I was"—Jason hesitated—"sort of watching to make sure Cedric got to bed all right. He'd been down in the dumps ever since your father jumped on him at the rehearsal we never got to hold." Jason was avoiding Sir Emlyn's eye, which was the sensible thing for him to do in the circumstances. "I heard the rest of you come up, but I didn't hear Cedric and I didn't hear Dave."

"How indeed could you have heard Mr. Gabriel? Mrs. Shadd has already mentioned that he never talks."

"Well, I know his step."

"Ah, I see. So failing to hear his step, you went back down to check on Mr. Rintoul?"

"No! No, I didn't."

"Why not, if you were worried about him?"

"Well, I figured Dave was with him, so—" Jason let his voice trail off into silence.

"You assumed Gabriel was offering cheerful conversation to alleviate Rintoul's gloom? Notwithstanding the fact that Gabriel is known for his lack of loquacity?"

"He'd be a warm body anyway, wouldn't he? Something's better than nothing, isn't it? Look, for God's sake, I don't know what I thought. I was tired and hungry and fed up with the whole damned business. I was wishing to God I'd never"—for some reason Jasper paused—"that I'd stayed the hell home and studied to be a druggist or something. I didn't go down again because I went to bed and fell asleep. What's that supposed to be, some kind of crime? I'm sorry I opened my mouth."

"Please don't feel that way, Jasper. It's your duty to assist the police in the performance of their duties, you know. When did you go to sleep?"

"How do I know? I wasn't timing myself."

"Was there a lamp burning in the room? Had you been reading to while away your wait for Rintoul? Or perhaps playing solitaire? Or just twiddling your thumbs?"

"I—don't remember. I'd had a few drinks, I wasn't feeling too sharp. That's it, I was drunk!"

"Jason Jasper, you were not drunk." That was Helene Dufresne at her most schoolteacherish. "What sort of nonsense are you handing us here? You've never taken more than two drinks together in your whole life."

"How do you know I haven't?"

"I know your wife and I know she'd snatch you baldheaded if you ever tried it."

"My wife isn't here. For God's sake, Helene, I've never been marooned with a pack of murderers before. A man can slip once in his lifetime, can't he?"

"Certainly he can, but you didn't last night and you needn't try to make us believe you did. Look here, Jason, you know perfectly well you and Joe Ragovsky were playing euchre with Corliss and me from the time we finished the supper dishes until about fifteen minutes before we decided to call it a night. You had one drink before we ate, like the rest of the crowd, and one after we quit playing, to help you sleep. And those were mostly water because we were running low on whiskey. What are you trying to play at here?"

"I had more than two," Jasper insisted. "After you went up, I sneaked out to the—" He stopped so short they could almost hear the screeching of brakes.

Frieda Loye broke in, her voice high and shrill. "To the kitchen, Jason? To get another drink, or to get hold of that icepick?"

"Frieda, for God's sake!" he yelled back. "I told you I went to get a drink. There was about an inch left in the bottle and I picked it up and drank it right down."

"You're a liar, Jason Jasper! Liar! Liar! You did it, you killed them. It has to be you, there's nobody else left. You wanted it worst of all, and we weren't dying fast enough for you. Were we, Jason? Were we?"

For the second time that day, Frieda Loye was hopelessly out of control. Her voice was like the scraping of a madman's bow across a loosened E-string. Her face was stark white, her eyes blazing red, her mouth a ghastly, writhing grimace. "It has to be you, Jason. There's nobody else left!"

Jason Jasper became quite calm, strangely dignified for one who a moment ago had been determined to play the drunken buffoon. "Oh yes there is, Frieda. There's somebody else. There's you."

Chapter 20

"What are you trying to do, drive me crazy?"

If that was the case, Jasper wouldn't have far to drive. Frieda Loye was all to pieces: shaking, sobbing, barely able to talk, much less to scream. If Corliss Blair hadn't put an arm around her, she'd have toppled out of her chair. Nevertheless, Madoc bored in.

"Why should Jasper want to do that, Frieda?"

"For God's sake, Madoc!" snapped Lucy Shadd. "Let up on her. Can't you see she doesn't know what she's saying?"

"Then she has in fact been driven crazy?"

"Of course she hasn't. That is—oh, all right. Frieda's been having some problems the past few months."

"What sort of problems?"

"Oh, nightmares, spells of hysteria. Getting strange notions, delusions that somebody's chasing her, trying to hurt her."

"Trying to kill me, she means! Lucy, you bitch!"

"Watch that mouth, Frieda. You know what I told you last time."

Madoc intervened. "What did Lucy tell you, Frieda?"

"She—she—"

Frieda couldn't go on. They were all glaring at Madoc now, even Lady Rhys. "Really, Madoc," she protested, "do you have to do this?"

185

"Yes, Sillie, he has to," said Sir Emlyn. "Loye, pull yourself together. Here, Madoc, give her a sip of this."

He pulled a brandy flask out of his coat pocket and passed it to his son. Lady Rhys looked a bit startled, but made no move to intervene. Madoc took off the tiny silver cap, poured a tot into it, and held it to the distraught flautist's lips. Passive now, Frieda swallowed, coughed, and sucked air in shuddering gulps.

"Thank you, Madoc. They're not delusions. I can't tell you any more. They said they'd kill me if I talked, and they will. You know they will."

"I see. All right then, Frieda, let's just leave it alone for the moment. Here, take the rest of this brandy. Now Lucy, once more, who tried to strangle you?"

"Do I have to answer that?"

"I'd prefer that you did."

"All right, if I must. My story about the masked man was a cover-up. Don't you cops have some theory about the most obvious explanation usually being the right one?"

"Lucy, you can't mean Frieda!" Corliss Blair protested. "That's a crazy notion if anything is. Frieda couldn't possibly strangle anybody."

"Well, she didn't, did she? You can see I'm still here. With a damned sore throat where she tried."

"But why did she try?" said Madoc. "Was there a particular reason? Did you also catch her among the castor oil plants?"

"Yes, as a matter of fact, I did. She was picking the beans. I didn't think much of it at the time, I thought she might be planning to make her own castor oil or something. Frieda's one of those nature's remedy freaks, you know. She's got some kind of fancy grinder thing and she's always messing around with herbs and raw vegetables. I made the stupid mistake of asking her about the castor beans after what happened to Wilhelm."

"When did you ask her? Ace Bulligan didn't bring the news about Ochs's having been poisoned with ricin until quite a while after that episode in your bedroom."

"So what? Wilhelm had been dead since the night before, hadn't he? Look, Madoc, I've got a few brains, too. I saw how Wilhelm died. I watched you take that sample from the floor, though you didn't see me watching. I knew who you were, and why you were doing it. Even if you hadn't done that, I'd still have suspected poison from the way Wilhelm was having convulsions and spewing all over the place. He'd had stomach troubles, sure, but never like that before."

"Was that when you thought of Frieda and the castor beans?"

"Then or a little later. I couldn't say, exactly. I was pretty busy, as you may remember, getting the show on the road."

"And yet you didn't mind sharing a room with her when we got here?"

"Why not? We'd roomed together plenty of times, and she'd never tried to kill me before."

"But you'd never taxed her with murdering one of her colleagues before."

"I didn't accuse her of murdering Wilhelm. I simply brought it up about the beans in a conversational way, to see how she'd react."

"When was this, on the plane?"

"Yes, of course. That was the only time I'd have had a chance, wasn't it?"

"Lucy, you did no such thing." Frieda was feeling the brandy now and she'd got her voice more or less under control. "You never said one word to me on the plane except did I want my coffee regular or decaffeinated."

"Frieda, you simply don't remember. Look, why don't you just try to relax, let your mind go blank. Forget the whole thing. It's all right, we're going to get you out of here as soon as we can and take you to a doctor. You're going to be fine. Isn't she, Madoc? Tell her."

"Yes, Frieda," Madoc said, "I think you're going to be all right. Did you grind up castor beans and feed them to Wilhelm Ochs?"

"Of course I didn't! She's lying about my picking the beans. I wouldn't have touched the things, and I certainly wouldn't have had them in my kitchen. For heaven's sake, there are all kinds of ways to get hold of plant poisons, if I wanted any. Lucy herself keeps a great big croton plant in her flat. Croton oil is horrible stuff."

"But Wilhelm Ochs was not killed by croton oil."

This was the first time in the session that Jacques-Marie Houdon had said a word, and he surprised everybody by speaking now. "I agree with Sir Emlyn that we must not ourselves beguile with irrelevancies. If in fact the poison that caused Wilhelm Ochs's death has been abstracted from my garden, I demand to know who has so grievously abused my hospitality."

He waited for an answer, got none, and shrugged. "All the same, it is logic there, what Loye has said. With her knowledge of plants, why should she have risked at a public gathering to acquire that which she could so easily have obtained in private?"

"A further question." Now that her lover had spoken out, Madame Bellini was emboldened to add her bit. "If Madame Loye is indeed a maniac as Madame Shadd alleges, how had she not the ability to complete the strangling? In the *roman d'horreur*, always the maniac displays superhuman strength."

"But I haven't said Frieda was a maniac," Lucy protested. "All I meant was that she's—"

"Kind of a weirdo like me?" David Gabriel finished for her. "This is the biggest load of crap I've ever heard in my life. Flautists don't stab people with icepicks, for God's sake! But any man who can stand there laughing while his buddy burns up somebody else's reeds fifteen minutes before a performance would do anything. Why in hell don't you arrest that punk, Madoc, and get this crazy farce over with? Jason's the guy, you know he is. He's got to be."

Lucy began to protest, but Gabriel cut her short. "Knock it off, Lucy. You're only trying to make Frieda look bad because Jason's one of your pals from the brasses.

You said yourself it's usually the likeliest person, didn't you? So how about Cedric's roommate, eh? Go ahead, Jason. Admit you killed him so we can get down there and meet our plane. If we have to stay here another day, we'll all be nuts."

"Gabriel has a point," said Madoc. "What about it, Jasper? Are you going to confess? Or shall we do this the hard way?"

"What do you mean the hard way?" Jasper was not a happy man.

"It starts with my arresting someone and goes on from there. Lawyers, inquest, arraignment, trial, all that."

"And the press everywhere you turn," Sir Emlyn added with understandable rancor.

"Oh, definitely the press," Madoc agreed. "This will be meat to them now that the Wagstaffe is already on the news."

"Oh my God! You can't do this. What about my family? I've got kids growing up, for God's sake. My wife— Madoc, I swear to God I never killed anybody. I never meant to get mixed up with it in the first place."

"That's a lie, and you know it," shrilled Frieda. "You were all for it, more than anybody else."

"But I thought it was a joke! I never thought it was real!"

"What wasn't real?" Madoc prodded. "Come on, Jasper, let's step out into the woodshed so you can take a look at your pal with that icepick rammed into his neck. That may help you understand how real this is."

"No! Oh God, I'd die if I had to look at him. You can't make me go. It's against the law."

"Right now, I'm the law. Talk, Jasper. What did you get yourselves into? Some kind of tontine?"

Jason Jasper shied back like a spooked horse. His face was pale chartreuse, streaked with rivulets of sweat. He looked about the way Wilhelm Ochs had looked just before he collapsed. "How did you know?" he croaked.

"I'm a clever man, Jasper," Madoc replied sweetly.

"I'm not." Now that David Gabriel had discovered he could talk, he evidently intended to keep on doing so. "What's a tontine?"

"Strictly speaking, a tontine is an annuity arrangement," Madoc explained. "Each member of a group contributes to a common fund, then receives a yearly payment out of the earnings. As each member dies, the shares of the others are increased until finally one person obtains control of the whole amount. They haven't always been very safe investments. Nowadays the term is sometimes used to refer to an object that's owned in common by several people until the last one alive takes possession of it. What sort is yours, Jasper?"

The trumpeter shook his head. Either he was refusing to talk or else he was physically unable. Madoc turned to Mrs. Loye.

"Then you tell us, Frieda."

"I—I—all right, I'll tell. I don't care what happens to me, I can't stand this any longer. It started when Samson Flogger was—you know."

"No, I don't know. Unless Flogger would be that member of the Wagstaffe Orchestra who was caught some years ago with a trombone full of—cocaine, wasn't it?"

"Heroin. It was ghastly. We were just going into rehearsal and all of a sudden there were police coming out of the woodwork. Samson ran into the conductor's room and shot himself. We were all right there. We saw them carry his body out."

"That must have been dreadful for you. But this situation now is even worse. Am I right, Frieda?"

She ran her tongue over her lips. "Could I have some water?"

"I'll get it!" Lucy Shadd sprang up, but Madoc restrained her.

"Please stay where you are. We may need you. Mother, would you mind?"

"Of course not, dear."

Puzzled but game, Lady Rhys went to the kitchen. The

rest of them waited. Madoc could see Lucy trying to catch Frieda's eye, and Frieda taking pains not to let her. Everyone else seemed to be holding his or her breath. He himself felt quite ridiculously relieved when his mother came back with a tumblerful of water.

"It's tepid, I'm afraid. I had to get it out of the kettle; that pump is quite beyond me."

"That's all right." Frieda gulped at the water as if it were lifesaving plasma. "You're right about the tontine, Madoc. I didn't want to do it, but I had to. I was there, you see."

"We quite understand, Frieda," said Lady Rhys. "Or rather, we don't, but we're prepared to. Do go on. You'll feel much better once you've got it all out to air."

"Do you honestly believe that, Lady Rhys?"

"Does that matter, Frieda? It has to be done anyway, hasn't it? This sort of thing can't be allowed to go on, you know. Corliss, would you mind letting me sit there?"

"Not at all," Corliss replied in some surprise.

Lady Rhys took the seat next to Frieda and held the obviously terrified flautist's hands for a moment in both of hers. "Now you see you're quite safe, Frieda. I shan't let anything dreadful happen to you. Trust me."

"Yes, Lady Rhys." Frieda Loye was like a child at the dentist's, not really believing it wasn't going to hurt, but knowing she wasn't going to get out of the ordeal. She straightened her thin shoulders, wiped her eyes and nose with the tissue Lady Rhys handed her, and began.

"You see, Samson and I had been—well, we'd been living together. What they call nowadays a relationship. At least that's what it started out as. Or so I thought at the time. Am I making any sense?"

"You're doing just fine, Frieda. Please go on."

"The reason I was afraid to marry him was that Samson gambled. I don't mean a few dollars playing poker with the fellows, I mean real gambling. He'd go to a casino and drop ten thousand dollars at roulette in one night. Or else he'd win a few thousand and come back all excited, and then go back the next night and blow it all. He had this mania about big money, he wanted to be filthy rich. I never could figure out why. He was really a good trombonist, he had a safe gig with the Wagstaffe. He was making a good living, or would have been if he'd been able to hang on to his salary, but that wasn't enough. It drove me crazy, seeing him always in hot water, having bookies calling to threaten him for not paying the debts he ran up. I knew he wasn't going to change, but I—well, I suppose I loved him. I've never had much luck with men." She dabbed at her eyes again.

"I'm so sorry, Frieda." Lady Rhys handed her a fresh tissue. "Please go on. Then Mr. Flogger began to—"

Madoc glared at his mother, but it was all right. Frieda didn't need any prompting.

"So anyway, Samson began having this big winning streak, or so he claimed. He'd come home with a wad of money and stuff it into this fake mute he had in his instrument case. I never knew how much he had in there; he kept the case locked. Anyway, I suppose most of it went right out again to the bookies and the croupiers. But he bought me this"—a handsome star sapphire set in platinum that she'd been wearing on her third finger left hand ever since Madoc first noticed her at the concert—"and a diamond bracelet I never wear, and a few other pieces of expensive jewelry I needed like a hole in the head."

She mopped her eyes again. "I keep them in a safe deposit box; I don't know what else to do with them. Samson bought things for the apartment, too, and he was talking about a boat and a Ferrari and—oh, I don't know. He was just throwing money right and left."

"And he kept on gambling?" said Madoc.

"I suppose so. Mostly on horses, I expect. He used to say there wasn't always a casino handy, but one could always find a bookie. He was doing a lot of traveling that summer, he had a temporary gig with a brass ensemble. They spent a lot of time in Central and South America. Apparently the Latinos are crazy about brasses."

"So now you assume that he was smuggling drugs back in his trombone all the time his alleged winning streak was going on?"

"He must have been. I don't know whether you're aware of it, but most professional musicians have more than one instrument. We usually play our best ones when the orchestra's at home, and take our next-best on tour. We're always concerned that an instrument might get lost or stolen, or damaged in one way or another. It's not all that unusual for a musician to carry a spare, for that matter. And that's what Samson did. Remember, Lucy?"

"Not offhand, no. Does it matter?"

"Yes, of course it matters. Samson had to have an instrument he could play on, didn't he? And a mute that wasn't crammed full of thousand-dollar bills. I didn't know that was why he was taking the extra trombone; it seemed a reasonable enough thing for him to do. South America's a long way from Wagstaffe, and I just assumed Samson was afraid he wouldn't be able to get hold of another instrument that suited him if anything happened to the one he was using. Doesn't that make sense to you, Lady Rhys?"

"Perfect sense, Frieda. Sir Emlyn always carries a spare baton. But you finally did find out why Mr. Flogger needed the extra?"

"Oh yes, I found out. The hard way. That day—the day it happened—he'd just got back from what was going to be the ensemble's last South American tour. There was some mixup about the planes; they'd had to change I don't know how many times and go through customs and all that. Anyway, we had our first rehearsal for the fall season and they'd promised faithfully to be back in time for it. They'd already missed a couple on account of that brass ensemble gig, and Maestro Pettipas was getting pretty hot under the collar about it."

"Why do you say they, Frieda?" Madoc asked. "Who else was with Flogger?"

"Oh, didn't I mention that? It was Wilhelm Ochs."

"Thank you. And was any other member of the Wagstaffe in the ensemble?"

"No, just the two of them. They were only filling in, you know. A couple of the regular players had been hurt in an automobile accident or something. I forget. Anyway, the ensemble needed a horn and a trombone so they hired Wilhelm and Samson to fill in. Samson jumped at the offer because it was a chance to get away from the bookies who were after him. Of course the regulars didn't know that, and I don't suppose they'd have cared one way or the other. It was strictly business with them, Samson said, they weren't a bit friendly. Not that it mattered. He and Wilhelm had each other for company."

"Was Ochs also a gambler?" Madoc asked her.

"Heavens, no. Wilhelm had only two interests in life. One was playing and the other was eating."

"Have you any reason to suppose he could have been involved in your friend's drug-smuggling activities?"

"I'm sure he wasn't, or the police would have nabbed him, too. They'd had their eyes on Samson for some time, I believe, because of the way he'd been throwing money around. Wilhelm wouldn't have gone for anything risky, he preferred life to be slow and easy. I expect he only signed on for those South American appearances because he was curious to find out what the food was like down there. But I do think he had at least a hunch about what Samson was up to."

"Why do you say that?"

"It's just a feeling."

"The hell it is," Jasper growled. "Wilhelm knew perfectly well where Sam was stashing the loot. Frieda knows that as well as I do."

"What makes you so sure?" Madoc was pretty sure himself by now.

"Look, Inspector, Wilhelm and Cedric were real buddies, not like Cedric and me. Whatever Wilhelm knew, you can bet your bottom dollar Cedric knew, too. And as soon as the police put the arm on Sam, Cedric switched the mutes."

"Do you mean he took the mute with the money in it and exchanged it with the mute from Flogger's other instrument case?"

"Hell, no. Cedric was too smart for that. He swapped it for his own mute."

"How did he manage that?"

"Easily enough. You see, we were all set to rehearse when the cops blew in. Cedric had his instrument out of the case and the mute stuck in the bell; that's how we usually go onstage. We can't very well take our instrument cases with us because they'd make the floor look messy and people would be tripping over them, so we have to carry whatever we're going to need during the performance. Sam had already opened one of his cases to get his instrument out, and they made him open the other one, too. Naturally we all started crowding around to see what was up."

"Excuse me," said Madoc. "Where were these cases? On the floor?"

"No, on a long table backstage. The cops started yelling at us to get back. That caused a little confusion, which was all Cedric needed. Then Sam broke away and ran into the conductor's room—that was a bad scene. A couple of the cops stayed to guard the cases, but it was all over by then. They never knew the mutes had been touched, but I knew Cedric. He was a real whiz at sleight-of-hand, in case you didn't know."

"Yes, Frieda mentioned that earlier on. Did you also realize the mutes had been switched, Frieda?"

"Oh yes, it was obvious enough to me. I knew Samson's mutes, you see, and I knew Cedric's. Brass players are funny about their mutes; they'll use almost anything that gives them the sound they want. Samson had come across some oddly shaped pudding molds in one of those shops that sell fancy cooking utensils. I forget just when, but he'd had them awhile. He worked them over till he got them to fit nicely into his trombone. I couldn't see why

they were any better than the mutes he'd been using, but
Cedric went crazy over them."

She sniffed again. "Cedric liked anything gadgety, of
course. So Samson bought another pudding mold and fixed
one for him, only the design wasn't quite the same because
the store had run out and he had to buy it somewhere else.
The big thing about the pudding molds was that they had
lids, you see. You could put stuff into them. Samson would
experiment with wadded-up paper towels, newspaper, all
sorts of things. Once he played an entire concert with two
pairs of my black panty hose stuffed into his mute."

"God that was funny!" For a moment Jason Jasper forgot he was in trouble. "Sam pulled them out when we were
going offstage after the performance, and we all laughed
ourselves sick, even Pettipas."

"I can imagine." Madoc was growing extremely tired of
brass players' humor. "But getting back to the money.
What happened after Rintoul bagged the mute?"

"Well, we had to stick around awhile answering questions and all that. Frieda was pretty upset about Sam, naturally, and the maestro was in a big flap about having his
rehearsal turned into a drug bust. So when the cops finally
said we could leave, the maestro said go ahead, and we
went. We decided we'd better go back to Frieda's apartment with her."

"Whom do you mean by we?"

"Cedric, Bill, Lucy, and myself. So anyway, while Lucy
was making Frieda a cup of tea and getting her calmed
down, I said, 'Hey, Cedric, let's see what Sam had in the
mute this time.' I didn't know anything about the money,
see. I just thought it might be something for a laugh. God
knows we all needed one by that time."

"But Cedric pretended he didn't know what you were
talking about," said Frieda.

"Oh, sure. You know old Ceddie, he always had to kid
around about everything. But anyway, Bill said he wanted
to see, too, and I told Cedric I knew damned well he had
Sam's mute because I'd watched him make the swap.

Frieda said she knew it, too. She'd noticed right away that the mute in one of Sam's cases wasn't his."

"Did she mention anything about Flogger's habit of keeping money inside his spare mute?" Madoc asked.

"Yes, but I think that was after Bill and I had hounded Cedric into opening it. Then, when all those thousand-dollar bills came flying out, she said something like, 'I thought so. That's where his big winning streak came from. And look where it got him.' By that time, you see, we all knew Sam had shot himself."

Chapter 21

"So that was when you decided to form the tontine?" Madoc was feeling the urge to hurry this along; he was getting nervous about the time.

Jasper was not to be hurried. "Sam had that mute jammed tight as a tick. We counted the money and it came to two hundred and fifty-six thousand dollars American, which was more than any of us had ever seen before in one lump. Bill and I thought it should go to Frieda, but she wasn't having any part of it. She was all for turning it over to the police, but Lucy said we couldn't do that unless we wanted to land Cedric in jail for having swiped it out of Sam's case."

"A point to consider," said Madoc. "So then what?"

"We had a few drinks and thrashed it over. We didn't feel like just throwing all that money in the fireplace, but we realized we'd better not go trying to spend it around Wagstaffe. Finally Bill, of all people, came up with an idea. While they were in South America, he and Sam had run into this chap who had an island to sell. It's a little one, down in the Antilles. I'd have to show you on the map. But anyway, Sam had been stringing the chap along, making believe he was interested. So we all got to thinking, why not? It was one way to use up the money without getting in trouble with the Canadian government."

Madoc wasn't so sure about that, but he held his tongue. Jasper went on.

"We got to gassing about how we'd build ourselves a colony of holiday camps we could either stay in ourselves or else rent and divide the income. So then Cedric drew up this agreement and everybody signed."

"I didn't want to," cried Frieda, "but they made me."

"Frieda, we were looking out for your own interests," Jason protested. "You were in no condition that day to think for yourself."

"Some interests. You just wanted my name on the deed so I wouldn't be able to squawk to the police about your stealing the money."

Frieda was trembling again, working up to another outburst. Lady Rhys slipped an arm around the thin little body and began patting Frieda's shoulder as if she were a child with a tummy ache.

"Please go on, Jason. We are all intrigued about the island. How did you go about negotiating the purchase?"

"We sent Lucy. Bill had the chap's business card and all that but he couldn't go back again because the orchestra's fall season was about to begin. Anyway, it stood to reason the authorities would be on him like a bunch of hawks if he so much as stepped foot outside the country, after what happened to Sam. But Lucy doesn't have all that much to do when the orchestra's not touring and she's a good organizer. So she took the money and sewed it into her girdle or something—she never would tell us how she managed to get it through customs—and found the chap with the island and beat him down to two hundred and fifty thousand dollars. He'd wanted quite a lot more, but I expect all that cold cash on the barrelhead was fairly persuasive. The upshot was, she came back with the deed and we had ourselves an island."

"And have you ever gone there yourself?"

"No, I haven't," Jasper confessed. "To tell the truth, I haven't wanted to. I've been sorry ever since that I let myself get sucked into it."

"Sure you have," snarled Lucy. "You didn't hesitate to let me risk my neck carrying all that money down there to pay for it, or to put my name on the papers as agent for the tontine. Jason, I don't know what you're trying to pull here, but you needn't think I'm going to let you get away with it. By the way, Madoc, did you know Dave Gabriel happens to be Jason's nephew?"

"Would that make Gabriel eligible for the tontine?"

"It could put him in a position to benefit if he helped his uncle kill off other participants."

"But since this appears to be very much a nonprofit venture, where's the benefit going to come from?"

"From three million dollars, that's where," shouted Frieda. "That's what they're after me about. They've been trying to force me to sign, but I won't."

"Sign what? Are you saying that someone else has offered to buy the island from the tontine?"

"Yes, one of those big resort developers. They offered a million at first, but Cedric's been bidding them up. He was furious with me because I refused to consent to the sale and they can't put it through without my signature. That's why he's been plaguing me, trying to wear me down. But I'm not going to profit from that drug money Samson killed himself over. They can kill me, too, I don't care. I'm so sick of it all I'd as soon die right now."

"Oh, blow it out your ear, Frieda," said Lucy wearily. "I don't think you're fooling anybody."

This had gone quite far enough. "I don't think she is, either," said Madoc. "Lucy, will you please take off your scarf?"

Lucy grabbed at the scarf and pulled it tighter. "Of course I won't! Why should I?"

"To show them what a liar you are."

Frieda tore free of Lady Rhys and leaped on her roommate. The chair Lucy was sitting in toppled over backward, the two middle-aged women with it, scratching, pounding, screaming. Frieda clawing at the scarf, Lucy defending it literally tooth and nail. But Frieda had got the jump. She was on top, she had the scarf.

"Look, Madoc!"

Madoc looked, everybody looked. Lucy's bare throat was not lovely. Neither was it marred by any contusion that would indicate a serious attempt had been made to strangle her.

"See, Madoc!" cried Frieda. "I caught on as soon as you told her to take off the scarf. All she did was put that violin string around her own neck yesterday morning, pull it tight enough to make a red mark, and start yelling so we'd come and see. That's why I never saw her masked murderer. There wasn't any. Am I right, Madoc?"

"Oh, yes." The scarf was making a convenient substitute for the handcuffs Janet hadn't thought to pack. Madoc borrowed another from Madame Bellini to tie up the feet as well. He'd known from the start of the battle that Lucy was going to be a kicker.

"You're quite right, Frieda. I wondered at the time whether she might have done just that. You ought to have hidden that string under the mattress or somewhere, Lucy, instead of just dropping it on the floor. Also, it was a bit unconvincing to have that red line go all the way around your neck."

"Why is that, dear?" Lady Rhys gave Frieda's skirt a final dusting and handed her another tissue to wipe the blood off her scratched cheek. "How else would one go about strangling oneself?"

"One would do it just the way Lucy did. However, a killer who meant business would be less apt to risk waking his victim prematurely by slipping the garotte under her head. In fact, he probably wouldn't have strangled her at all, but simply jammed a pillow down over her face to muffle any outcries, and held it there until she smothered."

"Then why did she do it?" demanded Helene Dufresne.

"I wondered the same thing," Madoc replied. "I wasn't sure whether Lucy was simply trying to gain attention, since her conduct on the plane and afterward had made it fairly obvious that she liked to be at the center of the action. There was also the possibility that Frieda had tried and failed to strangle her, perhaps impelled by one of those nightmares she'd been having. Lucy could have been playing the loyal friend, trying to cover up for her. The fact that Lucy was willing to stay in the same room with Frieda indicated to me that she herself wasn't taking the incident any too seriously. I therefore saw no reason to take action, and in fact there was none I'd have been justified in taking without something more than a violin string to go on."

"And so you let her kill Cedric," snarled Jason Jasper.

"Madoc didn't let her." There could be no question now as to whose side Frieda was on. "You let her as much as anybody. How was Madoc supposed to know about the tontine? I know why Lucy pretended she'd been attacked. She did it so she could threaten to pin it on me if I didn't quit holding up the sale. Once she'd got me sewed up, she figured she might as well get rid of Cedric before the deal went through, so there'd be that much more for her. And how good do you think your own chances of getting back to Wagstaffe alive would have been?"

"She's crazy!" Lucy was still fighting. "All right, she did try to strangle me, if you want to know. Try to be a pal, and see where it gets you! My word's as good as hers in front of a judge. You can't make a case against me out of the fact that I'm a quick healer."

"No," said Madoc, "but I have every hope of making one out of what the police in Vancouver are going to find when they open the orchestra's trunks. I've been rather intrigued by the fact that you shipped Helene Dufresne's cello on the train while insisting that she ride in the plane. Taking a leaf out of Flogger's book, were you?"

This time, Lucy didn't answer back. She was finished, she must know it. She'd gone too far, tried too hard, moved too fast. Somewhere along the line, she'd made a whopping great howler of a mistake, and she'd just remembered what it was. Maybe that orchestra manager who'd so opportunely been put out of commission so that

Lucy could run this show by herself would have something to contribute. Madoc didn't have to worry about that. From now on it would be routine police work, and somebody else, thank God, would have to do it.

Through the front window he could see Ranger Rick's green wagon driving up to the hotel. Behind him was another wagon, a brown one with a big gold star painted on the left front door. A woman in a high-crowned sheriff's hat sat behind the wheel. The law had come to Lodestone Flat, and about time. Madoc deputized the much-maligned David Gabriel and the ever-resourceful Joe Ragovsky to keep an eye on the prisoner, and stepped out to greet the sheriff.

"Understand you've got a present for me here."

Sheriff Lettie Bassock was a jolly soul, got up for her role in a buckskin jacket and high-heeled boots, with that broad-brimmed felt hat riding atop her frizzy gray hair. Instead of the Levis Madoc expected, she had on a wraparound buckskin skirt, fringed at the hem.

"Can't stand pants on a woman," she remarked as she slid out of her car. "Not on me, anyways, they always bind at the crotch. Hell of a fix to be in when you're chasing a rustler on horseback. Any idea who killed your chap?"

"Yes, as a matter of fact we have a woman named Lucy Shadd all gift-wrapped and ready to deliver," Madoc was glad to be able to tell her. "I don't have any written statement for you yet, but I do have eighteen witnesses, including myself, all set to testify."

"Well, I guess those ought to do me, for the time being. You're lucky Rick happened to catch me when he did. I was just heading out to take a look at my granddaughter's new baby. Okay, I know you folks have a plane to catch, so let's haul 'em down to Rick's and take a few of those statements. We'll tape 'em on his machine, save me the bother of writing 'em down. I can't spell worth a plugged nickel, anyways. Got your grips together?"

"I believe most of us are packed, and I expect the rest soon will be."

"Then how about if I take you, the prisoner, the stiff, and maybe one or two more if they're not too proud to ride with us? Rick can lug the lame, the halt, and the disinclined in his buggy there, while the leftovers clean the place up and make damned good and sure the fires are out. That set all right with you, Inspector?"

"You're in charge, Sheriff." Madoc gave Mrs. Bassock one of his shyest and winsomest smiles. "I'm sure my parents will be willing to stay and supervise the cleanup crew. Come in and meet them."

"Glad to. Say, Rick tells me your father's Sir Emlyn Rhys. I've got a little bone I've been wanting to pick with that fellow. How come in *Judas Maccabaeus* when they sing 'See the conquering hero comes,' he always makes his chorus keep the volume down? Hell's fire, if I ever saw a conquering hero coming, seems to me I'd be out there giving 'er the old fortissimo like a he-elk in rutting season."

"I'm afraid I can't help you on that one, Sheriff. You'll have to take the matter up with the maestro, and here he is. Mother, this is Sheriff Bassock, who's going to be handling the case from here on. And my father, Sir Emlyn Rhys. Tad, the sheriff wants to pick a bone with you."

"That can wait," said Sheriff Bassock briskly. "Business before pleasure, not that I'm not mighty proud to meet you, Sir Emlyn. I'm a big fan of yours, mostly. Howdy, Lady Rhys. Must be quite a treat for you, watching your son pinch the bad guy."

"It's been a revelation, I have to say," Lady Rhys answered. "Would you like to see Madoc's prisoner?"

It might have been her son's butterfly collection she was offering to show, Madoc thought, not that he'd ever had one. Mildly entertained, he waited until the sheriff had fished around in the back of her wagon and extracted a pair of handcuffs from among a good many children's toys, a picnic basket, a lap robe, a bag of groceries, and a roll of knitting that looked as if the family cat had been at it.

"Don't suppose I'll need my shootin' iron, do you?" she asked him. "I hate toting the cussed thing. Always seems to me any woman worth her salt ought to be able to manage without it."

"My mother would be the first to agree with you," said Madoc. "She never carries one, either. Right, Mum?"

"Absolutely," said Lady Rhys. "Mind that top step, Sheriff, it's a trifle wobbly. On the whole, though, I must say we've found the accommodations quite satisfactory, considering the circumstances."

"The Magsworths will be glad to know that," Sheriff Bassock replied politely as she followed her hostess inside to the lobby and walked straight over to the woman Joe and Dave were guarding. "So this is your murderer, eh? Doesn't surprise me any. She's got a mean mouth. Okay, sister, upsy-daisy. You want to walk out to the wagon by yourself, or do I have to sling you over my shoulder?"

"We had to tie her feet," Madoc apologized. "She was kicking everybody."

"One of those, eh? I don't mind the kickers so much as I do the biters. If there's one thing I hate, it's being gnawed by an outlaw. If you're planning to keep those teeth in your mouth, lady, you'd better not try to use 'em on me. Here, let me get this scarf off your hands so I can handcuff you proper. And don't try any funny business while I'm doing it. Like the poet says, the older I grow, the meaner I get."

"I'm sure you do," Lucy snapped back. "I just hope you're prepared to lose a lawsuit for false arrest."

"Oh, pooh! You needn't try to con me, girlie. Inspector Rhys doesn't make mistakes, and neither do I." The sheriff whipped the scarf away and clamped on the handcuffs practically in one motion. "Now sit there and behave yourself till I get back, or you'll be sorry you didn't. That's not a threat, that's a promise. Where's the victim, Inspector?"

"We had to put him out in the woodshed so we could get breakfast. Through here."

"Hell, son, I know this place a damned sight better than you ever will. My grandma was a dance hall girl here. Married a traveling evangelist, settled down in the valley, and opened a wedding chapel with an undertaking parlor on the side. Yup, they got 'em coming and going, Grammy and the Reverend. I don't suppose you'd remember that old song about when Mother played the organ and Daddy sang a hymn? That was them; they used to put on a real good show, whichever way the customer wanted it. Too bad they're not still around, they could have given your friend in the woodshed a bang-up sendoff."

"We don't care," David Gabriel told her. "He was no friend to anybody, as it turned out. More like what Lex Laramie would call an ornery varmint, if I employ the epithet correctly."

"Shucks, I suppose that means his folks won't want him back and the county'll get stuck with the burying costs."

"I'm sure the Wagstaffe Orchestra will stand the expense," Sir Emlyn reassured the sheriff. "Rintoul was, after all, their first chair trombonist."

This was probably the closest thing to a eulogy that Cedric Rintoul was going to get.

Chapter 22

Loading the two wagons took some time. The wayfarers' luggage had to be brought downstairs and stowed aboard. Delicia Fawn had to take a tempestuous farewell of Steve MacVittie, now a palsied wreck of his former stalwart self. He looked more relieved than bereft by the time Delicia had torn herself away and climbed in beside Rick. The ranger insisted Helene Dufresne join them in the front seat as chaperone, he being a married man with a growing family.

Corliss Blair, Ainsworth Kight, and the by now quite recklessly entwined Norma Bellini and Jacques-Marie Houdon made up the rest of Rick's passenger quotient. Joe Ragovsky and David Gabriel were staying behind with the elder Rhyses and the two pilots to do what tidying they could before the ranger came back. Everybody was sorry that Steve and Ed were to be left alone, but it wouldn't be for long. Rick had brought a message from Mr. Zlubert that new parts for the plane and a team of mechanics to install them would be arriving before dark and that they'd be bringing supper with them.

Despite the harrowing scene they'd just sat through, the crew in the ranger's wagon were in fairly high spirits as they left Lodestone Flat. For those in the sheriff's vehicle, the ride down to the ranger station was naturally a quiet one. Cedric Rintoul's body lay stretched out in the back under one of the hotel's rattier blankets. The manacled Lucy Shadd sat between Madoc and Carlos Pitney in the middle seat, none of them saying a word. Frieda Loye was up front with Jason Jasper and the sheriff, still sniffling now and then. Even the prisoner must have felt some relief when they were able to climb out and go into the house.

Ellen Rick had the kettle at the boil and a chocolate cake ready to cut. Better still, she had transcribed radio messages to hand out from some of the passengers' kith and kin. Madoc read his from Janet at a glance, read it again, then stowed it with exquisite care in the secret inside pocket of his waistcoat. After this, Ellen's chocolate cake would be an anticlimax.

Madoc ate a piece anyway, and found it good; then he taped his deposition. Rick would have liked to stay and listen, but he'd been told the rescue plane was less than an hour and a half away after a late takeoff and he'd promised to have the full complement of refugees at the ranger station by the time it arrived. The interval would be taken up by Sheriff Bassock recording other depositions, particularly those of Frieda Loye and Jason Jasper. Lucy Shadd probably wasn't going to talk, but no matter.

Ace Bulligan's comic *Moxie Mabel* was still cluttering up Rick's landing field; she'd have to be got out of the way or the incoming plane wouldn't have room to come in. Rick had said this would be a twenty-seater similar to the one that had dumped them on Lodestone Flat. Madoc spied the old flyboy across the field, chatting with Rick's children. He strolled over to say hello.

" 'Bout time you showed up, Mountie," was Ace's civil greeting. "I already brung down your murderer."

"Did you?" said Madoc. "That was neighborly of you."

"Yup, I sure did. Last night, me an' *Moxie Mabel*. Ugliest-lookin' bugger you ever seen. Little black-haired runt with a mean mouth, just like you. Cussed an' swore somethin' awful all the way down. An' he drunk up all my whiskey."

"Good Lord! How could he do a thing like that?"

"Ah, he'd o' done anything, you could tell to look at 'im. Rotten all the way through, clear down to 'is toenails. Tried to gimme a hard time, but I fixed 'im. Guv 'im that ol' one-two punch. Like this, see. Hold up your dukes."

Madoc sidestepped the flailing fists easily enough. "You'd better watch it, Mr. Bulligan, I could have you run in for assaulting an officer. Sheriff Bassock's over in the house, you know."

"Oh hell, her an' me's ol' buddies. Any time I feel like havin' myself a little vacation, I get pinched for disorderly conduct an' Lettie beds me down in the lockup. Don't cost me a cent an' the grub ain't bad, considerin'. Lettie's awfully stingy with 'er whiskey, though. Don't s'pose you got any you'd like to get rid of?"

"I'm afraid not, Mr. Bulligan. What I'd really like to get rid of is your plane. Could you just taxi down to the end of the field and park over behind Rick's hangar? We have a big one coming in to pick us up and take us on to Vancouver, and you're right in the way."

"Hell, you ain't leavin' already? You just got here." Ace Bulligan sniffed and rubbed his grimy knuckles into his bloodshot eyes. "Cripes, I'm goin' to miss you."

"The best of friends must part, Mr. Bulligan. When duty whispers low, 'Thou must—'"

"Ever tried not listenin'?"

"Yes," Madoc replied sadly, "but it never seems to work. You have gas in your tank, I believe."

"How the hell would you know?"

"It's my business to know things, Mr. Bulligan. Would you like me to twirl your propeller for you?"

"What the hell kind o' talk is that to use in front of innocent kids? Stand aside, you sneaky little bugger. I don't need no help from nobody."

Bulligan went over and gave *Moxie Mabel's* propeller a few heaves, raced to the cockpit and fiddled with the controls, raced forward and heaved again. The engine started to pop and sputter. He raced back and climbed into his seat, pulled his goggles over his eyes, fastened the flaps of his helmet, flipped the long ends of his dirty white scarf back over his left shoulder, and gave her the gun. He circled the field once, taxied straight down the middle, pulled back on the stick, and took off.

The children waved, Madoc waved. *Moxie Mabel* tipped her fragile wings in farewell and headed for the ridge. Presumably Ace knew what he was doing. Madoc got involved in a game of ball with the children and was still at it when Rick came back with the elder Rhyses, David Gabriel, and Joe Ragovsky.

"What's happening, Madoc?" was Rick's greeting.

"Ace Bulligan just left. I'd asked him to move his plane down to the end of the field, but I gather he was so pleasantly surprised to get the contraption started that he chose not to stop."

"Yes, Ace is like that. I filled his tank while I was waiting for Ellen to cook your spaghetti, so I expect he'll make it home all right. Here, Sir Emlyn, don't you bother about those suitcases. It isn't every day I get to play porter for guests as distinguished as you. Hey, kids, come over here. I want you to meet a real live knight and his lady."

The younger Ricks were polite enough, but unimpressed. "Where's his armor?" demanded Brian.

"And where's her crown?" said Annie.

"Oh, silly me," cried Lady Rhys. "I forgot to pack Sir Emlyn's armor. He doesn't like it much, you know. It creaks a lot, and it has no pockets."

"And if I get wet, I rust," added Sir Emlyn. "Then I stiffen up and Lady Rhys has to oil me. But she does have her court jewels with her. Why don't you put them on for the children, Sillie?"

"Oh, Emlyn, really!"

"Please?" begged Annie.

Lady Rhys wilted. After all, the Ricks had been more

than kind to them. "Very well, then. I'll need the gray bag, and a place to change."

Naturally the arrival of the elder Rhyses sent the household into a tizzy. Sir Emlyn was appropriated by the sheriff. Lady Rhys vanished into a tiny bedroom full of stuffed animals and doll furniture. Ellen hurried to get the used dishes out of sight and find some real cloth napkins.

Lady Rhys, used to quick changes, emerged in less than ten minutes wearing her black satin gown and all her diamonds. She'd even managed to fasten one of her bracelets in her hair. It wasn't much of a crown, but Annie was ecstatic. Even Brian was impressed. Admittedly, Lady Rhys was a trifle overdressed to be sitting at the Ricks' kitchen table eating chocolate cake with a stainless steel fork off a plate that had teddy bears dancing around the rim. However, she was having such fun that the rescue plane's landing took her unawares.

"Good heavens, I must change!"

"I'm sorry, Sillie," Sir Emlyn told her. "They're running late and they want us on board at once."

"Emmy, not like this."

"Why not? It's the way you came in."

"So it is. Oh, well."

Lady Rhys allowed Sir Emlyn to slip her tweed coat over her elegance, kissed Annie, shook hands with Brian, thanked the Ricks for their kindness, and sailed out to where the plane was sitting with its engine still running. As Madoc and Sir Emlyn paused to let her go up the steps first, she hesitated.

"Madoc, I've been wanting to ask, did you hear from Janet?"

"Yes, a short message. She's glad we're all right and sends her love to the grandparents."

"To the—Madoc! Is she really? Emmy, did you hear?"

"I heard, Sillie. Madoc, I cannot tell you how much your mother and I appreciate what you've done. We'd love to keep you with us as long as possible. In the circumstances, however, we think you should go straight home to Jenny. It will mean your missing the Fraser River Festival, I'm afraid."

Sir Emlyn smiled his shyest smile. Madoc smiled back.

"That's quite all right, Tad. Fun's fun but we family men have to put our responsibilities first."